MISSING BOY

RICK POLAD

**CALUMET
EDITIONS**
Minneapolis

**CALUMET
EDITIONS**

Minneapolis

THIRD EDITION MARCH 2026

10 9 8 7 6 5 4 3

Cover and interior design: Gary Lindberg

ISBN: 978-1-960250-49-0

To my brother, Mike, who made the
most mysterious and wonderful phone call
I have ever received.

Other Spencer Manning Mysteries

#1 Change of Address
#2 Dark Alleys
#3 Harbor Nights
#5 Cold Justice
#6 Death's Door
#7 Drug Affair
#8 A Grave Matter

About the Author

Rick Polad worked as a geologist, taught Earth Science and Astronomy at a junior college for twenty-nine years, and volunteered with the Coast Guard Auxiliary on Lake Michigan. Rick edited the English version of Living With Nuclei, the memoirs of Japanese physicist, Motoharu Kimura, and currently works as chief editor for his publisher, Calumet Editions. Rick also worked at Fermilab, the country's highest energy particle accelerator, and currently volunteers at Microtrace, one of the world's premier forensic chemistry labs. You can find more information on the Spencer Manning mysteries at rickpolad.com.

Acknowledgements

This book would not exist without the help and support of several special people. To my first readers and friends, Mike Polad, Carol Deleskiewicz, Gary Lindberg, Jonathan Roth, Ellen Tullar Purviance, and Helene Tipa Morrison. Thanks for your edits and input. Any remaining errors are the property of the author. And, as before, to all my friends and readers who have asked for more Spencer, my undying thanks.

MISSING BOY

RICK POLAD

His skin had peeled
And thus revealed
A creature more beast than man.

—Rick Polad and Mark Zelman

Breathes there a man with soul so dead,
He never to himself has said,
I'd like to kill that sonofabitch.

—Bruce Rubenstein, *The Family That Couldn't Sleep at Night*

Chapter 1

Very few people knocked down all the bottles, even after three tries. Martin figured that had everything to do with how they were set up. When there were no players and Meatstick wasn't looking, Martin held a ball up to the bottles. In order to hit the outside bottles, the ball had to hit perfectly in the middle of the bottom row.

Martin Lisk had worked at the baseball-throw booth for two weeks. At sixteen years old he felt lucky to have a job. He spent eight hours a day setting up milk bottles when people knocked them down and thought working at the Freak Show across the Midway would be a lot more fun. His boss, whom he knew only as Meatstick, treated him like he was stupid, taking way too much time explaining that the bottom row of three milk bottles had to go exactly on the circles. Then he had to balance two bottles on top of those and one more on the very top, making a pyramid. For that he got paid five dollars an hour.

On his second day at work, Martin had kept track of how many people played and won by making a tiny notch in the wooden counter with his fingernail. Sixty-three people played—only six won. The next day, he moved the outside bottom bottles off their circles, just a little closer to the center bottle. Of the first twenty people to play, five won—far better than the day before. When two in a row won an hour later, Meatstick came over with a scowl on his face. With big shoulders and biceps, arms covered with tattoos, and a big scar on his cheek, the scowl on his face only added to Meatstick's tough look. He was someone Martin didn't want to anger.

"Hey, kid. Lemme see you set up the bottles. You putting them on the circles like I showed ya?"

"Yes, I am, Mr. Meatstick. I'm very careful about that."

Meatstick watched and then shook his head. "Givin' out too many prizes. Must be a lucky stretch." He pointed his finger at Martin. "Make sure those bottles aren't coverin' up the lines."

After that, Martin set up the bottles inside the circles. But if there was a pretty girl next in line, he moved them in a little.

Martin got a fifteen minute break every two hours, and he used it to explore the park. Riverview Amusement Park was one of the most popular attractions in Chicago. With over thirty rides, including five roller coasters, every kid in town wanted to visit the park. But Martin's family didn't have much money, and the park was on the north side. He lived on the south side, so he hadn't been there until now. When one of the boys in his apartment building got a job at the park and told him how wonderful it was, Martin applied and got a job. It took him an hour to get there on the bus. His parents worried about him being out by himself late at night but had decided to let him do it. His mother always looked so relieved when he got home.

***

The lights started to come on at dusk, Martin's favorite time. The Midway lit up in a marvelous display of colors as thousands of light bulbs on the rides came alive. Laughs and screams from people on the rides filled the air. People came here to forget their cares and live out the motto of the park on the sign by the entrance: "Laugh Your Troubles Away."

Martin took his last break of the day at eight-fifteen and strolled up the Midway toward the river. Employees could ride for half price but Martin saved his money for Skee Ball. He was saving his winning tickets to get something nice for his mother. But once he got something, he wanted to ride the Fireball and see the Freak Show. Meatstick yelled at him sometimes because he was distracted by the display across the Midway as the barker for the Freak Show tried to lure people in with a tease of the Bearded Lady and the Snake Lady. Martin longingly watched the Fireball and then weaved through the crowd back to the booth.

The park officially closed at ten, but sometimes earlier. Meatstick told Martin that the managers would ride the gondola and see how big the crowd was. If the crowd was small, they would close early. Martin's last duties were to pack up the milk bottles and balls and help Meatstick close the booth. A little after nine, Meatstick told Martin to start cleaning up. A few minutes later he turned to ask Meatstick a question, but Meatstick wasn't there. When Martin turned back around, the barker from the Freak Show was leaning on the counter.

"Hey, kid, come on over here."

Martin walked up to the counter, and the man explained he was one of the managers.

"Meatstick tells me you're a real good worker. How would you like to work on one of the coasters, maybe the Bobs or the Fireball?"

With wide eyes, Martin replied, "Sure! That'd be great!"

The man nodded. "Okay. Come with me to the office, and we'll fill out the papers."

"Sure, but I have to close up the booth."

"That's okay, kid. Meatstick will do it."

Martin vaulted the counter and joined the man, who bought him some cotton candy.

With sticky mouth and fingers, Martin followed the man into the shack under the first drop of the Bobs. The room was dark, and he could barely make out a woman sitting behind a rickety wooden desk. As Martin took a bite of candy, the man grabbed his collar and roughly led him to the desk where the woman sat with a notebook. A bracelet on her wrist sparkled as she wrote. With a bored look, she asked him what his name was.

With a shaky voice, Martin said, "Martin Lisk. Is this where I get the job?"

As she stared at him with a blank expression, the man reached around from behind Martin with a rag that smelled funny and clamped it over his face. Martin struggled for only a few seconds.

The screech of the roller coaster got louder and louder until it was deafening. It roared past the shack and climbed the last hill, leaving behind the happy screams of the passengers.

Chapter 2

Her lips were moving so there must have been words coming out of her mouth. But all I could hear was the constant snapping of her gum. Each snap was a spike driven into my brain. When her lips stopped moving, I told her I would call her and thanked her for coming.

The year 1984 had started out cold and snowy with me wondering if George Orwell was paying attention. As spring had started to raise its head, I had bought a building on Montrose to use as an office. It consisted of a storefront that used to be a music store with an apartment on the second floor that I'd rent out at some point. I had a large room divided into a reception area and a separate office for me. Next to the office was a hallway that led to the back door, passing the bathroom and a closet. The only thing hanging on the wall was a plaque that read: "I Don't Believe in Coincidences."

I needed a secretary and had been interviewing candidates for the last week. The gum snapper was the latest reject. She was far from the best of the group, but amazingly she wasn't the worst. I had two more appointments, the first in an hour—Miss George.

The office was ten blocks from the police station, only a twenty minute drive from home, and even less to McGoon's, my favorite Irish pub. A few pieces of furniture had been delivered yesterday morning, and a sign company had stenciled "Spencer Manning,

Private Detective" on the window to the left of the door. There were two parking spaces on gravel behind the building off the alley.

Fifty minutes later, a tall blonde drifted through the door.

"Miss George?"

"Yes. Mr. Manning?"

"I am." I motioned to the chair. "Please have a seat." She crossed some very nice legs and handed me a folder.

"Here's my resumé. My father and I just moved here from Georgia. I worked for a lawyer as his office manager. I had a pretty nice package. I assume you offer benefits?"

I smiled and opened the folder. She seemed a bit pushy, but she was the best I had seen by far, and I was tired of interviews. I assumed that if I hired her the legs would be a fringe benefit.

"Do you have relatives here?"

"No, we don't know anyone."

"Then what brought you to Chicago?"

As she started to talk, the door opened again and another woman walked in.

"Oh, am I early?" She stuck out her chin and walked up to the desk. "I didn't know there would be someone else." She gave Miss George a dirty look.

"Yes, you are early, Miss…?"

"Perkins. I—"

"Miss Perkins. I'm in the middle of an interview, so if you'd come back in, say, a half hour?"

She gave me a look of dismay and ignored my request. "So, I assume you're going to do some decorating because this place is pretty boring I've worked in boring before and I just wouldn't last do you expect me to sit in that chair?"

"Do you always talk in run-on sentences?" I asked. She had no idea what I meant.

"How much vacation is there?"

I waited but just heard silence. Evidently vacation was something that needed an answer. She was looking at me defiantly.

"There is no vacation."

"You've *got* to be kidding." With hands on her hips, she looked like a petulant five-year-old.

"No, not kidding."

She stuck out her chin again. "Well!"

And she walked out in a huff. Problem solved.

"Miss George, I'm so sorry."

She laughed and uncrossed her legs. "That's okay. But I have a question."

"Sure. But if I may, I made up the part about no vacation."

"I thought you might have. Quick thinking."

She cocked her head and hesitated. "So, *are* there any benefits?"

"Well, I really haven't given it much thought. If you're willing to work it out as we go, I think you'll be okay."

She smiled and folded her hands in her lap. "You look trustworthy. Sounds good to me."

"Great! Would you wait here for a minute while I make a few calls?"

"Of course."

I called her two references from my office. One was the lawyer, who spoke highly of her—efficient and pleasant. He was sorry to lose her. The other was a jewelry store owner who was just as positive. The hunt was over. We chatted about pay and benefits, and she agreed to start in the morning.

"Please pardon the office," I said. "It'll get better."

She smiled and waved a hand. "Not a problem. I'll be glad to help."

I watched her walk out and let out a deep breath. Interviewing had been no fun.

I had started unpacking another box when I noticed a woman looking in through the window. She made eye contact and then turned and started to walk away. I was thinking of going out when she stopped, straightened her shoulders, and walked with great determination back to the door. A few seconds later my first customer walked in. I had dreamed of a beautiful, sultry blonde walking through my door ever since I had opened my first office across the yards from Beef's diner.

With brunette hair down to her shoulders and brown eyes, she didn't match my dream, but she had her own brand of beautiful, the kind fifties singers found in the girl next door. She looked somewhat shy and nervous, but there was also that spark of determination that had made her open the door. I motioned to the wooden chair in front of the desk and invited her to sit down.

"I'm Spencer Manning. Please pardon my clutter. I'm just getting settled."

She smiled tentatively and sat on the edge of the chair. "I know," she said. "I live in an apartment across the street, and I've been watching you move in." She looked around. "I was wondering what business it would be."

I sat behind the desk. "Well, nice to meet you, Mrs....?"

"Baker. Caroline, but I go by Carol. And I'm not married. My husband died a year ago. Just me and my son, Billy."

"Nice to meet you, Carol. Do you work in the neighborhood?"

"No, I don't work, Mr. Manning. I take care of my son."

Wondering how she survived, I gave her a friendly smile. "Please call me Spencer."

She nodded.

I broke an awkward silence with, "Well, nice meeting you, Carol. Thanks for stopping in."

But instead of showing signs of leaving, she said, "I'm not sure what detectives do."

A friendly chat would be nice at some point, but I had boxes to unpack, and I hadn't had any lunch.

Looking off to the side, she made it a question.

"Almost anything. But I'm trying to get unpacked. Maybe we could have lunch one day."

The mailman came in and welcomed me to the neighborhood. As he started telling me about my neighbors, I glanced back and saw Carol unpacking a box. She had made three neat stacks of files on the desk and separated the pens and pencils from the rest of the supplies.

"That's more work than I've done all day," I said with a smile after the mailman left.

"Oh, I hope you don't mind. I get nervous when I don't have anything to do."

"Not at all—thanks. Don't go away… I'll be right back."

From inside the bathroom I heard the phone ring and thought the hell with it, they'll call back. But it only rang twice, and then I heard: "Spencer Manning, Private Detective Agency, how can we help you?"

Chapter 3

B y the time I got out, Carol had hung up and was making notes on a yellow pad.

"That was a man named Johnny. He wouldn't give me his last name—said you'd know who it was. He'd like you to call back."

"Thanks, Carol. I'll call in a bit."

She looked hesitant. "I don't mean to tell you what to do, but he sounded anxious. I can wait."

"Okay, thanks." While I was dialing, I wished I hadn't hired Miss George. Carol was doing a great job.

Johnny Ray was the bouncer at the Blue Note, the club where Dad had introduced me to jazz. Johnny answered on the second ring.

"Hey, Johnny, people behaving themselves?"

"Spencer. If they don't, it never happens again. I heard you were gettin' yourself a real place of business. Hadn't heard about the secretary."

"Neither had I." I watched Carol picking up a box.

"Don't mean to bother you, Spencer, but I'd like to run somethin' by you."

"Whatcha got, Johnny?"

"Well, I don't know if there's anything in it, but my sister called, worried that her kid hadn't come home last night."

"Is that your godson?"

"Yes. Martin. He went to work on Monday and didn't come home."

"Has she checked friends?"

"She has. He often stays overnight with someone if he's workin' late, but he always tells her. She checked with the friends, and no one's seen him."

"Where's he working?"

"Riverview."

I was a bit surprised. Riverview amusement park is on the north side of the city. Johnny and his sister live on the south side.

"Long way for the kid to travel," I said.

"Yup. That's why he sometimes stays with friends up by the park."

"Did she call the police?"

"They're looking, but it's only been a day. They told her to call friends. They say they get a lot of calls about kids who just forgot to tell their parents what they were doing. But that's not like Martin. He's a great kid."

"What would you like me to do?"

"Would you check with the lieutenant?"

"I will, Johnny. But give me your sister's number. I'll give her a call too." I turned to look for a pencil and saw Carol with one already in her hand. She wrote as I repeated the number out loud.

"I'll make some phone calls and look around and get back to you, Johnny."

"Thanks, Spencer. Probably nothing, but…"

"I know. Try not to worry."

I hung up and looked at Carol.

"What?" she asked, with raised eyebrows.

I shook my head and smiled. "I've been interviewing people for a week, looking for a secretary. Coulda saved me a lot of trouble if I had known she was right across the street."

She laughed, and her gaze went to my left as she squinted.

"What?" I asked.

"I may be mistaken, but I think an unmarked police car just stopped in front."

I turned around. "Oh crap, only been here a few days and already they're looking for a donation." I folded my arms across my chest and waited.

Sporting a worried look, Carol sat down as the cops came in.

Ronny Steele held the door for Rosie Lonnigan—my two favorite detectives. The noise of car traffic increased.

"Well, well," Rosie said, "a new gumshoe in town."

"You guys have nothing better to do than harass hard-working citizens?"

"We're the welcoming committee," said Steele without a smile.

"Well, welcome me, and get back to fighting crime. I pay your salary, you know."

Carol looked nervous.

"Mr. Manning," she said slowly, "perhaps I should go. I—"

Rosie held up her hand. "No problem, ma'am... we're leaving." She turned to me. "Are you about done?"

I scrunched up my lips. "About."

"Good. Give it to him, Steele."

Carol tensed in the chair.

Steele reached into his back pocket and pulled out a magnifying glass with a red bow around it.

Carol's jaw dropped and she looked confused.

Rosie came over and gave me a kiss on the cheek. "Good luck, Spencer. Door's always open."

"Thanks, Rosie." I looked at Steele.

"You think I'm going to kiss you, you're nuts."

Everyone laughed except Carol. She was trying to figure this out.

Rosie nodded toward the door.

"If you guys have a minute…" I said.

"Sure," Rosie replied.

"I got a call from Johnny over at the Blue Note. His nephew didn't come home Monday night after work at Riverview. You guys have any missing kids?"

Rosie looked at Steele who shook his head. "I'll check with Missing Persons when we get back to the station."

"Thanks. I'll call you tonight." I looked at them through the magnifying glass.

Rosie laughed and headed out.

I turned the magnifying glass on Carol. "I'm detecting that you could use an explanation."

She smiled a pretty smile. "You're really good at your job."

"Yeah, I'm a genius. Short story is my dad was chief of police. I've known Rosie for a long time, and I have a lot of friends on the force."

Her smile got bigger. "Well, at least two. Is there a long story?"

"Yup. If you accept my offer, I'll tell you over dinner."

"What offer would that be?" She looked worried again.

I sat on the edge of the desk. "I'm going to take a ride over to Riverview this afternoon. If you'd like to come, we could get something to eat." I looked around. "And I need to do something to pay you back for organizing my office."

She blushed. "I'm sorry."

"Don't be sorry. You're wonderful. I wish I had met you an hour ago—you'd have a job."

"Thanks for the vote of confidence, but I'm not really looking for one, and I have my son."

"Where's your son now?"

"He's with my sister. Her son is the same age as Billy."

"When do you get him?"

"Sometime after dinner."

"Can I have you until then?"

She shrugged. "Sure. Sounds like fun."

"Great! Have you had lunch?"

"Yes."

"Okay. I'm going to grab a sandwich from the deli and make a few calls. Can you come back in a half hour?"

"Sure. See you then."

I called Martin's mother, Gloria, and told her the police would do all they could. As we chatted, I asked for the names and numbers of his friends on the north side where he stayed after work and if she knew where Martin worked in the park. She didn't. I hoped one of his friends would know. I also asked her for a recent picture of Martin in case I needed to spread it around the neighborhood. She said she'd get one to Johnny.

Carol was back right on time. I locked up and ushered her out the back door and into my baby-blue Mustang.

Chapter 4

Riverview Amusement Park was located on Western Avenue, between Belmont and Roscoe, just south of Lane Tech High School. Dad had taken me there at least once a summer since I was four or five. My goal in life had been to grow tall enough to be able to ride the roller coasters. That took five years. Wherever we went on vacation, Dad had me go to the library and learn about the history of the place. Riverview was no different. So, while we drove, I shared some of the local history with Carol.

"The park opened in 1879 and was originally called Sharpshooters Park." We stopped for a taxi letting out a passenger.

"Strange name for an amusement park," she said.

I pulled around the taxi and explained. "The land, which used to be a garbage dump, was bought in 1879 by William Schmidt, a wealthy baker. He invented the soda cracker." I turned onto Western. "He used the land as a shooting range for his friends and set up targets in the Chicago River, which ran along the western property line. Every Sunday, he and his friends would shoot and drink."

"So how did it become an amusement park?"

"Well, the wives complained their husbands were never home on Sunday. The men weren't going to give up their shooting, so they cut a deal. William built a picnic area and put in a carousel for the families to ride."

"So, another case of women changing history," Carol said with a smirk.

I laughed. "Yup, but then his son, George, became interested in amusement parks. He convinced his father to lease out six acres to an east coast syndicate for an amusement park, and in 1904 the park became Riverview Sharpshooters Park. By 1910, it was the largest in the world."

I moved into the right lane and turned into the parking lot.

***

As we looked for a spot, Carol asked what I hoped to find.

"Nothing in particular. So far, this is the last place we know of where Martin was. You can learn things just by keeping your eyes open. Let's just walk around and see if anything pops out."

I got a spot in the first row right next to the special parking area for motorcycles, paid, and we walked through the arched entrance gate which was painted with red, white, and blue stripes. "William was quite the entrepreneur. Before each season he mailed out free entrance passes to get people into the park, where they then had to pay for the rides and food."

"Smart."

"In the 1920s he also paid the streetcar fare for kids. The car ran down Western Avenue and stopped at the park. The fare was only a couple cents but that was a lot to people back then."

We stood inside the gate and talked about a plan. I asked Carol what her favorite ride was.

"Well, I don't know. I've never been here."

"Really? Well, then we'll just have to go on all of them!"

She laughed. "Hmmm. Don't know about that. Unless you want to take a chance on being thrown up on, I suggest we skip anything that spins around. And I'm not too thrilled about dropping out of the sky in a parachute."

I laughed. "Okay. We'll stick to the merry-go-round. But the best way to see the park is on the train or the Space Ride."

"What's the Space Ride?"

"Kind of a gondola that travels over the park."

She gave me a nervous look. "Let's stay on the ground."

"Okay, the Riverview Chief it is."

The station was to the left, not too far down the Midway at the edge of a park. We started in that direction, but Carol stopped in her tracks when we turned a corner and saw what I had always called the evil genie. It was the huge, wicked face of a smirking genie with a beard, thin moustache, wide eyes, and turban. When we were kids we used to say that if you looked at the face, the genie would get you in the middle of the night.

"What the heck is that?" asked Carol.

I laughed. "Officially, Aladdin's Castle." I told her about the evil genie. We stopped and watched the crowd gathered in front of the entrance.

"You have to walk through the castle where nothing is as it seems." I told her about the maze of screen doors with no handles you had to go through to get into the castle, the distorted mirrors that made you thin and tall or fat and short, the dark passages, the tilted floors, and the magic carpet that whisked you out of the castle over bouncing rollers.

She told me she could live without all that.

"Well, not if you were five."

I nodded toward the crowd. "What do you notice about the crowd?"

She cocked her head, scanned the fifty or so people in front of the entrance, and shrugged. "Nothing special." Then she squinted and looked confused. "I would think they're waiting to go in, but they're not in line—they're just watching, but nothing's happening. Is there some show?"

"Sort of. What else?"

After a few seconds, she said, "They're almost all men."

"Exactly!"

She looked confused again.

"Keep watching."

In a few minutes, two couples walked up to the ticket booth, bought tickets, and started up the stairs, which went up along the genie's beard to the entrance door at the left of his face. The murmur from the crowd stopped. Near the top, one of the girls screamed as a blast of air blew up from the stairs, blowing her dress up around her waist. The crowd howled.

Carol looked shocked. "These guys stand around waiting to see some girl's underwear?"

I laughed. "Evidently. Pretty cheap thrills."

"To say the least. How did that happen? Did she step on something?"

"Look behind you."

She turned toward a minaret on the other side of the Midway from the castle. "So?"

"So, there's a man in there who triggers the air when a girl gets to the right step."

"You've got to be kidding. Some guy's job is to blow up women's dresses?"

"Yup. Wanna try?"

"I think not, Mr. Manning!"

The crowd started to thin out, and we headed for the train station.

"So, what does this kid look like?" Carol asked.

"Like a kid." I had only met him once and described him as best as I could.

We sat in the first of six cars, right behind the engine, and started the trip around the park.

As the train started, we chatted about growing up in Chicago. I held up my hand as we passed the Bobs roller coaster. It was screeching around the last turn, and I couldn't hear her over the screams of the happy passengers.

"Are you up for a roller coaster?" I asked.

"I think so, but perhaps one of the others. I heard the Bobs actually leaves the tracks at some point."

I laughed as we made a turn that put the Parachute Drop directly in front of us. "Well, the Bobs covers more than a half mile in a little over two minutes, but I think it stays on the track the whole time."

"Just the same, I'll work my way up."

The train whistle blew as we came up to a walkway crossing, and we swung around a curve where the tracks started to follow the river.

"The land you're on now wasn't part of the original park, and the river wasn't where you see it. They rerouted the river so they could expand the park."

She nodded, took a deep breath, and looked up at one of the other roller coasters. I asked about her family.

"My mom died a few years ago, and Dad several months after. I think he died of a broken heart. They were like Siamese twins. I miss them a lot." She looked sad.

I knew how she felt.

"My husband died not long after that in a car accident," she said.

I resisted the urge to take her hand and tried not to think about car accidents. "Sorry to hear that."

She nodded. "Thanks. Billy was devastated," she said as we entered a tunnel.

Thirty seconds later we came back into the sunshine, and I asked how she got by.

"Oh, there were insurance policies and a small legacy from my folks... enough to make ends meet as long as I watch it. But I get lonely and bored when Billy's not there. I can't imagine what Martin's folks are going through. If it were Billy, I'd..."

I touched her arm.

"What do you think happened?" she asked.

"I have no idea. There are so many possibilities."

"So how do you find him?" She looked hopeless.

"I start talking to people here and asking questions and crossing off possibilities."

The horn sounded as we came to a crossing.

"Do you think you'll find him, Spencer?"

"I have to assume that I will. The plan is to be successful."

"And how often are you?"

I smiled. "So far… every time. But I've only been doing this for three years. Given time, the odds will catch up with me."

"Well, I hope you have at least one more time before that happens. If there's anything I can do, just ask."

"Thanks."

As we rounded a curve, she pointed toward the merry-go-round. "Now that I can handle!"

"Great! We'll get off at the stop coming up and go take a ride. And then we're going on my favorite ride."

"What's that?"

"It's a surprise."

"Well, okay, but remember the throwing up part."

I laughed. She didn't.

As we walked away from the station I told her about the merry-go-round. "I already told you it was originally installed to appease the wives. The horses were hand-carved and painted wood, and the organ music was from paper music rolls. Other animals were added over the years and the wooden horses were replaced by aluminum ones. Dad got us a tour of the sheds where a few of the old horses are stored. They're wonderful."

We got on and flew around and around at fourteen miles per hour.

As we made our way to the exit, Carol asked, "So what's this favorite ride?"

"You'll see," I said with a smile.

We cut across the center of the park through the game arcade, and as we reached the east side I could see the top of the Shoot the Chutes. I was pretty sure Carol wouldn't agree if I told her that's where we were going.

When we reached the entrance, I took her hand and led her into the line. She looked at me like I was crazy, but she kept walking.

As we stood in line I told her about the ride. Boats were lifted to the top of a tower by an elevator where they then ran down a water chute to splash into a lagoon at the bottom. I explained that the first

chutes ride was at Chutes Park on the south side. When that park
went out of business in 1906, the ride was built here at Riverview.

After ten minutes we were first in line for the next boat and we'd
be able to sit in the front row, my favorite spot. But, while she was
willing to go on the ride, Carol insisted on sitting near the back so
she wouldn't get wet.

She held tightly to the bar in front of us as we rode up the elevator. When we got to the top she gave me one quick look of apprehension and squeezed the bar all the way to the bottom where the boat
splashed into the lagoon, throwing up a wall of water. Everyone got
wet, especially those at the back.

She turned to me with a look of amazement and asked, "Can we
go again?"

I broke out laughing as the boat was funneled back to the load-
ing platform. "Well, all the rides except this one have a second ride
for half price deal. We'd have to stand in line again."

"Then let's come back sometime when Billy's tall enough."

As we walked back to the entrance, Carol asked about my dad.

"How about I give you the long story over dinner?"

She accepted.

***

I took Carol to an Italian restaurant on Clark Street. After we ordered, I told her about the "car accident" that had killed my mom
and dad. It was no accident and was meant as a warning to back off
from a drug case Dad was working on. It was just supposed to scare
him. But the kid who was driving lost control of his car and ran Dad
off the road and into a tree that killed my folks.

"Oh, Spencer, I'm so sorry."

"Thanks." I took a drink of wine.

"Was that the drug story about the race track?"

"Yes."

"Manning. I remember. Was that you who figured it out?"

I laughed. "Well, I had a hand in it. But I had a little help."

She squinted. "There was something strange about that time."

"There was? What?"

She buttered a roll. "At the same time there was a very bizarre story about the mayor's wife. Seemed like she just disappeared."

I nodded. "It did seem that way, didn't it?"

She looked at me with a twinkle in her eye. "Why do I get the feeling you know something about that?"

I shrugged and swirled the wine in the glass. "Perhaps because you are a shrewd woman."

Taking a bite of roll, she asked, "And are you going to explain?"

"Maybe someday when I'm old and gray."

"I'll look forward to that."

"Well, don't hold your breath. I doubt I'll live to be old and gray."

She laughed. I didn't.

As we ate, she said, "I can't stop thinking about Martin. I wish there was something I could do."

I thought about the photo. "Well, I'm getting a photo of Martin, and I'll make posters to put up around the neighborhood. If you'd like to help spread them around?"

"I'd love to. And Billy can help."

She looked excited. It's always good to have something to do. Helpless is a bad feeling.

We finished eating, and I drove her to her sister's to get her son, Billy, a sandy-haired eight-year-old who beamed when he saw his mom.

Carol hugged him and introduced me to the family.

I gave them a ride home, and Billy shook my hand when we said goodbye. When Carol put out her hand, I gave her a hug. She hugged back.

"Thanks for a lovely day, Spencer. I had a great time."

"Me too. Drop in any time."

"I may just do that. Don't forget about the posters."

I watched her disappear into the stairway.

***

At a quarter to nine, I turned my Mustang south on Ashland and headed for chez Stosh. Lt. Powolski greeted me with his usual loving charm.

"Another peaceful evening shot to hell."

"Good evening to you too."

"I knew I was in trouble as soon as I heard the rumble of that Mustang."

"If you mean because I'd go to the kitchen and get two beers to save you the trouble of getting up, you are correct."

I handed him a Schlitz as he turned down the volume on the Cubs game. They were leading the Cards six to one.

"To what do I owe this visit?"

"To your charming personality." I took a long drink. "And to my having some questions."

"Of course." He sighed. He waggled his beer bottle at me. "Whaddya got?"

"A missing kid."

"Check with Stengel in the morning."

"Rosie already has and I'll call her later."

"So what do you need me for? I was watching the Cubs win for a change."

"The kid is a nephew of Johnny Ray." That got his attention.

"Okay, tell me about it."

"Sixteen-year-old kid named Martin. Got a job at Riverview a couple weeks ago. Lives on the south side and takes the bus to work."

"Long way to go," he said as he took a drink.

"Jobs aren't easy to come by."

"Yeah, glad I'm not a kid these days. But they weren't so easy when I was a kid either."

"You can remember back that far?"

"You'd be surprised what I can remember. If you want me to dig up some of your childhood and share it around the water cooler, just keep it up."

"Okay, truce. You ever have any trouble at Riverview?"

He took another drink, set the bottle on the table, and pulled his recliner upright.

"Not usually anything we need to get involved with. They have their own police force."

That surprised me. "How official are they?"

He shrugged. "They handle everyday things themselves. They can't make arrests, but they can detain someone and wait for us. I have a feeling they handle problems themselves in ways we don't."

"You mean strong-arm tactics?"

"Don't know what I mean. But there are rumors about troublemakers being dealt with." He spread his hands out, palms up. "We've never had a complaint."

"Hmm. Who's in charge?"

"Ex-Chicago cop named Tommy Walters. He made sergeant and then started to throw his weight around; he quit after being written up too many times for his liking... and ours. He complained about what he called the 'kid gloves' method of running the department."

I emptied the bottle. "Hence the rumors about tactics."

"Yeah, could be. But he did get the job done, and he isn't going to put up with any crap, wherever he is."

"I think I'll have a chat. Can I mention your name?"

"Sure, we got along. Mine's about the only one that'll get you anywhere. But don't expect that to buy you a friend."

"Just a foot in the door is fine. I have plenty of friends. Why are you on his good side?"

Stosh laughed and emptied his bottle. "I wouldn't call it a good side, but I had an opportunity to help him at one point."

He saw my raised eyebrows and continued.

"Walters got things done, but that sometimes involved bending the rules, not unlike someone else I know. I was able to cover his back when one particular bend ended up with questions, but also bad guys in jail."

"Sometimes the end justifies the means."

He nodded. "And sometimes not. Speaking of friends, did you ever have a chat with Rosie?"

"I always have chats with Rosie."

"Sure. I'll take that as a no. I repeat—she cares about you. You need to tell her."

"I know, Stosh. Just waiting for the right time."

"Okay. I won't say any more. Game of gin?"

"Sure."

We played for an hour and ended with him up only a dime. But anything on the winning side made him happy.

***

I called Rosie when I got home. Missing Persons had the report on Martin but had no leads.

"When's your next day off, Rosie?"

"Tomorrow."

"Perfect. How about a day at Riverview? My treat."

"Only if we can skip Alice in Wonderland. The rabbit scares me."

"Okay. We'll do the Tunnel of Love."

"You scare me too. What's your plan?"

"With the Tunnel of Love?"

"Nope."

"Just want to nose around."

"And you think you can do more than the Chicago Police force?"

"I have in the past."

"You don't wear modesty well."

"Just giving the facts, ma'am. Pick you up at nine-thirty. Wear one of your summer dresses."

She laughed one of her laughs filled with smiles. She and Maxine had laughs that could fix the world's problems.

"Hey, I know about the castle—nice try."

"Party pooper."

"See you in the morning, hot shot."

I had no idea what I would find at Riverview, but I knew that just stirring pots sometimes got people excited. I did want to walk through Alice in Wonderland. Mom had read the stories to me when I was five. I thought they were wonderful, especially the silly poems. And when I was under forty-two inches tall, the only things I could get into were Kiddieland, the castle, and Alice. I loved Humpty Dumpty and Tweedledum and Tweedledee. I never stopped to think they were just small people in costumes. And I wouldn't mind a trip through the Tunnel of Love. Then somewhere along the way I'd have a chat with Rosie and get Stosh off my back. A year of his nagging was getting on my nerves.

Chapter 5

I woke to an early morning thunderstorm a little before six Wednesday morning. I made breakfast and listened to the radio for the weather. Storms were supposed to move through by mid-morning, so my trip with Rosie was still on.

Miss George—I wondered if I should call her by her first name—was waiting at the front door when I got to the office at five to nine. Prompt—I liked that. I asked if I could call her Samantha.

"Of course," she said with a smile.

While we talked about what to do with the office, it crossed my mind that both of her names could be men's names—Sam George. The rest of her wasn't manly at all. I gave her a key and wished her luck.

I left at nine-thirty to pick up Rosie and drove west down the alley so I could drive back east on Montrose and look at my office from the street. I got kinda choked up seeing my name on the window and wished Mom and Dad could have seen it. I got excited when I noticed Sam on the phone. Business was booming!

***

As we walked to the main gate, Rosie asked if I had a plan.

"Of course! I always have a plan."

She gave me a skeptical look.

"It's just not always evident at the moment."

"Or ever."

"No cotton candy for you, young lady."

I had asked at the ticket booth where the police station was, and we made our way down the Midway. As we walked I heard a voice from the shooting gallery.

"Hey pal, step right up and win something for the pretty lady." The man behind the counter had a big smile on his face.

"No thanks," I said politely.

Rosie and I had been having a shooting competition for years. The winner was decided not by who had the most bullseyes but by whose hole in the middle of the bullseye was the smallest. I was trying to be fair to the guy behind the counter.

"Come on pal, the little lady deserves a prize."

We should have kept walking, but this guy was pissing me off, and I walked up to the counter. "What about *no thanks* didn't you understand?"

"Come on, pal... you're here to have fun. Lighten up and show the lady what you can do."

"That wouldn't be a good idea... pal. I'm trying to do you a favor here."

A crowd had gathered.

He laughed. "What you're trying to do is not embarrass yourself. Perhaps the little lady would like to try."

"That wouldn't be a good idea either," I said.

"Look at this, ladies and gentlemen," he said with the same smile. He was having a great time. "We have ourselves a male chauvinist here... won't let the little lady make up her own mind."

I looked at Rosie. She was doing everything she could to not burst out laughing. And I had had it with the jerk behind the counter. I held out my arm toward Rosie, and she walked up to the counter.

The counter man was playing the crowd for all he was worth. "Here we go, ladies and gentlemen. The little lady is going to see if she can shoot a gun."

I slowly shook my head. I would have felt sorry for him if he wasn't such a jerk. This was going to be fun.

Rosie put down a quarter and picked up a rifle. She aimed at a six inch metal circular plate standing on its side on a post like a sucker on a stick. The plate would spin if you hit it either side of center. To win you had to hit the dime-sized bullseye in the center and then the plate wouldn't spin.

Rosie took a shot and the plate spun to the right. She looked at me and we both nodded. The sights were off. And Rosie now knew in which direction. Her next shot also spun the plate to the right but it spun more slowly. The next four shots hit the center. She asked for a reload and the counter man handed her a new gun as she put down another quarter.

"I'll keep this one," she said in her best *little lady* voice.

Nervously, the man reloaded the gun, and she picked off six small targets. When she asked for another reload he said he was taking a break. He had stopped smiling.

Rosie picked out four of his best prizes and gave them to some kids. As we walked away I said, "Can't say I didn't try to warn him."

She laughed. "Some people just deserve what they get."

Just past the Fireball roller coaster was a small wooden building with a "Police" sign above the door. There was only one long, horizontal window at eye level to the left of the door, and a coating of tan paint was peeling and chipped. It looked like it had been squeezed in as an afterthought between the rides. But then the rides were the money maker—the police were an expense. I knocked twice and opened the door.

A small foyer was empty. The dingy main room held only a desk and a few chairs. A small, oval throw rug covered a wooden plank floor. Two doors opened to the right and left at the back of the space. A woman's voice called out, "Be right with you."

I glanced at Rosie and got a *What the hell is this?* look.

I shrugged.

A fireplug-shaped woman with very prominent cheekbones limped through the left door with an armful of files. She asked if she could help us, but it was obvious she'd rather not.

I gave her my best smile and said, "I'm looking for Chief Walters."

She dropped the files on the desk and sat with a grimace. "Not here. Do you want—?"

The front door opening interrupted her, and a large, imposing-looking man came in. He glanced at us without interest and continued into a room that had a sign above the door: "Chief Walters."

"I think we've found him," I said with a smile.

She just stared at me indifferently.

I glanced at Rosie who shrugged slightly with a tiny smile.

As the lady opened a drawer, I noticed a diamond bracelet on her right wrist. It sparkled in the little light in the room. She pulled out a form and handed it to me.

"What's this?"

"Can you read?"

It was a request for an appointment. "Yup, since I was as tall as this desk. I was an early learner."

"Good for you. You can use the table."

Rosie's smile was widening. I put the form on the desk. "He's in there and I'm here. How about we skip this step and move right to you asking him if I can see him for a few minutes?"

"Fill it out, don't fill it out, means nothing to me. But if you don't fill it out you won't be seeing the chief."

I filled out the form with my name and the reason for my request and NOW on the date line.

She looked it over and handed it back to me. "Need your phone number."

"Not if I get the time I requested," I said with a bit of frustration.

We stared at each other. She kept staring as I filled in my number. She sighed and walked it in to him and was back in five seconds holding out the form. NOW was crossed out.

"Listen, Miss…" I looked for a nameplate. There wasn't any.

She gave me a penetrating stare. Her face was captivating, not because it was pretty but because it was commanding. Her features were harsh and slightly asymmetrical.

"And *listen* won't help," she said. "If you want an appointment, you need a time."

"What if this is an emergency?"

"Is it?"

"Might be."

She just stared.

"I was sent by the Chicago police to look into something. I would like to be able to tell them I actually spoke to the man sitting in the next room."

She glanced at the form. "Well, Mr. Manning, we're not part of the Chicago police here. Who sent you?"

"Lieutenant Powolski."

"I'm sorry. You still need to—"

"Send him in, Belva," came a gruff order from the next room.

"You can go in."

"I heard. Thanks."

Rosie and I started around the desk.

"Not her."

"It's okay, she's with me."

"Got that, but 'send him in' didn't mention a she."

"You've gotta be—"

Rosie put her hand on my arm and sat on one of the chairs.

Walters looked up as I walked in. I hadn't been properly introduced.

"Good morning, Chief Walters."

He nodded to one of the armchairs in front of a very nice oak desk, and I sat in a straight-back wooden chair with no padding. His chair swiveled and had hand-carved arms covered with dark brown leather. Most of the plank floor was covered with a dark green carpet, and the walls were nicely paneled and covered with photographs of Walters with several large fish. A bronze plaque with "Chief of Police, Tommy Walters" written in large letters hung behind his desk. It didn't mention anything about Riverview. An autographed baseball bat was propped up in a corner. I wasn't close enough to see if it was Cubs or Sox.

He looked at me without saying a word. His 'procedure' wasn't very friendly. I could play that game—I didn't say a word either. That was *my* procedure.

That lasted for about thirty seconds when he broke the silence.

"The only reason you got in here, Mr. Manning, is because you mentioned Lieutenant Powolski… that gets you one minute and you've already used up half of that."

I nodded and gave in. "A friend of mine has a sixteen-year-old nephew who is missing. I'm trying to help."

He shrugged. "And that brings you to my office?" He stared at me with a look that made it clear he thought I was wasting his time.

I was usually pretty confident about my attitude, but this guy had me intimidated.

"He's a kid named Martin Lisk. He worked here. Didn't come home from work Monday."

Walters shrugged. "So?"

I shook my head. "So there's a missing kid, and the last place we know where he was is here."

"Okay. But there's plenty more places in this city. I wonder where he went when he left work."

I tried not to let my frustration enter the conversation, but it was getting harder with every word he said. "He would have gone home. He had a long bus ride."

"To where?"

"South side."

He nodded slowly, pursed his lips, and lost a bit of the attitude. "Mr. Manning, we have enough problems here without trying to keep track of workers when they leave. I do have to admit, a lot of our problems are lost kids. Parents look away for a second and the kid's gone, but they show up sooner or later. I sympathize with you, but this sounds like a police matter."

"It may be," I agreed. "But could you at least look into it? Find out who he worked with and ask if they saw him on Monday?"

He folded his hands on the edge of his shiny wooden desk. "Mr. Manning, I will definitely ask some questions, but most of our workers are transient. We hire new workers constantly, and we don't ask many questions. I doubt this kid had any friends."

"I'm guessing your non-transient employees know who they work with. Wouldn't hurt to ask and see if he *had* any friends."

"It would not. But kids come and go almost daily. The part-time employees don't get time to make friends."

I took a deep breath and sighed. "Would you tell me where he worked?"

"No clue. I'm not in charge of that, Mr. Manning."

"Who is?"

He pushed back from his desk. "Probably the personnel department. It strikes me that if this was anything serious, the cops would be asking the questions, not some private dick."

I resisted the urge to tell him there was a cop in his outer office, gave him a card with my new phone number, and asked him to call if he discovered anything.

He nodded. It was a nod of agreement—and dismissal. He didn't offer his hand and didn't say goodbye. He just suggested that I wouldn't want to bother the employees with questions. I wasn't surprised. I left the splendor of his fancy office in a wooden shack and glanced at Belva on my way to the door. I was thinking about the name. She didn't look up from the file on her desk. Rosie followed me out.

I was glad to be back out in the sunshine and felt like I had escaped one of the levels of Hades. Rosie took my arm.

"That went well, don't ya think?" she said with a smirk.

"I think so," I replied without sarcasm and led her to a beer garden about fifty feet away.

"You certainly have a way with police chiefs, Mr. Manning."

We sat at a two-person wrought iron table. "How so?"

"I seem to remember a certain chief up in Door County. Not exactly a drinking buddy."

I really wanted to correct her. Maybe someday I'd be able to tell her the whole story. For now I only agreed and sighed.

"What do you mean, you think it went well?" Rosie asked. "Cuz it didn't sound so good to me."

"Well, in the past when I've stirred a pot something has crawled out."

"You have a plan just in case something crawls out?"

"Yup. Seeing as I just happen to have a plain-clothes Chicago cop with me, who Walters did not see because the troll at the gate wouldn't let her pass, I figured you could follow if he comes out and meet me back at the car."

"Easy enough. And something else. Belva and Walters seem to be cut from the same cloth. I wonder who really runs the office."

"Good point. I was wondering that myself. Any good boss will tell you that the secretary is the one who handles everything."

"What a strange name. Who would name their kid Belva?"

"Maybe someone with a twisted sense of humor, and history."

"Huh?"

I thought for a moment. "I don't remember her last name but back during Prohibition, Chicago had several famous murderesses. One of them was named Belva. She shot her boyfriend in the head."

"Lovely. The good old days."

"For some. Booze and jazz and gangsters. Belva was divorced from a rich society man. I believe it came out during the divorce that she whipped him as part of their love-making."

Rosie just gaped at me. "Bet he was glad to get rid of *her*."

"You would think. But I think *she* divorced *him*. He hired the best lawyers in town when she was arrested and said he'd take her back."

Rosie whistled. "Go figure. From society to jail. What a come down."

"Yes, but the ladies of Murderess Row thrived on it. They vied for the most press. Belva apologized to the reporters and said something like, 'Jails are such horrid places to receive guests.'"

"Chicago, what a place."

"And if I recall correctly, she had a good voice—was in the jail choir."

She looked at me with dismay. "The jail had a choir?"

"Yup."

"Wow. A bunch of murderesses who can sing. They should do a musical."

I laughed. "Yeah, right. Who'd want to go see that? But if I remember correctly, they did do a play many years ago that made it to Broadway."

"You're kidding."

"Nope. I remember Stosh talking about it when I was a kid. I was fascinated. Seems a woman reporter for the Tribune had been covering the ladies on the row, and she wrote a play that made it big."

"What was her name?"

I shook my head. "Stosh is the expert on Chicago crime."

"What did they call it?"

"What do you think?"

She laughed. "Chicago?"

"Yup. Nice publicity."

"And did you notice the jewelry?"

"Hard not to," I said with envy.

"Do you think it's real?"

"It's either real or a very good fake."

A mom went by with a kid whining that he didn't want to go home.

"Seem strange to you?" Rosie asked.

"No, I didn't want to leave when I was a kid either."

"I meant the bracelet, smartass."

I chuckled. "Not exactly the venue for it. Seems like she's trying to make a statement."

"About what?"

With a shrug, I replied, "Beats me. Someone whose ego needs a boost, or a sign of power, or who the hell knows what else." I thought for a few seconds. "Whatever it is, putting diamonds on Belva is like trying to get Cinderella's ugly sisters ready for the ball."

We watched the crowd and listened to the ride noises. Lots of kids were having lots of fun. I knew of at least one kid who wasn't and wondered about Martin.

Twenty minutes later, Chief Walters came out of the office and walked away from where we were sitting. Rosie followed him. I waited until they had disappeared and then headed back to the car. A half hour later, Rosie opened the passenger door.

"I followed Walters to the ball toss booth—the game where you throw at milk bottles. He nodded to a big burly guy running it who didn't respond. But five minutes later the guy left the booth when a kid showed up. He joined Walters, and they talked while they walked. Halfway down the Midway, they split up and the burly guy went back toward the booth. I followed Walters who disappeared into Aladdin's Castle."

"Hmm. What's the burly guy look like?"

"About your height, but a lot more of him, most of it muscle. Gray sweatshirt with the arms cut off. Tattoos on both arms, and a scar on his left cheek. Crewcut. About thirty-five."

I started the car and turned on the air. "Sounds like something that might have crawled out of a barrel." And now I was pretty sure where Martin worked. I shake the trees and Walters goes right to the ball throw booth.

***

I dropped Rosie at home and headed back to the office. I was eager to see how Samantha was doing. I was pleasantly surprised. All of the boxes were empty, and the desk tops were clear. I wondered what she'd do tomorrow.

"So, the phone been ringing off the hook?"

She laughed. "No calls, sorry."

"None?"

She shook her head.

There had been at least one. But maybe she had made the call... maybe to her father.

"How's your father doing? Did you check on him?"

"No. He was fine when I left this morning. I left him lunch, and I'll be home in time for dinner."

So she hadn't called her father, and she didn't know anyone else in town. Little things rouse my curiosity, but I had bigger things to worry about, like a missing kid and why I rub police chiefs the wrong way.

"How was your trip to the park?" she asked as she collected her things.

"Not very helpful, but you've got to start somewhere."

"Too bad. Do you want me to keep a daily journal?"

"No thanks. I tend to keep things in my head."

"Well, if you don't need me…"

"Nope. Have a good night."

"Will you be here in the morning?"

"Don't know. Probably not."

"I finished unpacking. What do you want me to do?"

That was a great question and I told her so.

"Let's just play it by ear. Feel free to bring a book or knitting or whatever you do to pass some time."

She looked puzzled. "I'd feel guilty doing that while you're paying me to work."

"I'm sure you'll handle the work if some pops up. If it doesn't, do whatever you like to do to get through the day."

She shrugged. "Okay. This is the strangest job I've ever had."

"Me too. You get used to it," I said with a smile.

She left by the front door, and I locked it behind her. I called Stosh and invited myself to dinner.

Chapter 6

Stosh was turning the steaks when I pulled in the drive.

"Grab a beer kid, and go see if the corn is done."

We ate on the deck while I told him about my afternoon. The sun was just dipping behind the house, and a light breeze kept mosquitoes away.

"Sounds like Walters has let his ego run away with him," Stosh said between bites. "He always was a pompous blowhard, but he didn't have the title to back it up."

"Well, I'd argue he still doesn't."

Stosh nodded as he picked up the corn. "In his mind, chief of police is chief of police. And he wasn't a bad cop, just a pain in the ass. He had his opinions and didn't mind sharing them. He pushed it too far and was offered a severance rather than a hearing."

"Great. Seems to be enjoying the new job. And he has a secretary who follows his lead on the pain in the ass part."

After adding more butter to his corn, Stosh said, "Rosie tells me you have a secretary. Coming up in the world."

"Yup. Name on the window and everything. Only one problem."

Stosh kept eating and asked a muffled, "Which is?"

"She wants to know what she's supposed to do to fill up eight hours a day. I have no idea."

"Tough being a big shot. What's your plan with the nephew?"

"Well, unless you guys turn up something else, I'm sticking with Riverview." I told him about the chat Walters had with the burly employee.

"I'm going back tomorrow to have a chat with the bottle guy. And I'll ask around about Walters. Something not right there. But now I think I know where the kid worked. I stir things up and Walters heads for the ball throw booth."

Stosh put down the stripped ear of corn. "As I said, he got things done. I'm betting you got the ball rolling, and he was asking all the right questions. Maybe you'll get a call from him."

"I doubt it. He didn't seem too anxious to help."

"No. I imagine not. But he knows he'll get a visit from Missing Persons at some point, and he'd rather we didn't poke into his affairs. So, he's likely to give answers before the questions are asked."

"And what do you think those answers are?"

"Probably that he looked around and came up empty. He's right about the other things that could have happened after the kid left the park."

"You get many missing kids?"

"Yeah. But one is too many."

"How many are found?"

He shrugged. "Some are, some aren't. A lot leave on their own, and some meet with foul play. Do you know what the family situation was like?"

I shrugged and laid my napkin on the table. "Tough, money-wise. Martin's brother died a few years back. I only met them all once, and they seemed like a tight family. Lots of love and respect. I don't think Martin left on his own."

"Well, hopefully he'll show up soon. Let's play some gin."

I cleaned up the dishes while Stosh closed the grill and got out the card table. By ten he had won back half of the twelve bucks he had lost.

Chapter 7

I wanted to have a chat with the bottle guy before the park got crowded so I got there at ten when it opened. Three buses were pulling into the lot as I paid. It was a beautiful early June morning. A skinny kid was setting up bottles when I got to the booth across from the Freak Show. I asked where his boss was.

"He went for money. Be right back." He looked at me curiously. "Don't ya wanna play, mister?"

I shook my head. The odds of winning were with the house. "Nope, just want to chat with your boss. What's his name?"

The kid shrugged.

"You don't know his name?"

"Not his real name." He balanced the last bottle on top of the pyramid. "Everybody calls him Meatstick."

"Meatstick."

The kid nodded.

"Odd name. You know why?"

"I guess it's because he usually has one in his mouth. He won't share, but I took one once. Tasted like pepperoni." He came over to the counter. "You sure you don't want to play, mister? I've never run the game by myself."

The kid looked hopeful—probably would feel like a big shot. I agreed and he set three balls on the counter.

As I picked them up, I asked if he knew Martin Lisk. He didn't.
I asked how long he had worked there.

"Just since yesterday. Meatstick said the last kid quit."

"What's your name, kid?"

"Anthony."

"Nice to meet you, Anthony."

I took aim and knocked down three bottles. The second ball got
two more and the last one missed.

"Sorry, mister. Wanna try again?"

I could spare the quarter but I declined. "I'm just gonna wait for
Meatstick."

"Suit yourself."

The barker at the Freak Show got my attention as a crowd started to gather. He stood on the stage in front of the painted backdrop
along with a lady with snakes in her hair and the tattooed lady. There
wasn't a square inch of bare skin visible. He lured people to the ticket window with promises of even stranger wonders inside.

***

Meatstick showed up ten minutes later carrying a canvas bag.
He had on shiny black pants and a sleeveless gray sweatshirt.
Riverview was a step above a carnival, but most of the employees
had the transient look that went with carny workers. Meatstick was
no different. Short and stocky with tattoos on both arms, he looked
like he would fight first and talk later, or not bother to talk at all. As I
walked back to the booth my pager vibrated with my office number.
I had set up a system with Samantha—the same as with Stosh and
Rosie. If it was an emergency that needed an immediate call, she
would put a 9 after the number. There was no 9.

As I walked back to the booth the kid said, "That's the guy I
was telling you about," and Meatstick shuffled up to the counter.
He didn't say a word—just stared through me with indifference.
Between him and Walters I was hard pressed to decide who was
more annoying. I didn't offer my hand.

"They call you Meatstick?"

He folded his arms on his stocky chest. "You got somethin' to say, say it."

I took a deep breath. "I'm looking for Martin Lisk. I understand he worked here."

"Lots of kids work here, if you call it that. Amazing they get paid."

"So how about Martin Lisk?"

"Doesn't ring a bell. What's it to you?"

"He's missing."

"Too bad. Hey kid… wipe off the counter and straighten the balls."

"So you're telling me you never heard that name?"

"Yup. I got enough trouble here without trying to keep track of damned kids. They go through here like water down that river out back. This ain't the best paying job in the world. Kids find something better to do, and we get a new kid. It's like a revolving door." He nodded to the new kid.

A dad and his son stepped up to the counter, and the kid set three balls down and took his quarter. The man's face was confident, and his son's eyes were wide open.

I turned back to Meatstick. "Do you—?"

"You wanna play, put down a quarter." He turned away.

The father knocked off the top bottle with his first ball and the two end bottles on the left with the second. He got the rest with the third and won a pencil with a rubber monkey stuck on the eraser. The kid didn't look at all happy.

A teenage boy with his girlfriend put down his quarter. Meatstick watched the kid set up the bottles. The barker at the Freak Show was hawking the next show in ten minutes.

I don't know why I did it because I knew what he'd do with it, but I put my card on the counter and asked Meatstick to call if he heard anything about Martin.

He didn't respond.

The teenager got all the bottles in two tries. The girlfriend picked out a small stuffed lion.

Meatstick was less than helpful, but I wasn't surprised. I was betting he wasn't all that well paid either. Why should *he* care?

I found a spot down the Midway where I could sit and watch the bottle booth. I watched for twenty minutes, but Meatstick didn't do anything other than his job. This time nothing fell out of the trees when I shook them.

***

I decided to head back to the office, but first I wanted to walk through Aladdin's Castle. It had been a long time since I dared the bizarre world inside.

I made it through the maze of screen doors with no handles, but it took a while. You didn't know whether they opened from the left or the right, or in or out. I was ready to get out my pocket knife and start cutting some screens. There were no laughs or screams—I was the only one in the place. The next room was full of mirrors that changed your shape to fat or thin or tall or short. I didn't care about that when I was a kid and I still didn't. As I turned the corner at the end of the hall the lights went out. Air jets blew from the sides, and scary faces lit up with ghastly grins. As I bumped into a wall and tried to make out which way to turn, I heard a voice from behind me.

"Don't turn around. I saw you talking to Meatstick. I figure you want to talk to me too."

"Why do you figure that?"

"Meet me at the hot dog stand across from the Bobs in ten minutes."

"How will I know who you are?"

"I'll know who *you* are."

I didn't hear anything except whooshing air. I turned around and only saw a face with a scar from eye to chin lit up in the eerie darkness, reminding me of a recurring dream I'd had when I was a kid. I would wake up in the middle of the night screaming at a grotesque face looking in my window. But my folks never came running, so the scream was part of the dream. When I screamed the face disappeared.

Now I wondered if the dreams had started after a trip through the Fun House. Not so much fun. Then I realized that wasn't the only thing I had seen this time. I'd also seen a very brief, tiny flash of light just before the face had lit up. It was at about the level of my waist.

***

I waited ten minutes at the hot dog stand… then another ten. Not being able to resist the smell of hot dogs, I bought one. Lunch with Samantha would have to wait for another day. I waited forty-five minutes before I gave up and headed back to the office.

I drove down Montrose and passed the office instead of turning early and going back to the alley. I honked at Carol who was just coming out of her building. She waved and smiled.

The water was running behind a closed bathroom door when I walked in. I read a note pinned to the small bulletin board outside my office door—"call Rosie." She didn't answer her phone but a gruff voice said he'd find her.

"Hey, Spencer. Still can't get over a real person answering your phone."

"Yup. If you look up 'big shot' in the dictionary you'll find my picture. How's things, Rosie?"

"Things are busy. Lots of job security. I spent some time this morning going through files on missing persons."

I crumpled up the note and missed the basket with my toss.

"I went back to the beginning of April, a month before Riverview opened. There are thirty-two cases, and six of those are kids under the age of twenty, including Martin."

"Interesting. Thanks."

"There's more. Of those six, five were after May first when the park opened and four of those worked at Riverview."

I paused to let that sink in. "Seems like a coincidence."

"And you don't believe in coincidences."

"Right."

Samantha came out of the bathroom and waved as she went by.

"So?" Rosie asked.

"So time to ask more questions. I assume Missing Persons looked into this already. Nobody was concerned about the Riverview connection?"

"No one saw it. Probably different people working the cases, and if you weren't looking for it, Riverview was just the place on the job line."

"Yeah, probably. You mention it to anyone?"

"Yes. They're going to look into it again."

"Any of those kids ever found?"

"No. Still missing. Who are you going to ask questions of? Your buddy Walters?"

I laughed. "Not right now. I think we both know how much I'd get from him. I'll find someone else."

"Good luck."

"Thanks. Dinner?"

"Sure. Pick me up at seven."

***

I walked into the front office and asked Samantha how the day was going. She tried hard to sound productive but there really wasn't anything to do. She apologized.

I gave her a reassuring smile. "Don't worry about it, I'm not expecting you to invent work. I'm hoping things will pick up over time. As long as you take care of whatever comes in, I'm happy. Looks good to have someone sitting in the office."

She didn't look too reassured. "I just can't believe you're paying me for doing nothing."

"Hey, my dad once told me if someone wants to give you money and it isn't illegal, take it. It really does help to have the door open and a person at the desk. Just don't complain when you're swamped."

She laughed and assured me she wouldn't.

"Did you get your phone hooked up yet?"

"No, I need to get that done."

"Give me your number when you get it."

She assured me she would.

"I do have something for you to do. Call Riverview and find out who the owner is and get a phone number and an address. I'd like to pay him a visit."

She looked excited. "Right away, Mr. Manning."

She came into my office five minutes later with a slip of paper. Charles Block was written on it in neat script with a phone number and an address downtown.

"Thanks, Samantha."

"Anything else?" she asked hopefully.

I shook my head. "Sorry. But you'll be the first to know when there is."

***

Charles Block had an office on the third floor of a building on the west side of Michigan Avenue in the high rent district. Riverview Enterprises was stenciled on the glass door. After telling the receptionist I didn't have an appointment, I explained who I was and asked if he could spare a few minutes.

After a blank stare, she said she'd check. I sat and studied the photographs of Riverview on the walls, some dating back into the teens. Ten minutes later, her phone buzzed and a deep voice said he would see me. She held the door open. Block was seated at a large desk with a giant aerial photo of the park on the wall behind him. One of the windows facing Michigan Avenue was open, and the sounds of Moody Blues drifted up from somewhere on the street: *Tuesday Afternoon*. Two days late.

Charles Block stood up behind the desk and offered his hand. "Please have a seat, Mr. Manning. How can I help you?"

"Maybe not at all. But I'd like to make you aware of something." I told him about the kids.

He obviously felt badly.

"And I want you to know I didn't get such a warm reception at your park," I said.

He looked concerned. "We try to be a customer-friendly place. Who did you talk to?"

I explained and he laughed.

"I should have guessed." He offered a cigar. I took it. "Chief Walters is very protective of the park. Doesn't think he needs outside help, and I have to say, since I hired him, he's handled things nicely without any."

"When did you hire him?"

"It's been a couple years. My secretary can get the exact date if you need it."

"Not at the moment." I put the cigar in my pocket and wondered what methods Walters used to get things handled so nicely. "Maybe he hasn't had a situation where he's needed any help."

He lit his cigar, took a few puffs and placed it in a large crystal ashtray. "Perhaps. And maybe that's because of him. We really didn't have a qualified person there before Walters. I felt we needed to be more official… you know, stop trouble before it gets started. So I felt we needed someone with police experience. Are the police involved in this?"

"Each case was investigated with no result."

"I see. Well, I hope the kids are found to be okay."

"Me too."

He folded his arms across his chest. He was done with me.

But I wasn't done with *him*. "May I ask a question?"

"Please."

"I'd like to find out where in the park Martin worked. Who would have that information?"

Pushing a button on his intercom, he said, "Miss Randel, would you come in, please?"

As soon as the door opened, Block asked her who was in charge of personnel at the park.

She glanced briefly at me and said, to him, "That would be Mrs. Meyers."

"Thank you, Miss Randel."

She left before I could ask where I would find Mrs. Meyers. So I asked Block.

He shrugged. "I have little to do with the running of the park, Mr. Manning. If things run smoothly, I don't hear about it. You could ask Miss Randel."

I nodded and gave him my card. "Please call if you hear anything."

"I will save your card, but I think it best that everything be handled by my Chief of Police. That's why I pay him."

"Understood. By the way, I'm wondering how a Block got to be sitting in that chair, seeing as how the founders were Schmidts."

"No male heirs who wanted to run the place. My mother was George's daughter."

"I see. Thanks for seeing me, Mr. Block."

"No problem, Mr. Manning."

I closed the door behind me and stopped at Randel's desk. I had to clear my throat before she looked up with a blank look. I must have left my charm at the office.

"Do you have a first name?" I asked.

"Yes." She went back to doing whatever it was she was doing.

I asked my question.

In a very business-like tone, she told me to go to the personnel department at the park. I thanked her and gave her my best smile.

As I opened the outer door, I paused and asked another question that suddenly popped into my head. "Does Mrs. Meyers do the hiring at the park?"

My smile was wasted because she didn't even look up.

"Yes. That's what someone in personnel does."

"And what is Mrs. Meyers' first name?"

"Belva."

My smile was gone before the door closed behind me. Evidently I had been ten steps from the personnel department and the answer to the question Walters didn't know the answer to.

Chapter 8

Martin woke up and found a wooden tray with a plate of food on the table next to the bed. He had no idea where he was or how long he had been there or whether it was day or night. His watch was gone, and all he had on was his underwear. He felt lightheaded, and when he reached out to pull off the covers it looked like his arm was moving in slow motion. His right arm hurt, and he noticed a tiny red mark on the inside just below his elbow.

After what seemed like a very long time, he found himself sitting at the table with the tray in front of him. The food didn't look appetizing, but he was hungry. Some sort of meat, corn, and mashed potatoes covered the plastic plate. It was all cold.

As he ate, he looked around the room; it was smaller than his bedroom. The bed and table were the only furniture in the room, which had bare white walls and two boarded up windows, and he could see the front of a toilet through the door in the corner. There was another door, this one closed, at the other end of the wall. As he ate, he drank water from a plastic glass on the tray. It tasted a little strange, but he was thirsty and drank it all. As he mixed the corn in with the potatoes, he realized he was watching himself eat from the other side of the table and thought that was great fun.

When he was done eating, Martin walked to the closed door and turned the knob. It was locked. He went to the bathroom and then laid down on the floor next to the bed and fell asleep.

When Martin woke up he found a new tray on the table. This one had a plate with eggs and toast. He remembered dreaming about someone walking around in the room. It was a woman with a hood dressed all in black. She had a stern-looking face and wrinkled hands. He thought it strange that he remembered his dream—he never had before. He got up to eat, this time with more assurance than before. As he reached out for the chair, he noticed another red mark on his arm.

Chapter 9

I picked up Rosie at seven and headed for McGoon's. I figured it was time I had a chat with her. She looked lovely in black slacks, a white blouse, and a loose yellow sweater. We both ordered chicken boxtys and Harp beer.

"Anything on the kids, Rosie?"

"There's somebody on it. Not much to go on. If they find something that points to Riverview, I'll be assigned to it."

"You and Steele?"

"Nope. Just me. Remember what I told you about Steele's missing son?"

"Yup. Never found. Don't know how you live with that."

"Me either. Probably not well, which leads to him not being assigned to a missing kid case."

I nodded and sipped the beer. "The whole thing is pretty damned sad."

"What's your plan?" she asked.

"I called two friends where Martin sometimes stayed if he worked late. Neither has seen him in a week, but one told me Martin worked at the baseball throw game with the milk bottles."

"Well, that's a start."

"And a red flag."

"Red flag?"

I told her about my chat with Meatstick, who said he didn't know Martin.

"Maybe not so strange, Spencer. Those guys don't exactly make friends with the workers. And it *is* a revolving door. It's a high-end carnival, but a carnival none-the-less."

"I suppose. But the guy is creepy."

She laughed. "They all are."

"I'm also going to check with the late-night bus driver and see if he remembers anything. I'm hoping you'll give me a hand."

"How so?"

"Well, I'd like to go tonight, and I'm thinking the driver isn't going to pull over to the curb and chat, so someone to drive the car and follow the bus would save me a walk."

"You'd trust me with the Mustang?"

"Yes, for a few blocks. And don't lose the damn bus."

"Sure. How would I lose a bus?"

"Overwhelmed and distracted at the pleasure of driving a real car."

"I'll give it my best. So you're hoping the driver is the same driver and remembers Martin."

"Yeah. The only other plan is to just nose around the park and stick my nose in where it isn't wanted. Martin is the most recent to disappear, so I'll concentrate on him and see what else I run into." I told her about the no-show at the hot dog stand.

She took a long drink.

"Be careful," she said with a slight smile. "I have a feeling Walters isn't on your side."

"No wonder you're a detective. Does appear that way, but appearances can be deceiving."

The food was as good as usual, and the beer was cold. What more could a guy want?

We finished eating and headed for the park. I had checked the bus schedule and found there were buses at the stop just outside the park at ten-thirty and eleven-twenty-five. The kid would've had plenty of time to catch the ten-thirty. We got there at ten-fifteen, switched places in the car, and waited. The bus was a minute early. I got on and paid. Four kids and three adults got on with me.

It didn't take long—the driver didn't have much to say. He was the driver on Monday night, but he laughed when I asked him if he remembered the kid, even with my excellent description.

"You have any idea how many people get on this bus, mister?"

"Sure. Just a shot in the dark. Have to be able to say I turned over all the rocks." I was quiet for two lights before I tried something else.

"There's another kid. Mind if I give you another description?"

"Nope. It's your fare."

"About five-foot-four, hundred and twenty pounds, pimply face, wearing a red jacket and a Sox cap."

The driver thought hard for about ten seconds before shaking his head. "Nope, doesn't ring a bell… sorry."

"That's okay, thanks for your time." It was a good test of his awareness of his passengers. The kid I had just described had gotten on with me and was sitting three rows back.

I got off the bus at Diversey and walked back to my Mustang. The baby-blue had a yellowish hue from the street lamps. I didn't like the effect.

As we drove, Rosie said, "Maybe he got off the bus."

I shook my head. "I asked his mother if there may have been somewhere else he went. She assured me there wasn't. He always came straight home."

"You never know, Spencer. Even the best of kids don't always do what they're supposed to do."

"I guess. But if he got off that bus the possibilities are endless. I'm sticking with Riverview. And the way Meatstick and Walters are acting, I think I'm right."

I drove to the lake where we took our shoes off and walked in the sand. I wanted to take Rosie's hand, but didn't. We found a flat slab of limestone and sat and watched a red moon rise out of the lake. After a few minutes, she moved close to me, and I put my arm around her shoulders.

"Rosie, I…"

"No need, Spencer. Just enjoy the evening."

I turned toward her and smiled. "I am. I like being with you. I've missed that."

She just looked at me with confusion. "If you have…"

I touched my finger to her lips.

"Remember last year… the night we discovered the diamonds?" I asked. "Stosh suggested I should ask someone up to the cottage and spend some time. He meant you."

"You didn't ask."

"No, I didn't. And he said if I didn't ask I should tell you why."

She was quiet and apprehensive.

I took a deep breath and took her hand, but I couldn't get the words out.

"Don't worry about it, Spencer."

"No, I want to tell you. Would you mind if we went back to your place?"

"Not at all."

We slid down off the rock and walked back to the car. It was a short drive to her apartment. She asked if I wanted anything to drink. I declined.

We sat on the couch. She had her legs tucked under her.

"I had a twin sister—Margaret," I said.

"You did? How come I never knew?"

"Well… we were both born with a congenital heart problem. It's got a long name, but basically there's a problem with the left side of my heart—the side that pumps blood to the body. Something wrong with the walls."

Both of us were silent for a few minutes.

"You *had* a sister?"

I let out a big sigh. "Margaret died when we were three."

She reached out and took my hand. "I'm so sorry, Spencer. They couldn't help her?"

"They can't help anyone. Almost all babies who are born with it die in the first year. Margaret was very lucky to make it to three."

"So you don't have the problem?"

I just stared out the window at the half moon. "I do."

Her jaw dropped, and she just looked at me with wide eyes. "Spencer! Why didn't you ever tell me?"

I shook my head. "I haven't told anyone. I don't want people feeling sorry for me or treating me differently. The only one who knows is Stosh."

She still looked shocked. "But you're almost thirty."

I nodded. "Yes. Margaret was in a very small percentage that live past the first year. I'm off the charts."

"Do you see a doctor?"

"I go every year for regular checkups, but there's nothing they can do about my heart. I'll just drop dead one day. I wake up every morning surprised."

"Pardon my asking, but does this have anything to do with your willingness to walk into dark alleys without fear?"

I laughed. "I've thought about that. Maybe subconsciously, but I think more to do with my lack of common sense when adrenalin kicks in."

She smiled.

I turned to her and put my hand on her knee. "But it does have a lot to do with my relationship choices."

"How so?"

"It wouldn't be fair to anyone to be in a relationship that could end any day."

She crossed her legs and leaned back on the couch. "There's another way of looking at that."

"Which is?"

"Which is, it's not fair to love someone and not be able to be with them, even for just a day."

I was staring out the window when a cloud drifted slowly across the moon. "You'd be willing to take that chance?"

She let go of my hand. "I would have been, if it was for you."

I thought for a bit. "Would have been?"

Running her hand through her hair, she said, "I've loved you for a very long time, and I've hoped all these years that you loved me too. We've had such great times but you never said anything."

"I was afraid to… It wouldn't have been fair…"

"I know. You told me. But you never gave me the chance to decide that for myself. Still, I kept hoping. And then there was that night last year when we went back to my place after looking for your pretend hooker."

I turned toward her. "Yes, that was wonderful."

She nodded. "It was. And I expected more." She shrugged. "When more didn't come, I started letting go of my hope."

"But you never told me how you felt."

"No, you're right. I guess I hoped you would figure it out."

I didn't know how to tell her how sad I felt.

She continued. "So I didn't tell you about loving you, and you didn't tell me about your heart."

"I'm sorry, Rosie. I was just trying to take care of you."

"I wish you hadn't, Spencer. I really do. I can take pretty good care of myself."

I reached out and touched her hand. "Are you saying all hope is gone?"

She slowly shook her head. "I'm not sure. I cherish our friendship, but the rest… I just don't know."

I felt empty. "That's sad."

"It is, in so many ways."

"What do you mean?"

"Well, this is sad. But I've also been sad when I went home alone, wondering why you didn't want me."

"But I did. I…"

"I know. I get it." She took a deep breath. "I had hope for a long time. The saddest part was when I realized I was letting go of the hope a little with every day that went by."

She just looked at me with tears in her eyes. Silence rolled into the room like fog on a beach, sudden and ominous. I remembered thinking I had nothing when I struck out with the bus driver. I was wrong—I had plenty compared to the nothing I had now.

I thought I should leave but I felt glued to the couch. I wondered if there was any hope left at all and asked again.

"I can't give you an answer, Spencer... other than to take some time. I'd like to see how I feel tomorrow, and the next day."

I nodded, knowing that was the best I deserved. I didn't want to leave.

"We could talk for a while, but not about this," she said with resignation.

I took whatever she offered. The night turned into morning and somewhere among the sentences she fell asleep. Eventually I did too, but not before I had spent hours just looking at her.

Chapter 10

The phone woke us up to a room filled with light. Reaching across the arm of the couch, Rosie answered and pressed the speaker button.

"Morning Rosie, Stosh."

"Good morning, Lieutenant. I've got you on speaker." She looked at me.

"Trying to find Spencer. He doesn't answer at home or his pager. You have any idea where he is?"

As I looked to the end table for my pager, I remembered I had left it in the kitchen.

"I do," she answered.

"This ain't twenty questions. Where is he?"

"That's a little personal, sir."

Stosh wasn't often silent, but he was now.

"Did he tell you about…?"

"He did. Doesn't matter."

"Didn't think it would. Can you put him on?"

She pulled the phone down onto the couch. "If you don't mind the speaker, go ahead."

"Hey, kid. Time to get up."

"Okay," I said with very little energy. "That wasn't in the plans yet."

"Change your plans. The early work crew found a body floating in the Tunnel of Love."

"Who?" I hoped it wasn't Martin.

"Don't know."

"A kid?"

"Nope, adult male."

I let out a sigh of relief. "Thanks, Stosh, I'll run over there."

"Okay... stay away from Walters."

"I'll try."

"Right. And Spencer—about time." He hung up. I knew he was smiling, but I also knew he didn't know there were two meanings to Rosie's *doesn't matter*. Those two words had just become the saddest in the English language.

"Rosie, I..."

"There aren't any words, Spencer. Go do your job. You're the best at it, and I'm very proud of you. And we'll always be friends, no matter what."

I could only nod.

"Do you want some breakfast?"

"No, thanks. I'd better just go. Thanks for letting me stay."

"Sure. Good luck with Martin. And I'll repeat the lieutenant's advice—stay away from Walters." She smiled.

I tried to return the smile, but couldn't.

***

The Tunnel of Love had become my ride of choice after discovering girls. It was a water ride with a decorated boat winding in a flume through a park and a tunnel where a kiss was guaranteed. The park had a good record as far as accidents but, as I remembered, one of the accidents resulted in the death of a worker who fell into the flume and was run over by a boat. Maybe this was another accident. Maybe not.

I showed my ID card at the gate and followed the commotion to the ride. Several officers were chatting with employees, and Detective Steele stood just outside the entrance to the tunnel.

"Hey, Steele."

"Manning."

"Got anything?"

"Not yet. Just a dead body."

"Got a name?"

"Benny Parker. Park employee."

I told him about the man who hadn't shown up yesterday. Unfortunately, I had no way of knowing if it was the same guy. I'd recognize the voice but this guy was done talking.

He turned to say something I couldn't hear to the officer guarding the boat.

"Could it have been an accident?" I asked.

"May have. Head bashed in and what looks like hair and skin on the bow of the boat. We'll know more after the coroner's report."

He didn't offer to let me know, and I didn't ask. We both knew Stosh would fill me in.

"Have you talked to Walters?"

"He's been called but he's not here yet. The Riverview Police Force is only here during park hours."

"Do you know him?"

He lit a partially smoked cigar he pulled from his pocket. "Haven't had the pleasure. But I know *of* him."

"Had a chat with him yesterday. He was less than helpful."

"Fits what I know."

I told him I was going to take a walk and would stop back. He just nodded.

***

I heard a curt "Excuse me, sir" from behind and turned to see a man a bit shorter than me in a tan uniform that didn't quite fit. A badge pinned to his left shirt pocket had "Riverview Police" and "Sergeant" stamped on it. It looked like a prize from a Cracker Jack box. The handcuffs clipped to his belt didn't look real either, but the gun on his right hip did. There was a nametag over his right pocket—"Mooney."

"The park isn't open yet. What are you doing here?" Mooney asked me.

"I'm with the police."

"You have ID?"

I sighed. Sometimes they didn't ask. And with all the police around I would have thought this guy wouldn't have either. I smiled my best smile and tried to win him over.

"Well, I'm not officially with them, just kind of helping."

He folded his arms across his chest.

This guy didn't look like he'd make decisions all by himself, and I knew Walters wasn't there yet but would be soon.

"How about we walk back to the Tunnel of Love and check with the detective," I suggested.

He nodded in that direction and I led the way.

As we approached the crowd I noticed Walters talking with Steele.

"Tell you what," I said as friendly as I could manage. "Looks like everyone is busy. I'll just check back in later."

"And I'll just see you to the gate," said my escort. He didn't even try to be friendly.

I found Steele's car and waited. An hour later he showed up with a smirk on his face when he saw me.

"You must be pretty important, PI. Not everybody gets an escort out of the park."

"Funny." I moved away from the car. "Walters and I aren't exactly best friends."

"Well, don't feel bad. He's not the friendly type. Hop in, we'll chat."

He started the car, checked in, and turned on the air.

"So, missing kids," I said. "I start asking questions and somebody ends up dead."

"People end up dead even when you *don't* ask questions."

"Yup. Maybe nothing, but maybe something."

"What?"

"Don't know. I'll ask some more questions. I'll start with you. Whadda ya got?"

He lit a half-smoked cigar and rolled the window down halfway.

"From what I've heard, not much. Missing Persons is looking into the Riverview connection."

I was getting more cigar smoke than I wanted, and Steele had no info I could use.

"I'm going to take a walk through the park," I said.

"I thought you were invited out."

"Yeah, but in ten minutes a coupla bucks gets me back in. See ya."

He waggled his cigar.

***

The park was clean and quiet. It had a certain feel that it didn't have when it was full of people—more like walking through a forest. Behind the piped-in band music, I could hear birds chirping, patiently waiting for the feast that would soon fall to the ground. Employees in the booths and at the rides ignored me. I watched them getting ready for the day as I walked slowly by. None of them looked happy. But my memories were of energetic barkers with big grins, luring me into whatever magic hid behind the wall. Everything here was a show—nothing was as it seemed.

As I watched the people, I thought about Dad's warning to stay close. Riverview wasn't as bad as the carnivals that moved through town because a lot of the employees here came back from year to year. For what it was, it was a good job. But this wasn't an easy life. And that started me thinking about the four kids who were missing and perhaps hadn't had dads to give them that warning.

I remembered those glorious days fifteen years ago as I walked past the Bobs and the Parachute Drop and the Tilt-a-Whirl. I thought I was walking aimlessly, but I ended up standing in front of a sign that read, "Wonderland – Come in and See What Alice Saw."

I learned to read by listening to Dad and Mom read to me and following along. While Dad read Dashiell Hammett and Rex Stout, Mom stuck with the classics. And one of my favorites was *Alice in Wonderland*, the magical world where nothing made any sense. She read my favorite parts over and over, and then one night said she had a new story. I was disappointed, but not for long. It was another Alice book, *Alice Through the Looking Glass, and What She Saw There*, where I met Humpty Dumpty and the rest of Lewis Carroll's wonderful characters. I was fascinated by Humpty Dumpty, the egg-shaped creature who fell off the wall and couldn't be put back together again. That made no sense to me—you'd never be able to piece an egg back together. That they would even try seemed ludicrous to me. And I never understood how the King's horses could be helpful.

A light rain started to fall as I stood outside the entrance to Wonderland. Little puffs of steam rose as the cool drops hit the blacktop.

"Come in out of the rain, mister. All it takes is a quarter."

It took me a second to pick the voice out of the background of characters painted on the wall. A man wearing a jester costume, with a large bulbous nose and droopy jowls was standing next to a painting of the Red Queen. The Cheshire Cat grinned just above his head. That cat had given me nightmares when I was a kid—something devilish about that grin.

I paid my quarter and entered through the looking glass door.

I usually find that the things I remember from childhood are different when I see them again. But Wonderland hadn't changed. Humpty Dumpty still sat on the wall, slowly twirling his legs in circles. He was just a giant egg, no taller than four feet. When I was a kid, I had decided there must be one of the midgets from the freak show inside the egg. There was the rabbit and the Red and White Queens having a tea party. I was still mesmerized by the Red Queen's bulging green eyes. A giant frog dressed in a bright-yellow sleeveless jacket and huge boots stood next to the giant chessboard.

All of a sudden there was a commotion, and I remembered what came next. I was the only one in the building, but even one person deserved a show. As Humpty started to flail his arms and wobble, the rest of the characters rushed over to him to help, but he fell backwards off the wall as the Red Queen recited the poem.

Dad fed me the real world with crime and murder, and Mom let me escape through the looking glass where everything was a mystery. I always thought Carroll was wonderfully crazy, but there was method to his madness. At some point Mom had pointed out that the poem at the end of the story held the real name of Alice, the person Lewis Carroll used for his stories. The first letter of each line spelled her name—Alice Pleasance Liddell.

When I got back outside, the rain was falling harder, and I stood under a canopy with the jester who was now smoking a cigarette. The Midway was empty. He nodded at me when I walked over to him.

"So what brings a grown man to Wonderland?" he asked.

"Just reliving some old memories. It hasn't changed in fifteen years."

He tossed the cigarette to the ground and stepped on it. "Nope. The book doesn't change so Wonderland can't either."

That was more wisdom than I expected from a carnival worker. I'd have to change my stereotype.

"Mind if I ask you a few questions?" I asked.

He lit another cigarette. "Not if I can ask you one first."

"Deal."

"Did you find your memories?"

I smiled. "I did. Just like I never left."

He nodded, and a look in his eyes said he had a few memories too. "I hope it rains all day."

"And why would that be?"

"Cuz they close the joint early if the crowds are thin. Round about dinner time I start tasting a cold beer."

The rain had turned back to a drizzle, and a man with a clipboard passed us as he walked down the middle of the Midway.

"My name's Spencer."

"Harvey. I'd shake your hand, but..." He reached out with a hand in a multi-colored glove with fancy sparkly attachments on the ends of the fingers.

"Not a problem, Harvey. Beats a white rabbit outfit."

He looked confused. "Pardon?"

"Harvey, the white rabbit?"

He still looked confused.

"Never mind. How long have you worked here?"

"Must be about eight years. I started on the cleanup crew."

"You like it?"

"It's a job. I've had worse."

"They treat you well?"

"For what it is… yup. No travel, steady pay, and this sure ain't hard work. Why do you ask? I gotta figure you don't care all that much about *me*."

"Well, that's not true, but I'm working too. Private investigator."

I didn't get the reaction I expected.

"Now there's a real interesting job." He turned and looked at me closer than he had. "You don't look old enough to be a private investigator."

I laughed. "Well, ya gotta start somewhere."

"What brings you here? You working on the missing kid?"

That stopped me cold for a few seconds. "You know about that?"

"Sure, we all do. The cops sent out the word that a kid was missing and told us that we should come across with information if we knew anything."

"Interesting." I hadn't expected any help from Walters.

"This might be more interesting. Also said not to talk to anybody about it but Walters."

That made more sense. "And yet here you are talking to me."

He looked disgusted. "Not a fan of Walters. I do my job, but I'm not going out of my way to help him. So what's with the kid?"

I told him about Martin. "Ring any bells?"

He shook his head. "Nope, sorry. That's on the other side of the park. We don't get around much."

"You have any kids working in your area?"

"Sure. They work all over. But I don't really know anybody here."

Changing the subject, I asked, "Does Humpty Dumpty ever get hurt when he falls off that wall?"

"Hah! Looks can be deceiving. There's a mattress behind the wall. He might bounce a little."

I smiled at the thought of Humpty bouncing. "Who plays Humpty? Pretty small egg."

Harvey shrugged. "Probably one of the midgets from the Freak Show."

"You've never seen them?"

Before he could answer, the goon who had thrown me out of the park came around the corner of Wonderland. He glared at Harvey and turned to me.

"Thought I made it clear you weren't wanted around here."

"What you want or don't want doesn't much concern me."

Harvey stifled a laugh and got another glare.

"How about what Chief Walters wants?"

"Same answer. My money is just as good as the next guy's."

"We'll see." Mooney turned and walked quickly away.

Watching Mooney, Harvey said, "You got a lotta nerve, Spencer. People around here don't mess with Walters."

"I'm not from around here." I stuck my hand out from under the canopy. The rain had stopped. "Did you know Benny Parker?"

He pushed the jester hat back on his head. "Not much more than I know the rest around here."

"But a little more?"

He shrugged. "We chatted more than others, but people here don't get to really know each other. It's just a job. Poor guy. Accidents happen, but I feel pretty safe in Wonderland. No moving parts."

I laughed. "Many accidents happen around here?"

He shook his head. "Nope, hardly any. They do a real good job. Each ride is inspected and run every morning. And at the start of the season Mr. Block rides each ride himself. That's one reason people like working here."

I watched a roller coaster with only one person in the front car pull up the first grade. "So, maybe not an accident."

"What?"

"Benny."

His brow furrowed. "Why would you say that?"

I told him about the voice in the castle.

"You think that was Benny?"

"No clue. Maybe. But I don't like coincidences."

"But accidents do happen, no matter how careful you are."

"They do." I started to put out my hand again and stopped. We both laughed.

"Watch out for Walters," he said.

"You too. He probably won't be happy you were talking to me. I hope it doesn't affect your job."

"Hey, how many grown men you think they can get to put on this outfit?"

"Point taken. Thanks for the chat, Harvey."

"No, thank *you*. Nice to have an adult to talk with."

I gave him a two-finger salute and walked farther into the park. The Midway wound past the Parachute Drop and Kiddieland, where it paralleled the train tracks and turned along the river. As I passed the police shack, I thought of stopping in but decided not to. I'd just wait and see what effect my pot-stirring would have. I could always stir some more. The sky was overcast, which would hold the temperature down, but the rain made the humidity pretty unbearable.

As I walked, I thought about Martin. He was a good kid who had just wanted a job, and what a great place to work. But the great place had turned to sadness. Maybe the great place wasn't so great. Just like Wonderland, maybe things weren't as they seemed. And maybe they were.

I had a couple of other things to try in my search for Martin, but my gut told me I was in the right place.

Chapter 11

I stopped to get a hot dog on the way back to the office. I got two in case Samantha wanted one. I had no idea if she liked hot dogs, but if she didn't I'd do the right thing and not let it go to waste. When I came in the back door I thought I heard sobbing. Samantha was dabbing her eyes with a Kleenex. Seeing me, she tucked it in her sleeve and reached for a phone note.

"Hello, Mr. Manning," she said with some hesitation. "Detective Steele called—he wants you to call back. And Johnny dropped off this envelope."

"Thanks, Samantha. Something wrong?"

"Oh, nothing I want to worry you with."

I sat on the edge of the desk. "I'm pretty low on worries. Try me."

She sniffed and pulled out the Kleenex. "I think my father is missing."

"Think?"

"Well, back in Atlanta, he'd go off with friends for a few days and not tell me. I got used to it. But he started to have trouble with his memory, and I had him move in with me so I could be with him. When I decided to come to Chicago I had to bring him with me. He wouldn't be safe by himself."

"Have you considered a retirement home?"

She shook her head quickly. "He'd never agree to that, and his memory's really not that bad."

"Okay. So he's either missing or he's not."

"I guess he is. He wasn't there when I got home yesterday, and he didn't come home last night. And he doesn't have any friends here."

"Did you call the police?"

"No. I did when he left in Atlanta. They said one day wasn't enough for them to get involved."

I agreed. "Maybe he hooked up with one of your friends."

"I don't know anyone here either."

I gave her my best understanding look. "I'm sure he'll show up. Probably be there when you get home."

"I hope you're right."

I slid off the desk.

"But what if you're not?"

"Then I'll look into it. And if he isn't home tonight I'll have a chat with my police friends."

She forced a smile. "Thanks, Mr. Manning. I'd appreciate it."

"Sure. And I'd feel better if you'd call me Spencer."

She nodded.

I seemed to have started a missing persons department. I got a Coke out of the fridge before calling Steele and drank half of it trying not to think about Rosie. I wasn't successful. I was usually pretty sure of myself, but I didn't even know what to think. I didn't like not being in control; it was such a helpless feeling, like being on a ship abeam of the pounding waves.

***

Steele answered on the first ring.

"Hey Steele, Spencer. You called?"

"Yeah. The lieutenant figured that as long as I had the dead guy I should look into the missing kids. You got anything on that?"

I wondered about that decision, given Steele's son who had disappeared, but he didn't seem upset.

"Rosie with you?"

"Nope. Pitcher is on this shift."

"I've asked some questions. But no—nothing. I'm just interested in Martin, but it might be easier to find four instead of one."

"Maybe. I'll go have a chat with Walters tomorrow."

"Hope you have better luck than I did."

"Well, I've got that shiny thing in my pocket. Tends to make people listen."

"Or pretend to. You have anything more on Benny?"

"Nope. Check in the morning."

The phone rang as soon as I hung up. I reached for it and then remembered I had a secretary. I heard her say whoever it was had the wrong number. At the moment I had enough business. But maybe it was wrong to think of it as business—neither case was going to make me any money. Thank goodness for trust funds.

I told Samantha she could have the rest of the day off to go home and check on her father. She seemed relieved.

"I'll be here till six or so. Call me and let me know if he shows up or not."

"Thanks, Spencer." She gave me her phone number.

I gave her my fatherly nod and walked her to the door.

My desk was too neat, the office was too quiet, nobody was honking their horn, and missing kids were hoping someone would find them. So far, that wasn't me.

I opened the envelope and pulled out a photo of Martin. I locked up and walked two blocks to a print shop where I ordered fifty posters: "Missing Boy, If you have any information, call the Chicago Police."

I spent the next few hours moving files around, trying to make some sense out of a file system that didn't exist. Just as I was ready to turn off the lights the phone rang. It was Samantha.

I listened to her sobbing for a minute. There was still no sign of her father. I told her I'd be over in a half hour. I left after calling Stosh to tell him something had come up, I'd be there whenever I got there, and to eat without me.

***

S amantha lived in a three-story apartment building in Evanston, just north of the Chicago border. Parking was no better than in Chicago, and I had to walk almost a block to get to her building. But it was a warm evening, and I needed the exercise.

Samantha buzzed open the door and met me at the top of the stairs. Her eyes were puffy, and she had made no effort to fix her makeup.

"Thanks for coming, Spencer. I don't know what to do."

It was a one-bedroom apartment with a kitchen built into one wall of the living room.

We sat on a beige couch that had a sheet and blanket draped over the back. She told me that was where she slept. As her lower lip quivered, she offered something to drink. I shook my head and asked when she had last seen her father.

She took a deep breath. "Well, yesterday morning when I left for work. When I got home he was gone."

I jotted down his name, Samuel George. I was willing to bet he wanted a boy to name after himself but got a Samantha. I asked for a picture. Samantha looked a little embarrassed when she said she didn't have one. I told her a description would have to do. What she gave me would have fit about any seventy-year-old man. I looked around the apartment—the walls were barren. I wondered how a place could be so empty of anything that showed someone lived there. I made a few notes and thought about the possibilities. I didn't like any of them. Her father was seventy-two years old, and there were no scenarios that would be okay. If I disappeared for a few days no one would worry. But Samuel was dependent on his daughter, who said he didn't have any money or friends in Chicago.

"Did he take his wallet?"

She nodded.

"Any unique features?"

"Like what?"

I shrugged. "Like scars, moles, one leg shorter than the other."

She smiled briefly and shook her head.

"How about teeth?"

She looked confused. "What do you mean?"

"Does he have a gold tooth or missing teeth or a lot of fillings?"

"Well, there are no gold teeth and none missing, but beyond that I just don't know. We had been separated for a while. I know he hasn't been to a dentist in the last couple of years."

I nodded. "Nothing that would distinguish him from the rest of the crowd?"

"Well, he does have a ring that I gave him."

"Tell me about it." I didn't tell her that the ring would be more helpful if we had to identify a corpse.

"It's a Masonic ring. I gave it to him twenty years ago. He wears it on his right hand, next to the pinkie finger."

She told me about the ring, especially an inscription that said "To Dad, Love Sam."

"Mind if I take a look in the bedroom?"

She shrugged. I took that for a no.

There was a bed with a worn yellow blanket and two pillows, a three-drawer dresser, and a cracked mirror on the wall. That was it. I felt even more lonely than I had all day.

After telling Samantha I'd get back to her in the morning, I gave her a hug and tried to offer some hope, but I didn't feel very hopeful.

Chapter 12

Stosh was sitting on the porch when I pulled into his drive. He lived on a quiet street on the north side. The sun had set, and a cool breeze made for a nice night to sit outside.

He nodded at me and said, "Apple pie in the kitchen." There was an empty plate on the wooden table between the two rocking chairs.

When I returned, he glanced at the plate and then stared at me.

"Two pieces?"

"No dinner."

"Yeah, the hectic life of a famous PI with his own secretary."

Someone driving by honked. Stosh waved.

"So what kept you from a steak dinner?"

"My secretary." I took a bite of pie.

"My my. Somehow I had assumed your relationship with Rosie had changed."

"It has." But I didn't want to talk about it, and I didn't want a lecture. "My secretary's father is missing."

He looked at me with a raised eyebrow. "Another one? Trying to take over my department?"

I stretched out my legs, put my feet up on the railing, and didn't respond.

"So, the kid of a friend's sister and your secretary's father. Good thing you're not doing this to pay the bills."

"Agreed."

"What's with the father?"

I filled him in on the details, and he shook his head. "You hear about older people having trouble. She's taking on a lot to try and take care of him given the history. Sad."

"Yes, it is. She has no one to turn to here."

"No friends or relatives?"

"Evidently not."

"Why did she move up here?"

"I asked her that but we got interrupted, and I never got an answer."

"Might help to get one."

"Can't imagine why, but if it ever comes up again…"

"Information is always a good thing, Spencer. You never know when you'll find the key to the puzzle. Maybe they were running away from something."

"And maybe he wanted to see the Cubs play."

"Yeah, that's it." He gave me a disgusted look. "Anything on the kid?"

"Nope. I'm going to look at a few other possibilities and pass out posters with Martin's picture. But I gotta think the answer is at Riverview."

"And what would that answer be?"

"No clue." I ate the last of the pie. "But I start nosing around and someone dies? Wouldn't you wonder?"

"I can wonder all I want, Spencer. Only thing that matters is facts, and I have some if you're interested."

I gave him my best inquisitive look.

"Got the coroner's report on Parker." He paused to wave to a neighbor.

"I'm still here."

"Yeah, I noticed. Lucky me. Let's go inside—getting a little chilly."

I sat in my favorite chair in the living room while Stosh took the plates to the kitchen. He returned with two bottles of Schlitz.

"Hair and blood on the boat match the victim, but there was no water in his lungs."

"So probably killed somewhere else. But he could have been hit by the boat and then stopped breathing before he went underwater."

Stosh nodded. "Could have. But the front of the boat is either pointed or flat. The dent on Parker's head is concave, like a baseball bat."

"So?"

"So we'll have people there in the morning."

I told him about the bat in Walters' office. "Sending Steele?"

He nodded. "And Pitcher and a few others."

"Walters isn't going to like that."

"Nope. I'll see if I can get around to letting that bother me."

"Anything else on Benny?"

"Team went through his apartment. A little dive." He paused for a drink. "Found an IOU for a little over ten thousand dollars. I couldn't read the signature, but Benny was into somebody pretty heavy."

I agreed and filed the IOU in my memory. I could think of only one person who would cover that kind of money. "You said Walters was a good cop and a bad cop. He seems to have his own little kingdom there at Riverview. I talked with the owner, Block. He didn't come right out and say it, but I got the feeling that he didn't care what Walters did as long as nothing ended up in *his* lap."

"And that surprises you?" He unfolded the card table and chairs and set them up in front of the couch.

I took a long drink. "Nope. But I wonder how far Walters would go to keep things running smoothly."

Stosh pulled out the top drawer of the desk and got the cards. "I wouldn't think too far. He knows what the rules are—just sometimes has his own interpretations. Kinda like someone else I know."

As he shuffled, I moved to the table and thought about Walters. Maybe he knew what the rules were, and I certainly didn't mind bending them myself, but I thought it possible that power would change bend to break.

After losing the first three gin hands, I asked another question.

"You said you assigned Steele to the murder case."

"Among others."

"Do you think that's a good idea?"

"I don't usually do things that I think are bad ideas. How do you mean?"

I arranged my cards. A run of three and garbage. "I think the murder has something to do with the missing kids."

"So?"

Drawing a card, I said, "With Steele's son disappearing, I wonder about involving him with missing kids."

He fanned out his cards. "I already thought of that. We had a chat. He assures me it wouldn't be a problem if it heads in that direction."

"You're the boss."

He laid down his cards. "Gin."

I threw mine onto the pile, and he left them there.

"It's your deal," I said.

He still left them there. "What's eating you?"

I pursed my lips and took a deep breath and said, "What makes you think something's eating me?"

He laughed. "You gotta be kiddin'. You've *never* lost four hands in a row."

I nodded. "Well, I suppose you'll find out sooner or later." I looked up at him to see if he had a clue. He didn't. "You have been misinterpreting a few statements."

"Hard to believe. I play a detective on TV."

I didn't smile.

He leaned forward. "Okay, I'm listening."

I took another deep breath. "When Rosie said 'It doesn't matter,' she meant she was okay with my heart thing." I paused. He just raised his eyebrows, and I told him about the other meaning.

He leaned back in his chair, and I waited for the lecture.

He just looked sad. He knew what it was like to lose someone he loved. Francine had died three years ago, and he still hadn't changed anything in the house and preferred to sleep in his recliner.

"I'm sorry to hear that, Spencer. I know you had your reasons for not telling her, and I felt bad about nagging you about it, but I hoped you would—"

I held up my hand. "I know. I appreciate it. I was just a fool."

"We're all fools at some point. But it sounds like there is still hope."

I shook my head. "Not much. She said she wants time, but I think she was just trying to let me down easy."

"Hey, that's been *your* MO. Rosie tells it like it is. Just wait and see. Sounds like she's still your friend. Remember, there's no gem as precious as a good friend."

"I know. Thanks, friend." I tried a small smile.

He picked up the cards. "You wanna try and get your money back?"

"I think I'll call it a night, Stosh. Thanks for the company. Always a pleasure."

"Agreed. Don't think too much about it, kid. The sun'll still come up in the morning. Go find your missing persons, and the rest will take care of itself. I'll call Evanston in the morning about the father. Tell her to go in and file a report."

"Will do."

He walked me to my Mustang, and I fought the urge to floor it after hitting the street. The chill in the air matched my mood, and I lay awake for a few hours trying not to think, but I wasn't successful.

I eventually fell asleep to the soft patter of rain on the roof.

Chapter 13

Second night in a row without much sleep. I woke up a little before six to a clap of thunder. The wind had picked up, and the western sky was gray. Early morning storms usually passed quickly, and I hoped this was not an exception. I wanted to spend some time at the park. I went for a run and concentrated on my breathing to stop myself from thinking. I had spent the night thinking and gotten nowhere. Every breath helped a little.

A shower and some eggs and bacon left me ready to start thinking about Martin. The only plan I had besides waiting for something to happen was doing some more pot stirring at the park, and that would have to wait until noon. I wanted to be lost in the Saturday crowd.

The storm moved out by eight and left a fresh smell in the air and a fresher outlook in me. Everyone needs a good storm once in a while. I called Samantha and told her to go in and file a report. After turning down my offer to go along, she agreed to meet me at her apartment at eleven. I wanted to offer some support… I knew what it was like to feel alone.

The kid across the street was shooting baskets in the driveway, and his mother was working in the front row of rose bushes. I waved as I walked to my Mustang.

Mom would have spent the morning puttering in the garden on a day like today, and the afternoon trying to get Dad to go shopping.

After he sprawled on the couch with the Cubs on the TV, she'd end up taking me. The lure of a triple ice cream cone was hard to resist.

Before I got into the car, I shrugged my shoulders to settle the shoulder holster that I didn't like wearing. It was never comfortable. A few months back I had a sport coat custom made with a little extra room on the left side. Today a wind breaker covered the gun. Even knowing that trouble could pop up anytime, I had decided I could handle myself pretty well without a gun, but there were times when additional peace of mind was worth it. How ironic that an amusement park would fit that category.

When I had decided to carry a gun, I'd spent many hours on the range trying different weapons and had chosen a Smith & Wesson snub-nosed .38 because of the small size, the powerful load, and my love of Smith & Wessons. I had Dad's .357 Magnum with the blued steel barrel in a case at home. The snub nose wasn't as accurate and took a lot of practice to shoot well, but I could put five shots in the center of a target in five seconds with either hand. It would serve the purpose. I had only needed it once, and I hoped that would be the last time. But my theory has always been, *if it comes down to him or me, it's going to be him.*

The sun was up over the buildings between me and the lake and the day promised to be warm. I took a short detour to pick up the posters. Samantha was just walking up to her apartment when I arrived. I told her I'd be back after I found a parking space. Street parking on the weekends was never easy. I got lucky—only a block away.

I had nothing to add to what she had done at the station. She told me they had an artist make a sketch and that they would distribute it and check with the hospitals and homeless shelters.

She made coffee, and we sat on the worn couch that had come with the place.

With a worried, exhausted look, she asked, "What do you think, Spencer? I mean, what are the chances…?"

I patted her arm and tried to reassure her. "The police are good at this. They'll find him." I took a sip. "If someone asked him his name and where he lived would he be able to answer?"

"Depends. His mind wanders. Sometimes he is perfect and others he acts like he's somewhere else… I have no idea what he's talking about."

"That must be hard. I'm so sorry."

She just nodded.

I took another sip and watched the steam rise from the mug. "I have a question, if you wouldn't mind."

"No, of course not. You're doing so much to help me. I can never…"

"Glad to help. I've been wondering why you moved up here, not knowing anyone. None of my business, so don't…"

"No, it's okay. My fault, I guess." She turned toward me with a forlorn look. "I had to get out of a bad relationship and leaving town seemed like the best way of doing that—start a new life. I really don't want to explain that."

"That's okay, Samantha."

She smiled and continued. "We had no ties in Atlanta and no more family left. When my boss couldn't talk me out of leaving he told me he had a friend in Chicago who would give me a job, and here we are." She paused and took a drink. "But then it turned out the friend was only interested in me, and…"

I took a deep breath. "I don't mean to butt in, but moving may have confused your dad."

She looked like she was going to cry. "He wasn't very bad in Atlanta. If I had known he would…" Her eyes filled with tears.

I reached out and put my hand on her knee. "I'm sorry, Samantha. It's not your fault. You couldn't have known. You were just trying to make your life better. And you still took care of your father. Many wouldn't have done that."

She nodded, sniffed, and got up to get a Kleenex.

I stood with her and said I needed to get back to work.

"Going to the park?"

"Yup."

"Do you have some theories?"

"Not really. Just going to nose around. I've been known to get people riled up who'd rather not have people nosing around."

She returned my smile and gave me a hug. I returned it.

***

I stepped into a puddle as I got out of the car. Patches of black-top were starting to dry as the sun evaporated the moisture. Not a cloud in the sky.

Stopping just inside the gate for a hot dog, I decided to make a circle of the park and then decide what to do next. Somewhere along the way I'd stop and see Mrs. Meyers and see if I could confirm where Martin worked. I ate as I walked and let the screams and laughter and screech of steel wheels on steel rails of the wooden coasters bring me back to when I was too short to go on most of the rides. The Tunnel of Love was taped off, and a policeman stood just outside the tape. As I passed, two cops in plain clothes lifted the tape and went inside the tunnel.

I finished my hot dog as I walked up to the Bumper Cars, one of my favorite rides as a kid. My memories lured me in, and I squeezed into the car. There were only two other riders and, for reasons beyond my understanding, they ganged up on me, and I spent five minutes trying unsuccessfully to get away from them. So much for memories.

When I reached the river at the back of the park, I had to wait for a train to pass and decided to make four stops: another walk through Aladdin's Castle; the ball-throw booth; Wonderland; and the chief's office. Having no idea what I would do at any of those, I headed for the castle.

On the way, I stopped to watch the barker at the Freak Show. I loved listening to his patter. He was standing next to the tattooed lady… it was hard to find the lady under the tattoos. As I scanned the crowd, I saw a floppy hat with five brightly colored spikes standing up and then falling over with a bell at the end of each spike. Hard to miss a jester—even in a crowd. My friend Harvey was standing next to my buddy Walters. Wondering what the conversation was about, I decided it was hard to know whom to trust. I waited for Walters to leave and then walked up behind Harvey. His floppy hat blocked my view of the stage.

I was surprised by his remark: "If it isn't my favorite private investigator." He hadn't even turned his head.

I walked up close behind him and examined his skull. No eyes in the back.

"Hi, Harvey. Nice trick. Something I'd expect *inside* the castle."

He laughed and turned his head sideways as I walked alongside. "Eight years of jestering has left me with special powers."

"Indeeeed." I drew it out.

"Yes, like being able to see reflections in glass." He nodded toward the panel above the ticket booth to our right. "I saw you come around the corner and picked you up in the glass."

I was impressed. Finished with his spiel, the barker and the tattooed lady made their exit. The crowd dispersed, some to the ticket booth. Harvey and I walked across the train tracks and south along the Midway.

"Looks like you'd be better suited as a detective," I suggested.

"Would I get to wear a snazzy suit like this?"

I had to double-step to avoid a kid running in front of me. "I'm thinkin' not. We're supposed to blend in with the crowd."

"Then no dice."

"Why aren't you at Wonderland?"

"Every couple of hours I'm supposed to walk around and show off the goods. Not every day you can get paid for making a spectacle of yourself. And on a nice day like this, it's a pleasure."

I admired Harvey. He seemed entirely satisfied with his station in life.

"Are you here every day?"

He laughed. "No, I get two days off like every other working stiff."

"Which two days?"

"Well, the park is closed on Monday, and the other day varies."

I nodded. "How much farther are you walking?"

"Just back to Wonderland."

That was just up around the bend at the south end of the park. He jingled as he walked.

"Mind if I ask a few questions while we walk?" Wonderland was on the way to the police station, and from there I could continue on to Aladdin's Castle.

"Not at all."

"Can you think of anything you can tell me about Benny?"

He shook his head, which set a few bells to ringing. "Nope. But Benny was a little odd. Always pretty nervous."

"Any idea why?"

"Maybe the same reason as some of the others."

When I didn't respond, he continued.

"I've been here for eight years and seen a lot come and go. Aren't many who have been here this long. Benny started just after me. Walters started at the end of the season, two years ago."

We walked a bit before he continued.

"The feel of this place changed after Walters showed up."

He paused, and we stopped and watched the Parachute Drop ahead of us at the bend. The parachutes had reached the top at one hundred eighty feet and were about ready to fall. When it let go, I knew the people in the car were screaming, but I couldn't hear them. They were too far away—like heat lightning.

"I could watch that every time," Harvey said with longing.

"Do you go on the rides?" I asked.

"We're not supposed to take the places of a paying customer."

"Too bad."

"Well, truth is that ride scares me to death. But I love watching."

"So what about Benny?"

He took a deep breath as we continued walking. Before he could say anything a kid grabbed the edge of his coat and rang the bells. The kid ran off. Harvey just laughed.

"I think there was something going on between Walters and Benny," he said.

"How so?"

"When Walters started, he insisted on doing all the hiring."

"I was told that Belva does the hiring."

"Same thing. The two are interchangeable."

"Meaning?"

He shrugged. "Seems to me she's the one who runs things over there. I think Walters had something on Benny."

"Why do you think that?"

"Nothing in particular. Just a feeling. Benny was a different man when Walters was around." Anticipating my question, after waiting for a roller coaster to scream past, he continued. "He would all of a sudden get nervous… kind of stuttered and paled. But to be honest, Benny wasn't the only one Walters had that effect on."

"Not hard to believe," I said.

Wonderland was in sight, but we had to navigate around a group of Cub Scouts coming out of Kiddieland to get there. One of the boys spotted Harvey, and he was quickly swarmed by wide-eyed kids who, when they discovered pulling various parts of his clothes rang bells, wouldn't stop pulling. Harvey went into his Wonderland act, and the kids ran on ahead with two moms trying desperately to herd them back into a group. Five minutes later we finally made it to the colorful front of Wonderland.

"Thanks for the company," Harvey said.

"My pleasure," I replied. "One more question. Was Belva here before Walters?"

Scrinching up his face, Harvey said, "She was—coupla years. Why do you ask?"

"Just something burrowing into my brain."

To Harvey's credit, he just nodded instead of asking what it was. I liked Harvey.

I turned to go but stopped for another question.

"You said you think Walters has something on a lot of the workers."

"Yup. But don't bet your house on it."

"And he's got nothing on you?" I asked.

"Nothing to get. Clean as a whistle."

I thought for a few seconds. "Might be interesting if we gave him something."

His eyes twinkled. "Might be. What do you have in mind?"

I shook my head. "Don't know… just a thought. You seem to know everyone. Can you give me a list of the workers who have been hired since Walters got here and where they work?"

"Sure. Call the number on your card?"

He had kept my card. Amazing.

"How about I buy you breakfast Monday?"

"Never turn down free food! And the park is closed on Monday so no work. Got some place in mind?"

"Family diner called Molly's on Fullerton about four blocks east of here. Eight?"

"See you then."

We nodded at each other, and he went back to work.

I took the long way around, passed the Tilt-a-Whirl and the Fireball rollercoaster, and stopped at the police station where Belva grudgingly confirmed that Martin did indeed work at the ball throw booth.

Chapter 14

Deciding to make another lap around the park, I got some pop-corn and ate as I walked along the river at the back of the park, imagining the targets out there that Schmidt had set out in the early 1900s for his friends. Ten minutes later I was at the little park across from the police station. As I threw the bag in a trash barrel my heart jumped. Rosie was sitting at a table close to the concession stand with her back to me.

I didn't know what to do. I had been wondering if I should call her, but didn't want to be pushy. I had decided she'd get back to me if she wanted to. If she was here, that meant she wanted to. I was happy and relieved. Wondering how she knew I was going to be here, I walked over and started to sit down next to her. In a split second I realized it wasn't Rosie, and my heart sank. I stuttered an apology and found my own table. I thought I'd been successfully not thinking about her. I guess not.

I tried to lose myself in watching the crowd but wasn't having much luck. I couldn't get my mind off Rosie until about a half hour later when a familiar face walked into the police station. I hadn't seen Joey "the Juicer" Mineo since a few winters ago when I was hired by a distraught husband to pay off his wife's gambling debts. She had been into Joey for four grand, and I was the delivery boy. The IOU for ten grand the cops had found in Benny's room suddenly clicked into place.

Joey was on the payroll of Larry Maggio, the current head of organized crime in Chicago. Larry was the grandson of Johnny Torrio, who had started running moonshine in Chicago during prohibition and handed off the business to Al Capone. Larry and I had met a year ago because of some paintings.

Joey was the type who didn't appreciate losing money that was owed him, and he had been known to teach lessons to deadbeats. He had very graciously accepted the four grand in cash and thanked me for helping him with his accounts. He had said he hated to have to deal with accounts receivable—bad for business. He had gone on to say he didn't really want to hurt anyone—he'd much rather have his money. And he certainly didn't want them dead... hard to collect. I could imagine that swinging a baseball bat hard enough to get a point across, but not hard enough to make it permanent, was an art. But Joey and his hired help were good at it. He was still walking around in eight-hundred-dollar suits. And for ten grand, Joey really wasn't going to be happy if someone else had swung the bat not so delicately. I sat staring at the door as it closed after him, wondering what business he had with Walters.

About twenty minutes later, Joey reappeared and stopped outside the door, squinting at the sun. He straightened his tie and reset the Stetson Homburg on his head at a fashionable angle. It was like he was admiring himself in a mirror, and he had every right to. Joey had no bad habits. He wasn't into drugs, alcohol, or gambling. But he had always dressed like royalty. His suit today was a light shade of blue, his gray tie matched the color of the Homburg, and the band at the base of the hat was the same shade of blue as the suit. A gray and orange feather stuck out of the left side of the hat band. When he came out I decided to just stay put. I wanted to have a friendly chat about business but would save that for another time.

Joey looked around to see if anyone was catching his fashion show. No one seemed to be, except for me. I was pretty sure Joey's scan had included me—Joey didn't miss much. After a crowd passed by, he walked in my direction and casually sat down at my table.

"Well, whaddya know. How's tricks, Shamus?"

I nodded. "Doing okay, Joey. Got a real office with a secretary. Looks like you're still operating above the poverty level."

He laughed. "Don't let looks fool you. Business ain't so good lately."

A kid started to cry after he dropped his ice cream cone. His mother was explaining that they had spent all their money and couldn't afford another. Joey got up, bought another cone and handed it to the kid. Mother and son were very grateful, although mom was the only one to say so—the kid was too busy devouring the treat.

Joey sat back down.

"Business can't be that bad if you can pop for ice cream cones for strangers," I said with a smile.

He shrugged. "I gotta soft spot for kids. I used to be one."

"Speaking of business, what brings you here?"

As he crossed his legs and smoothed the pants legs, the Rosie look-alike walked past our table without looking at me. My sadness was back.

"I was just wondering the same thing about you, Shamus. I come here to take care of a little item, and here you are. Helluva coincidence, and I don't like those."

"Neither do I."

He took a deep breath and let it out slowly, looking at me all the time. "Perhaps we're here about the same thing."

"Could be."

But both of us were talking in circles, and we silently agreed to call it a draw. He stood, touched the brim of his hat, and walked slowly away.

Before I had visited Joey, I'd done some homework and discovered two facts. One, not many people crossed him… out of respect for the age-old tradition of wanting four good limbs. And two, he never carried a gun. He hired people to carry them for him. Rumor was that Joey had the best bodyguard in town. Joey never went anywhere without him, but no one had ever seen the guy. One man described him as a shadow without the shadow.

It crossed my mind that maybe there *wasn't* a bodyguard. Maybe a good rumor did the trick. And rumors didn't cost much.

I wanted to follow Joey and find his bodyguard, but I also wanted to keep an eye on the station. If I knew who was inside I could figure out who Joey was doing business with. There were only two possibilities. So I just watched as Joey walked down the Midway. The crowds were thin, so I could follow him until he turned the corner at the Tilt-a-Whirl. I didn't see anyone following him.

Turning my attention back to the police station, I was thinking about how to find out who was there when a man who looked like an employee opened the door and went in. Two minutes later, he was back and walking in my direction. I joined him as he walked past.

"Pardon me," I said, "you look like you work here. I was just in the police station but no one was there. Do you know where they might be?"

He looked puzzled. "Well, I don't know where the chief is, but Belva is right there sitting at her desk."

"Strange, she wasn't there a few minutes ago."

"Probably in the can, mister. Go on back... she's there."

"Thanks. Much obliged."

He touched the bill of his worn out ball cap and kept walking.

I waited for him to get out of sight and then walked past the office and down the Midway to Aladdin's Castle. I now knew who Joey's business was with. If he had been looking for Walters, he would have been out in a few minutes because Walters wasn't there. Joey was in there for twenty. He and Belva had something to talk about.

***

The customer line leading up to the castle steps was short. I bought a ticket and followed a group of teenagers who screamed and yelled just like they were supposed to.

I spent an hour standing in exactly the same spot where someone had told me to meet him and saw everything I was supposed to. The scary face with the scar lit up every time someone came around the corner. The girls screamed and grabbed the guys. The guys laughed and let them grab. Blasts of air came out of slots in the side walls and a low-pitched, rumbling thunder came from the ceiling. But it was the thing I didn't see that got my attention. Something I'd seen before was missing.

Chapter 15

S tosh and I had spent almost every Saturday afternoon of base-ball season watching the Cubs in his living room with beer and sandwiches. I didn't get there until the third inning, and I was hungry. Rick Sutcliffe had thrown a one-hitter the day before, and the Cubs were in first place. I had been listening to the game on WGN on the way over. Steve Trout was on the mound. Cubs fans were always hopeful, but this year, with Sandberg and some good pitching, they had reason to be. They hadn't played in the World Series since 1945, and worse yet, they hadn't won since 1908.

"About time," Stosh said in his gruff, lovable way.

"Crime stops for no one. Mind if I help myself to your kitchen?"

"That's the only way you're going to get anything." He unmuted the TV as the commercial ended.

When I got back to the living room, the Cubs had walked the bases full of Reds.

As I handed Stosh a bottle of Schlitz he asked, "So who you been bothering on a Saturday?"

"Stopped by Samantha's and tried to get more information on her father. Not much there. Who doesn't have a picture of their father?"

He raised the footrest on his recliner. "Maybe someone who had to leave town in a hurry."

"Yeah, maybe. But the two references I called didn't make it sound like anything was wrong. I sent her to the station to file a report."

"I know. I talked to Evanston. They'll let me know if they find anything."

"Thanks, Stosh." After a few bites of a ham sandwich I continued. "Spent the rest of the time at Riverview. Guess who I ran into."

He just gave me a disgusted look. I wasn't sure if it was because of the bases-clearing double or he just wasn't in the mood for guessing games.

"Joey the Juicer," I said.

That got his interest. "Not someone you'd expect at an amusement park."

"No. We had a chat, but he wasn't talking about much."

"Never does. And neither does anyone else, which is why he's still walking around in expensive suits."

After finishing the sandwich, I stretched out on the couch and watched the game. The Reds finished their half of the third, but not before six runs had scored and Trout was headed for an early shower. I got up and went for more beer. When I got back, Stosh had his feet up and his eyes closed. I swiped at the bottom of his feet as I walked by. No reaction other than to reach out as I popped the top off a bottle.

"I need a favor," I said as I handed him the bottle.

"Now there's a surprise."

"Find out what you can about Belva Meyers."

"Belva? Really?" Lt. Powolski knew who Belva was. He knew more about Chicago crime history than anyone in the city.

"Really. Like to have a chat with her parents. Who would do that to a kid?"

"And where did you run into this version of Belva?"

"She sits at the front desk in the police station at Riverview and keeps people away from Walters."

"What are you looking for?"

I shrugged. "Nothing in particular. Anything that pops out. I've got nothing so far, and she seems like a good place to start."

"Okay, I'll look into it Monday. But it ain't on top of the pile."

"Even after my solving all your tough cases?"

He just humphed.

We watched a couple innings without conversation and then I asked another question.

"Can you tell me any more about Walters?"

"Like what?"

"Like why he was let go."

He straightened in his chair and put down the footrest. "First of all, he wasn't let go… it was a mutual agreement. And second, no."

I spread my hands palms up, and gave him a pleading look.

"The files are sealed."

"But you know."

He shrugged. "What I know or don't know doesn't matter. Sealed is sealed. Unless you have some damned good reason, they're going to stay that way."

"Maybe I'll find one."

"Always open to new information."

As we watched the game, he asked who was on my trust list. Dad had started the concept a long time ago. Who do you trust? Who do you think is telling the truth? Some of it is you just know down deep and some is a gut feeling. The down deep is a short list. For Dad it was Mom and me, and Aunt Rose, and Stosh, and probably a few people on the force. But you can't always trust your relatives.

My deep down trust was, of course, Stosh, and Aunt Rose, and Rosie. I was pretty sure about Steele but there was still something about him that made me hesitate. When I had first met him I didn't trust him at all. That had changed as I got to know him, especially after the rescue of Detective Pitcher a year ago, but I still kept my eyes open.

I thought about the case and came up with a very short list for my gut feeling. I told Stosh about Harvey. One of Dad's rules was you never totally trust a stranger, but he also acknowledged that sometimes you just have to trust somebody. Just keep your eyes open. For me, Harvey fit that niche. Stosh just nodded.

"And I think I can probably trust Block. He's owned that place for a lot of years. Why mess it up now?"

Stosh humphed again. "You're forgetting one of your dad's rules. Never trust someone with a lot of money. They usually don't get there by being nice guys."

I nodded. "Yup. But he seems so innocent. I think he just likes sitting in the chair and has no idea what goes on from day to day. He reminds me of Mr. Carlson on *WKRP in Cincinnati*."

"Things usually aren't what they appear to be on the surface, kid. You never know what skeleton is rattling in the closet."

I asked if they had made any progress on Benny.

"Not much. Other than that ten grand note, no motive and no witnesses. But plenty of possible murder weapons. The repair shop has a whole rack of pipes of various sizes. Doc says something rounded, two or three inches in diameter, so a pipe would fit. Gonna keep the lab busy for days looking at those pipes."

"And the bat?" I asked.

He smiled. "It was the first thing we tested. Clean except for Walters' prints."

I didn't expect them to find anything. If Walters had done it, he wasn't that dumb.

The Cubs pulled within a run in the ninth but left the tying run on.

"You got plans for dinner, kid?"

"Nope."

"Let's go get a steak. And Buddy Guy is playing at the Blue Note."

"Steak sounds good," I said, grabbing my jacket. "I'm going to give Johnny a call before we leave, but I'd like to wait to see him till I have some good news."

He shrugged. "Some mighty fine blues."

***

Over steak and baked potatoes we chatted about many things before Stosh came around to Rosie. He was sad to hear we hadn't talked and added his two cents.

"Give her a call."

I swirled beer in the bottom of the glass. "She said she wanted time."

He nodded. "How long are you going to wait?"

I shrugged. "I don't think it's up to me. She's the one who wanted time."

"If you get any more stubborn I'm gonna start looking for two more legs and long ears. Keep it up and you may lose a friend too."

I took a deep breath and admitted he was probably right.

As we walked to the car, I noticed a haze around the moon—cirrus clouds blown off the tops of a thunderstorm to the west. I hoped it was slow moving. I was taking Carol and Billy to the Cubs game Sunday.

Chapter 16

I woke up early Monday thinking about Rosie. It would have been easy if she had called me. But life wasn't always easy. I put on sweats and sat on the deck and looked at the stars. The deck faced south and I had a view of the sunrise over houses to the east and a view of the sunset to the west over trees. If it hadn't been for the case, I'd have left for Door County and been waiting for the sunrise over Moonlight Bay. The birds were singing as I watched night melt into the first hints of dawn. Other than birds, the first sound I heard was the paper hitting the driveway. I walked to the front, picked it up, and went back to my chair on the deck to catch up on the news.

Billy's first ball game had been a win for the Cubs… and the vendors. That kid could eat. When I picked them up I gave Carol the posters, and she said she and Billy would start passing them out today.

***

I walked into Molly's a few minutes before eight. I had wondered if I'd be able to spot Harvey without the costume. He solved the problem. In a booth halfway up the middle aisle was a guy wearing a jester's hat. I slid into the booth opposite him.

"Nice hat."

He laughed and took it off. "Wanted to make it easy for you to pick me out of the crowd."

"Mission accomplished."

I ordered my usual two eggs over easy, pancakes, and bacon. Harvey chose a Greek omelette.

When the waitress left, Harvey slid a piece of paper across the table with three names listed along with where they worked in the park: Percy Humphrey—Bobs; Chester Zardis—Tilt-a-Whirl; and Frank Knight—Bottle Booth.

"There are certainly more," he said, "but that's all I know for sure that have come since Walters took over."

"Great. Thanks. So Knight is Meatstick. I saw him talking with Walters. What's your opinion of him?"

Harvey finished his orange juice and answered, "We're friendly when we're together, but I don't go out of my way to be cordial. He's not the nervous type like Benny… likes to push people around, especially the kids."

"You think he bows to Walters?"

Harvey shrugged. "Don't think he bows to anyone, but if Walters has something on him he may have to obey."

The food arrived. I peppered my eggs and took a bite. "What makes you think Walters has something on these people?"

"Well, the people who work at amusement parks aren't usually rubbing elbows with the social elite. Most are down on their luck and have had some sort of trouble along the way."

"Not unlike most people. That doesn't make them bad."

"Nope. Not saying that. But it makes them vulnerable."

"I noticed Benny isn't on the list."

He shook his head. "Nope, he'd been there almost as long as me."

We ate in silence for a few minutes before Harvey continued.

"You asked if I wanted to give Walters something to hold over me."

I nodded.

"Any ideas?"

"I've given that some thought. If you were arrested and spent some time in jail, that would put you on the same footing as the others."

He looked surprised. "We'll come back to the arrested part, but I assume you're thinking Walters would approach me with some scheme?"

"That would be my hope. But who knows."

"And what makes you think Walters is involved in something?"

"Just a hunch. I don't trust him, and neither do you."

He pursed his lips and nodded. "Now back to the arrested part. I've never been arrested... never even had a traffic ticket. Not something I need on my resumé."

I laughed. "Agreed. But it would just be for show."

"So we have to get some fake cops? Walters would know."

"Yup. Which is why we use real cops—people Walters knows."

"And how do we do that?"

The waitress filled our coffee cups and took away Harvey's plate.

"I have friends in high places."

He gave me a sideways glance.

"Another slight problem," he said. "I don't get paid for being arrested."

I laughed and soaked up the last of the egg with wheat toast. "No, not usually part of the benefits package. I'll make up whatever you lose in pay."

He looked at me like I was nuts. "Really? So, I *will* get paid for being arrested?"

"Yes, you will."

His eyes narrowed, and he stared at something over my shoulder.

"What if he decides not to let me come back?"

"I'll cover your pay as long as this goes on... and there *is* something going on. Either he takes you back and you have a heart to heart, or when you *do* go back, Walters won't be there."

"And what am I being arrested for?"

I took a deep breath and let it out slowly. I had thought about this while waiting for dawn. "I'm not sure. Any crimes you've always wanted to commit?"

"Nope. Not something one usually thinks about."

"I'll think more about it. Not entirely sure this is a good idea."

He burst out laughing. The people across the aisle looked over at us. "Well I'm sure it *isn't*! I can think of a lot of things I want, and none are a criminal record."

"You wouldn't have a record. It would all be smoke and mirrors."

"Have you talked to your friends?" he asked.

"Not yet."

He grimaced and nodded. "How about you do that before we go any further with this? And even then, I'm not making any promises."

"Understood."

My pager went off as he wiped his mouth and laid the napkin on the table. The message was 911, Stosh's code for *call now*.

I asked Harvey if he would mind another free breakfast on Wednesday. He said he never turned down free food, thanked me for breakfast, and donned the jester hat. I laughed quietly. I had no idea why, but the hat was part of why I trusted him.

I used the restaurant phone and called the station. They had found a body that matched the description of Samantha's father. There was no ID on the body, and his pockets were empty.

"Ring?" I asked.

"Nope, but maybe someone stole the ring."

"Where was he found?"

"Alley over by Clark and Montrose. Looks like a hit and run. Lots of broken bones."

I told him I'd pick up Samantha and head to the morgue.

***

Samantha was understandably shaken. She was flustered and tried to think about what to shut off before we left the office. I told her to just grab her keys and not worry about it. In the car, she asked non-stop questions. I tried to keep her calm and figured her asking questions was the best way to do that.

"It's probably Dad, isn't it, Spencer?"

"There's no way of telling, Samantha. There's just as much chance it isn't. That's pretty far for him to have wandered from Evanston."

She started to cry. "I've been trying so hard to keep up hope. But, I mean, he matches the description. What are the chances it's some other man who was out wandering the streets?"

I shook my head and turned into the parking lot of the morgue, a two-story brick building with very few windows. "There's always a chance. Would you like to wait a few minutes?"

She sniffed and wiped her eyes with a handkerchief she had taken out of her purse. "No. It's not going to change if I wait."

I had a hard time opening her door. Feeling like I was leading her into hell, I did it slowly and offered my hand. I put my arm around her and led her into the building.

After telling the man at the front desk what we were there for, we sat for a few minutes before another man in a white lab coat asked us to follow him. I didn't dare look at Samantha. I was out in the middle of nowhere hiking when my folks were killed, and Stosh had handled this part. I couldn't imagine what Samantha was going through.

The attendant pushed open a pair of metal doors, and we entered a white room with a wall of drawers. He pulled open one of them, slid out a tray, and unzipped a gray cover. Samantha was squeezing my arm. As the man pulled back the sheet, she collapsed against me and started to tremble. I put my arms around her and held her for a minute before gently pushing her away.

Looking up at me with tears in her eyes, she said, "It's not him."

As the man zipped the cover, I pulled her back to me and we turned toward the door. I heard a gentle whoosh as the attendant slid the drawer back into the wall with a peaceful finality.

She was still holding my arm as we walked back out into the sunshine.

"I never gave up hoping, Spencer."

"Good to have hope." I opened the car door and let her in. As I walked around the front of my Mustang, I thought of Rosie. I had some hope left for her and me but not much.

On the drive back to the office Samantha asked what my plans were for the day.

"Well, I'm going to pay another visit to Mr. Block. I'd like to go back to the park, but it's closed on Monday, so that'll have to wait until tomorrow. How about you?"

She smiled. "Just waiting for the phone to ring."

I patted her arm. "Thanks for doing that. I know it must get boring."

"It'll be a lot better than it was an hour ago."

"Glad it worked out this way." I was happy for Samantha, but there was someone else whose life was going to turn upside down. I asked Samantha to call Block's office and see if I could get an appointment for sometime today. I felt perfectly okay just walking in unannounced, but this gave Samantha something to do. As I pretended like I was busy at my desk, she called out that I had an appointment at two. I pretended some more and then took her to lunch. There was a Martin poster in the deli window.

Chapter 17

When I walked in the office, Miss Randel nodded to a chair and said Mr. Block was on the phone. I could see her phone from where I sat. There were no lights lit. I listened to WGN from the radio on her desk. I had cleared my throat three times before she told me, ten minutes later, that I could go in. What had I ever done to deserve *her*?

I sat in the same cushioned chair in front of Block's desk.

"Well, I didn't think I'd be seeing you again so soon, Mr. Manning. Actually I had hoped not to see you at all."

I gave him a disappointed look. "That seems to be the mood around here."

He looked confused. "What does *that* mean?" He picked up a pencil and rolled it between his fingers.

"Miss Randel is none too fond of me either."

His look changed to surprise. "My remark had nothing to do with you personally. I had hoped all this would be cleared up." He laid the pencil down parallel to the right edge of the blotter. "What do you mean about Miss Randel?"

"Not too friendly. Treats me like I was serving a summons."

He laughed. "My apologies. I'll have a chat with her."

"No need. I won't take it personally. Has she been with you a while?"

"Depends on what you consider a while. Her first day was the fifth of July two years ago."

My surprised look got an answer to my question without asking.

"Not easy to forget the fifth of July. The fourth is a huge day at the park, and she had to hit the ground running. Jumped in with both feet. She's been a blessing."

"What happened to your previous secretary?"

"Just up and quit. No notice. Just called that morning and said she was quitting."

"Did that surprise you?"

He spread his hands palms up and laughed. "You bet. And I could use several other words that I won't mention. She left me high and dry."

"Why do you think she did that?"

He slowly shook his head. "No idea. Must have gotten a better job. But people usually don't behave like that."

"Had she done a good job?"

"Excellent. No complaints."

"What's her name?"

With a look of surprise he asked why I wanted to know.

"Just curious. I gather facts, especially odd ones, and then let them roll around for a while. Once in a while some of them stick together."

After a deep breath, he said, "Gertrude Morgan."

"Do you have an address?"

He shifted in his chair. "I'm sure we do, but I see no reason for sharing that. I'm glad to help with what's going on at the park, but that can't have anything to do with Gerty."

I actually was happy about that. Tracking down Gertrude would give Samantha something to do.

"Well, how about this? I'd like a list of full-time employees hired after Walters."

"Again, what does that have to do with the kids and the murder?"

"Again, just collecting information and following a hunch. I can have the police make it a formal request if you'd prefer."

He sighed and pressed a switch on his intercom. My favorite secretary answered.

"Miss Randel, would you please put together a list of full-time employees hired at the park after Walters started?"

"Yes, sir."

He gave me a hard stare. "I don't think you'll find any problems with my employees. Most have been with me for a long time. I take good care of them." He turned his stare out the window. "This all started when my grandfather held shooting parties for his friends. Then he added a carousel for their families, and now it has grown into this." He pointed to the large aerial photo of the park. "Once a year I close the park and have a day just for employees and their families. Everything is free." He looked back at me and shook his head. "No, you won't find any problems with employees."

"Good to hear, Mr. Block. I'm sure you're right. But it's not the ones who have been there a long time that I'm wondering about."

He straightened in his chair. "Now, if you're finished…"

"One more question. How did you find Miss Randel?"

He looked like he was trying to remember. "I guess it was just pure luck. I was in a bind and got a call from Chief Walters about something else. When I told him I had just lost my secretary he said he had someone who would be perfect. She was in the office two hours later, and she was."

"Was what?"

"Perfect. As I said, she's been a blessing."

"Okay. Thanks for your time."

He nodded. It was a pretty warm nod compared to what I knew was waiting for me in the outer office.

Miss Randel was concentrating on something in the typewriter when I walked out. I sat in a chair along the wall opposite her desk. She stopped concentrating and started typing. I assumed it was my list, but it would have been nice of her to mention it.

Ten minutes later she was still typing. I had decided to ask her about it when the phone rang. Her responses were terse but polite. When she hung up I asked about the list. She disgustedly pulled what she was working on out of the roller, put in another piece of paper, opened a file, and started typing again. Two minutes later she pulled out the paper and handed it to me.

I had told Block that I didn't take her treatment personally, but it was hard not to. It was *me* standing there being ignored.

Without thanking her, I folded the sheet in half and left the office. As I waited for the elevator, I looked at the list. Harvey had given me three names. This list had six, and two of them were women. Harvey's three were also on the list. Block was right about his loyal employees. Any company with that little turnover was doing something right.

A warm breeze was blowing from the south as I walked out into the noise and bustle of Michigan Avenue. Just to the south was the water tower that had been the northern limit of the fire that had wiped out most of the city in 1871.

I stood for a minute and thought about Rosie, but my thoughts quickly went back to a summer up in Door County some fifteen years ago when I had assured Dad I was old enough to take care of the rowboat. He had walked up to the cottage with the fish we'd caught and left me to tie it up for the night. I hadn't done such a good job. When I looked back from the top of the hill, the boat was drifting out into the bay. My only thought was to swim after it, but I knew my folks were real serious about not swimming by myself. I had no idea how I was going to get it back.

A honking horn brought me back to the city, and I headed for my car.

Without a plan for the rest of the day, I decided to drop the list off with Samantha and put her to work on addresses. I'd stop by her apartment building and start knocking on doors, asking if anyone had seen her father. I added Gertrude Morgan's name to the list and handed it to Samantha. She was thrilled to have some work to do and told me she'd leave the completed list on my desk in the morning. I thought she was being optimistic.

Chapter 18

Halfway to Evanston my pager went off. Stosh's emergency number again. I was close enough to the office to go back and save a dime. Samantha was surprised to see me. She was doing something in the file cabinet and seemed a little flustered. I explained why I was there and told her it was tough being so popular. She agreed.

I had to wait five minutes before Lt. Powolski came on the line.

"Another kid is missing, Spencer. Worked at Riverview. I'm putting together a task force, and we're meeting in my office in thirty minutes."

"I just left."

***

As I pulled into the police lot I wondered what I would say when I saw Rosie. She would probably be at the meeting. Six people were already in Stosh's office when I got there. I knew three of them, one being Steele. Rosie wasn't there. I found a spot on the wall to lean against as Lt. Powolski introduced me to the three I didn't know and passed out a list with the missing kids' names. There were now seven on the list. Five had a capital R next to them, including the latest, Rodriguez. All were boys.

"As you all can see," Stosh began, "we have seven missing kids going back almost two years, and five worked at Riverview. That connection was made by a case Spencer is working on... that would be Martin Lisk. All are males between the ages of fifteen and seventeen and there is no particular ethnic bias." He paused as the door opened. My heart skipped a beat. I had actually felt relieved that Rosie wasn't there. It was another detective I didn't know. Stosh nodded to her, and she found an empty spot against the wall opposite me.

"Spencer has done some legwork on Martin, and Steele and Jenks have been working on the others, but we have very little. And then there is the murder of Benny Parker. Steele is working on that also, and we also have very little on that. Please share information and consider the two related. They may not be, but I'm not a fan of coincidences." He leaned on the desk and asked Steele and me to share what we had.

The basic information was that five of the kids, including the two not from Riverview, were from group care facilities where they were waiting and hoping to be placed in a foster home. But older kids rarely found a home. Most people wanted babies or younger kids. Two, including Martin, had families, so there was more information in the file, but it wasn't of much help. In all cases, the kids had just disappeared without a trace.

When we had finished, Stosh assigned names to pairs of detectives and asked that we meet again after more legwork. They all left, leaving behind an air of hopelessness. It was always hard not having any leads to follow, but being about kids made it worse. I stayed and sat on one of the wooden chairs.

Stosh let out a sigh and slumped in his chair. "Always sad when kids get caught up in adults' screw-ups, but when it's all about the kids..."

"And what the hell is it all about?"

He closed the file. "Damn good question. I assume you have nothing to add to what you said."

I shook my head. "Just as frustrated as you. But I have a feeling I'm making some enemies, and that's always a good sign."

"Well, you've always been good at that. Just be careful who they are. Any particular plans?"

"Not really. But I have an inside man who may be helpful." I told him about breakfast. "Meeting again Wednesday."

He nodded. "I know your gut says you trust this guy, but keep your eyes open. Many a man has been stabbed in the back while their gut was smiling. You don't have eyes in the back of your head."

"Will do." I pushed my chair back, but before I stood up I asked about Rosie. "Kinda thought Rosie would be here."

"She's on a night assignment. Probably sound asleep." He gave me a disappointed look. "I assume you still haven't called her."

"No. I think I'd rather not know."

"Yeah, that's the easy way out. Good luck with that. Now get the hell out of here and find out if all this is connected."

As I stood up, I thanked him for the call about Samantha's dad.

"Sure. Not easy. And as time goes by... Sometimes I hate this job."

I started to walk out and turned back. "Don't mean to be a pest, but did you get a chance to check on Belva?"

He closed his eyes and leaned his head back. "Oh hell, Spencer. I completely forgot. Sorry. I'll get someone on it this afternoon. I must be getting old."

I smiled. "Last I checked we all are, just some are getting there faster than others. I'll close the door so you can get a nap."

He picked up a vase, but I was gone before he could throw it. When Francine was alive the vase had always held fresh flowers. Now it was empty.

Walking down the stairs, I thought about Rosie with mixed feelings. Not approaching her meant I didn't have to hear her answer, and the more time went by the more I was sure of that answer. Thankfully, I had other things to think about, but getting sleep was not going to happen for a while.

***

The sunny day had disappeared as the sky clouded over. I decided to use what was left of the afternoon to do some legwork for

Samantha and parked right in front of her building at about three. I rang the eight bells in the building and got three answers. All three were willing to chat, but none had seen Samantha's father. They didn't even remember seeing Samantha. Not much community spirit in apartment buildings, but there's usually at least one watchdog who collects all the gossip. Maybe I just hadn't found that person yet—but that person was usually home all day.

I checked the two adjacent buildings and the stores across the street with the same result and then took a walk around a few blocks, hoping that some miracle would occur. It didn't. The closest I came was a brief chat with an older couple who assured me they hadn't seen any lost old men. It was strange that he hadn't turned up somewhere by now. Either he was confused—and someone would surely help out a confused old man—or there was something else going on. I felt pretty helpless, but this was something the police did well, and they were doing it.

When I got back to the building it was almost five, and I tried the bells that hadn't answered before. Two more answered. Still nothing, but one woman did remember Samantha moving in.

I vacated a great parking spot for some lucky commuter and stopped to get a frozen pepperoni pizza on the way home.

I read on the deck until I lost the sunlight, then just sat and listened to the crickets until the moon rose in the east. My plan for Tuesday was to check in at the office to see if Samantha had come up with any addresses and then pay another visit to the park. And maybe Stosh would have something on Belva. So far I was getting a whole lot of nowhere.

Chapter 19

Gertrude Morgan's phone rang at three in the morning. She groggily answered after six rings. A female voice simply said, "There's a bus leaving the Grayhound terminal at seven-ten. Be on it. You'll get further instructions." The line went dead.

She stared at the phone and shook her head, trying to wake up. The voice sounded the same as on past calls, but it had been months since the last one so she couldn't be sure. All she knew was that she was getting free rent and a nice monthly check, and there was nothing keeping her in Chicago. Her children were grown and had moved away, and she had no real friends.

As she hurriedly packed two worn suitcases, Gertrude wondered where she was going—and why.

Chapter 20

There was another plate of eggs and toast on the tray. Martin tried to think about how long he had been in the room. He vaguely thought he could figure it out by how many trays there had been, but as he tried to remember he decided he didn't care. It was too hard to think. But he did remember another dream. He was sitting at a bench on a stool filling small plastic envelopes with white powder and passing them to the boy next to him. He couldn't remember what happened to the envelopes after that, but he did remember a man with a large red nose who would suddenly be standing in front of him like a ghost that just appeared out of thin air. As he fell back asleep he wondered where his mother was.

Chapter 21

Samantha only had one address so far. I had given her a couple of names to call for help, and she hadn't heard back from either. She had found the one by herself. Percy Humphrey lived just west of the loop on North Avenue. Not one of your best neighborhoods, and it might be a different Percy, but I doubted it. I told her I'd check back in the afternoon. She apologized for not having had more success, and I told her to get what she could. As I turned to leave, she stopped me.

"Mister, um, Spencer. Have you...?" She looked at me with sad eyes.

"I'm sorry, Samantha. They have nothing. And I asked some of your neighbors about him, and they haven't seen him. But the police will keep looking. The word is out."

She frowned and looked like she was going to cry.

I walked back and put my hand on her shoulder. "I know it's not easy, Samantha. If there's anything else I can do..."

She just nodded, covered my hand with hers, and struggled to hold back her tears.

***

The barker at the Freak Show was just getting started when I walked up. A crowd of about twenty had gathered out front. He was dressed in white pants and shirt with bright red suspenders and a red and white polka dot bow tie. I liked the look. He was accompanied by the lady with three arms and the five-hundred-pound man. I questioned the extra arm, but the man looked like every pound was real. Across the way, three teenage boys were trying to coax their dates into the fun house. But the girls didn't seem to buy into the *fun* part. The boys gave up and led them to the baseball throw booth to impress them with their skills. I could hear the far-off screech of one of the roller coasters and the screams of the riders.

The barker finished his patter and another man herded people to the ticket booth as three men helped the fat man off the stage. Even as a kid I had been struck by the sadness of the poor people who were the attractions in the Freak Show. I had never gone in. About half the crowd bought tickets. I had watched the people walking down the Midway for about ten minutes, wondering what my plan was, when the barker came out of the front entrance and walked south toward the Bobs. I followed. He stopped and talked to two people at concessions before turning into a shack under the coaster. I bought a hot dog and waited.

Five minutes later he returned and headed back toward the Freak Show. As he passed a cotton candy booth I caught up with him and made a comment about the weather. He glanced at me and kept walking. Figuring he had no interest in meteorology, I tried again.

"Can we walk and talk?"

Without looking at me he said, "I'm sure we can. But I see no reason to talk to you."

"Really?" I tried to look hurt. "You don't even know me."

"You've made my point." Despite the happy tie he was good at surly.

"Well, if that's all that's stopping you, I'm Spencer Manning. I'm looking into some missing kids and would appreciate a few minutes."

He stopped and turned toward me. He was six inches shorter and at least thirty pounds lighter than me but made up for it in belligerence. "My mother taught me not to talk to strangers, especially ones named Spencer Manning. So I suggest you take a hike."

"Nice to know you had a mother. Don't you think she would have been concerned if you were missing?"

"You don't know my mother. Now blow." He left me standing there wondering why suddenly no one liked me. Maybe Randel was his sister. I considered catching up to him to ask, but just sat on a bench to finish my dog.

As I got up to throw away the wrapper, I was joined by my favorite pretend cop… Mooney.

"Boss wants to see you," he said with a snarl.

"About?"

He didn't answer, and he certainly didn't have what it would take to get me to the boss if I didn't want to go. But if you shake trees and fruit falls out, you have to pick it up, so I started walking with Mooney at my side trying to pretend he was important. He nodded at the door when we got to the station.

Belva was at her desk. Walters' office was empty. Mooney waved me to a chair against the wall. I stared at her while she fumbled with papers on the desk and then looked up. I had no doubt her parents knew what they were doing when they named her. There was nothing friendly about her look.

"You were told not to bother our employees."

"As I recall, Walters made a suggestion. I don't always follow suggestions."

She gave me a hard stare and continued. "It's *Chief* Walters, and people who don't follow suggestions have been known to find trouble."

I was supposed to be scared. "I've found trouble before. Hasn't been a problem."

She slowly said, "So far."

"Yup. I may be mistaken, but that sounds like a threat."

"Just an observation."

I stood and walked to the edge of her desk and looked down at her. "Here's an observation for *you*. Kids are missing, and you don't seem to be concerned. And Benny Parker is dead. I can't help but wonder why you're *not* concerned. And I'm not going to stop wondering."

"We certainly are concerned, and we've cooperated with the police on both matters. Now I strongly suggest you mind your own business." But despite the bravado she seemed a bit flustered.

I put both hands on the desk and leaned forward. "Missing kids *is* my business."

"You've been warned, Mr. Manning. I'm just trying to do you a favor. If you continue to bother our employees we'll call the police."

"Well, thanks for the favor. Maybe I can do you one someday." I gave her a two finger salute and walked out with another person added to my list of admirers.

Mooney was leaning against a post across from the office. I strolled over to him and tried again.

"Nice weather for June, don't you think?"

He didn't respond.

I gave him my best tough guy stare and walked away with him following. When we got to the entrance, I walked past and kept going back toward the Bobs. About halfway there I turned around and headed for the exit. Mooney followed me all the way to my car and watched me pull away.

Driving north on Western, I felt I was making progress. Shaking the tree had made people nervous... at least it had made Belva nervous enough to threaten me. And as I crossed Montrose, heading home, I remembered Mooney had said the "boss" wanted to see me. The only one in the office was Belva.

If nothing else, I had some topics for conversation with Harvey in the morning.

***

I threw a burger on the grill, made a salad, and sat on a deck chair with the evening paper. The headline on the front page was "First McDonald's Restaurant To Be Torn Down." The article ran two columns and talked about the restaurant Ray Kroc had brought to Des Plaines, a suburb of Chicago, in 1955. Ironically, Ray Kroc had just died four months ago, in January. It was the first fast-food burger restaurant in Chicago and the ninth in the chain of restaurants named after the McDonald brothers in California. They planned to build another more modern restaurant across the street and a museum on the site of the old one.

I had made my own history at that McDonald's. A month after I got my driver's license, I had a car full of friends who wanted a cheeseburger, so we headed out to Des Plaines. As I was about to pull into the parking lot, another car came out of the lot and cut me off. Aside from hitting it, my only option was to cut up short of the driveway over the planted area. After we all calmed down, we went in and were met by the manager who saw me cut through his flower bed but didn't see the other car. He told me to get out and never come back. We left, but I did go back. I made a mental note to go and watch the demolition.

I turned the burger and the page and started to read an article that caught my eye. A woman was found dead in the ladies' room of the Grayhound bus station. And then I felt the punch in my stomach. She was identified as Gertrude Morgan. A narrow red mark around her throat made it appear she had been strangled. Another lady had found her at six-thirty this morning.

I shut off the grill, added a piece of cheese, and called Stosh.

"Hello, kid."

"Hey, Stosh. I just read about Gertrude Morgan at the bus terminal."

"Yeah, never a dull moment. Why does that rate a call?"

"Because two years ago Gertrude Morgan was the secretary to Mr. Block, the owner of Riverview."

"Come on over." He hung up. Still no manners.

***

Lt. Powolski was sitting on the porch lighting his pipe when I pulled into the drive. I sat in the rocker next to him. It was warm enough to enjoy the evening without a jacket. A light breeze out of the west held the sweet smell of lilacs.

Stosh worked the pipe a bit and then said, "Tell me again."

"I was in Block's office yesterday talking about his secretary."

"Of course you were. Can I take a wild guess about her looks?"

"Her looks have nothing to do with it. We were talking about the fact that she doesn't seem to be a fan of mine."

"A woman with taste. And?"

"And I asked about his previous secretary. He said she had quit without reason or notice and left him holding the bag at a busy time. It was Gertrude Morgan. The day after I ask about her, she's murdered."

He puffed slowly, letting smoke lazily move in my direction.

"Do you have any more than what was in the paper?" I asked.

"Still had her purse and wallet, but there were pale skin lines where a ring and watch or bracelet used to be." More slow puffs. "Could very well have been a robbery gone bad. Not exactly the safest spot in town."

"How about if you add Benny to the picture?" I asked.

"Then it looks a lot less like robbery… and a lot more like you should let us take care of this."

"Thanks for your concern, but I have some more people to talk to."

"Such as?"

I told him about the lists of employees.

"And why do you think that's important?"

"No idea. But it beats doing nothing, and the first person I talked to got me a chat with Belva, who reminded me I was supposed to mind my own business."

"You probably should." He knew I wouldn't.

"Sure." I stretched out and put my feet up on the railing. "I'm having breakfast again with Harvey in the morning. I'm worried about him. He's been seen talking to me."

"Not afraid of Walters?"

"Doesn't appear to be."

"Maybe that's because he knows he doesn't have to worry about Walters because he's Walters' stooge."

"Could be, but I doubt it. I like him."

"Sure you do. Just keep it in mind. Speaking of Belva…"

We went inside as the night started to chill.

Stosh settled in his recliner, and I sat down on the couch.

"So?"

"So Belva is clean. Not even a traffic ticket. With that name, who'd figure?"

"That doesn't fit my theory."

He looked at me with raised eyebrows but didn't ask what my theory was.

"But Belva's kid isn't."

"Kid?"

"Eighteen years old, name is Albert. The usual couple of speeding tickets and an arrest for burglary and resisting arrest four years ago."

"Interesting. What happened?"

"The case was thrown out. Evidence was somehow compromised."

I gave him a puzzled look. "Compromised how?"

"Don't know, but I could dig a little deeper if you want."

"Not at the moment, but I'll let you know."

He had a playful look in his eyes. He knew something I didn't and was enjoying it.

I just stared at him for a good minute, which is a long time if you're just staring. I finally gave in. "Okay, you're dying to tell me. Don't make me beg."

Folding his arms across his chest, he said, "Guess who the arresting officer was."

"Don't have to—Walters."

"Yup."

"You thinking something wrong there?"

"I just gather facts. Fact one… Walters books Belva's kid. Fact two… the kid gets off with bad evidence. Fact three…"

I finished for him. "Walters gets a job as police chief where Belva works."

"Yup. Starting to smell bad."

"Like Limburger cheese."

He rubbed his forehead. "The question is... did Walters do a favor for Belva cuz she could get him the job, or did Belva get him the job because he could help with her kid? Who did a favor for who?"

"Whom."

I got a dirty look and continued. "Maybe there was something else she needed him for."

"Like what?"

I shrugged. "No clue. I need to do some more detecting."

"Two people dead, Spencer."

"Understood."

"We still doing our normal Wednesday night, or is two in a row too much excitement for you?"

"Sure. I'll get a nap tomorrow."

He laughed, turned on the news, and we talked until almost eleven-thirty when his phone rang. That was never good. He rolled his eyes and shook his head. I let myself out.

As I headed home, I wondered what Rosie was doing and how this was going to end. I had to get up early to meet Harvey, so I tried to stop thinking and looked forward to getting some sleep.

Chapter 22

I stopped at the office on the way to Molly's. The list of addresses was on my desk—two copies. I was happy with Samantha's work and felt worse and worse about her father. There was little chance that he was alive, but it was pretty strange that the police had found nothing.

Harvey was waiting for me, sipping coffee in the same booth but without the hat. He looked happy to see me. Who wouldn't be happy about free food?

"So what's new, PI?" he asked with a smile.

"Nothing good." I slid into the booth and turned my cup over. The waitress was right behind me with the pot. "Do you know Gertrude Morgan?"

With scrunched lips and a slow shake of his head, he said, "No, the name isn't familiar."

I sighed and took a sip.

"Why?"

"She was killed yesterday. Strangled at the bus station."

"Yeah, it's a fun city. But why do I suspect she's not just a statistic?"

"Do you know Block's secretary?"

The waitress stopped and we ordered.

"I know he has one. Don't think I could tell you her name. She shows up with him at events once in a while. Not bad on the eyes. She's Gertrude?"

"No. But do you remember the one before her?"

He looked thoughtful again. "Probably saw her but I couldn't give you a description—you're going back a few years."

"And I assume you don't know either's name."

"The only reason I know Block's name is because he signs my checks," he said with a smile.

Looking straight at him, I almost whispered. "Gertrude Morgan."

His eyes widened and he took a deep breath. "And you're assuming it's somehow connected to all this?"

"There's a plaque on my wall that says *I don't believe in coincidences.*"

He encircled his cup with both hands. "But they do happen."

"Yes, they do. But I err on the side that they don't until I get proof otherwise, and the list of coincidences is growing." I didn't tell him about Belva's kid. Most of me trusted him, but I was paying attention to the part that needed more time.

"Have you noticed anything at the park?" I asked.

"Nothing out of the ordinary. But there's a meeting tonight after work."

"For what?"

He shrugged and answered after finishing his eggs. "Nobody knows."

"How did you find out about it?"

"Word just spread around that management wanted to talk to us lowly employees."

"Do you have to go?"

"I wondered that, but asking the fellow who told me would have been useless. Normally I would ignore it, but with what's been going on I think it might be interesting."

"Might indeed. You willing to meet again tomorrow morning?" I finished my pancakes and sat back.

"Sure. As long as you're buying… I'm hungry."

I thought for a minute about how to word the next question.

"Harvey, when we first met we were talking about Humpty Dumpty and I asked who was inside the egg. You said probably one of the midgets from the Freak Show. Do you remember that?"

"Sure. What about it?"

"I'm wondering about the *probably*. Wouldn't you know for sure? I can't imagine that someone shows up for work in an egg costume."

"I would if I saw them, but I don't get inside much, and if they use midgets they probably bring them in through the tunnels. They wouldn't want the show walking down the Midway."

"Tunnels?"

"Sure. When the place was built, they dug tunnels to move supplies and food for the stands. It's like a tiny city down there."

I was amazed and wondered if Stosh knew. Dad certainly didn't or he would have told me. "How do you get into the tunnels?"

"There's entrances leading down from the major attractions and the supply shacks. And there's a hidden opening out onto the river."

A busboy cleared the table, and the waitress asked if we wanted anything else. We didn't and she left the check.

"Have you been down there?"

"Yes, but not often, and not in a while."

"Can you get me down there?"

"Be tough. Why do you want to?"

I smiled. "Because it's there. I'm still a little kid at heart. And when I don't have answers to questions I keep poking around till I find them."

"And where are you poking today?"

"I already started," I said with a smile.

Harvey smiled back, but with a knowing look like an adult putting up with a wayward child that they loved anyway. Since Harvey would probably never join my inner circle of trusted people, I didn't want to share everything with him, even though my gut told me I could.

"I'm going to start checking on employees. Block gave me a list of six in the last two years that includes your three." I gave him the names. "I'd like to catch them at home. Do you know any of them?"

He nodded. "I know all of them, but I know Percy best. I like to hang around the Bobs. I help him pick up souvenirs."

"Souvenirs?"

He smiled. "When the coaster flies around the last turn, all kinds of things fall out of the sky… coins, watches, even a set of false teeth."

"Don't people come looking for them?"

"Sometimes, but usually not. Percy has kind of a museum of items in the shack under the Bobs."

"Interesting." I looked at the list. "Where does Harold work?"

"He runs one of the trains."

After finishing my coffee, I said, "I was going to come to the park and nose around a little more, but my presence isn't exactly welcome so I don't want to be there long. If I stop by Wonderland around eleven would you be able to tell me who's at work? If they're not working, I'll drop by their house and have a chat."

"Sure. Why don't you wear a disguise."

I smiled. "Like what?"

"How about a jester hat?"

"Yeah, nobody would notice *that*! Thanks for the suggestion."

"Just trying to help."

"Did you notice anything different about Benny recently?"

"Different how?"

"Don't know… the way he acted, or things he said."

"Not that I recall. What are you thinking?"

"Well, he was there before Walters, so he and you differ from that group of hires in the last two years. If something is going on with Walters and those people, Benny wasn't involved. But Benny was the first to die. So something changed. There's gotta be a connection there somewhere."

"Sorry, Spencer. I can't…" He pursed his lips and looked like he was thinking. "There was something he said a few weeks back." He thought some more. "I don't remember what we were talking about, but somewhere in the conversation he said he was going to be free."

"Free from what?"

Harvey shook his head. "I have no idea. Sorry."

"Okay, thanks. If you think of more, remember it."

"Sure thing."

I picked up the bill and asked for his phone number and address.

"Why are you asking?" He looked suspicious.

I shrugged. "In case I have to get ahold of you before breakfast or cancel if something comes up."

"Okay, but keep it to yourself." He wrote the numbers down on a napkin as he explained. "I want as little to do with the world as possible. I don't bother it… I don't want it bothering me."

That didn't seem to fit with the carefree jester, and I told him so. He just stared at me with what I thought was a bit of sadness. Made me wonder what had come before the jester.

As we walked to the door, I decided to stop by the office and check with Sam, then head over to the park and play it by ear from there. Sure was nice not having to punch a clock.

Chapter 23

An accident kept me from getting to my office without backtracking down side streets, so I parked a block away and walked. The exercise wouldn't hurt. I entered by the front door for a change and admired my name on the window. Samantha hung up the phone as I walked in.

"If that was new business, I've got enough at the moment," I said with a grin.

"Good morning, Spencer. I got all the addresses. The list is on your desk."

"Yes, thanks. I picked it up a couple hours ago."

I was almost to my office when she said, "Spencer."

I knew by the tone what was next. I didn't know how to handle it.

"It doesn't look good for my father, does it?" She was staring down at her desk.

I walked back to her and touched her shoulder.

"At least there is no bad news. Someone could be trying to find out who he is and having as little luck as we are." I knew how stupid that sounded, but it was all I had. If someone found a confused stranger their first call would be to the police.

She looked up at me with tears in her eyes. I felt helpless and had trouble keeping my own tears back when I thought of my folks. I needed to get to work.

Harold's was the closest address on the list. If he wasn't home I'd ring some doorbells.

***

At eleven o'clock, Harold and Barbara Reid still weren't at work. I thought I saw Mooney but was pretty sure he hadn't seen me.

Harold lived in the middle of a block on Paulina, north of Fullerton… a short, one-change bus ride from the park. The building was an old wooden rooming house that had been turned into an apartment building and ignored for quite a while. The gate in the chain link fence was missing, and rotted siding told a story of neglect.

The front door screeched open, and I stepped into a dingy foyer with remnants of old wallpaper on plaster walls. Mailboxes were on the left wall, but none were locked. They all had a number but most didn't have names, and all of the buzzer buttons were missing. 2D did have a name—Harold Dejan. When I saw the missing buzzers I wondered how I would get in, but the entry door wasn't locked—it wasn't even closed all the way.

Standing inside the door, the only sound I heard was faint music coming from the first floor hall. Sounded like Glenn Miller. I walked down the hall and back, noticing a "Manager" sign on one of the doors. I took a deep breath, patted the gun under my left arm, and started up the wooden stairs. Apartment 2D was in the middle of the hall on the right. I listened at the door, heard nothing, and then knocked. No answer. Another three knocks had the same result. A few seconds later I heard a door open and close on the first floor. I couldn't tell if it was an apartment or the entry door, but no one came up the stairs.

Pulling my hand up into my sleeve, I tried the door knob. As I tried to turn it the door opened a crack. I listened another minute, wondering if I should enter the room. I heard nothing except my heart beating. It took some deep breaths to slow it down. I was dreading what I might find. If Harold was dead I shouldn't be in the room alone with him in case someone saw me there. But if he wasn't home I wanted to look around. Deciding to take a look, I pushed the door open and stepped inside.

The blinds were down, and it took a minute for my eyes to adapt. I was the only one in the room. Aside from a few meager pieces of furniture and a worn throw rug on the floor, the room was even more bare than Samantha's apartment. I opened the drawer in the table next to the bed and found only a Bible. There were a few dingy shirts and pants hanging in the closet. Dirty dishes filled the sink. I quickly looked in the kitchen drawers and under the bed and found nothing of interest. I pulled the door shut and headed back down the stairs. When I got to the bottom, I heard a voice.

"Can I help you, mister?"

A scruffy old man was mopping the linoleum floor.

"No, I was just looking for someone," I said. "But he wasn't in."

"Who?"

"Just a friend, have a nice—"

"I'm the manager here. I know the comings and goings if you're looking for someone."

"Well, I'm looking for Harold Dejan. Have you seen him?"

He shook his head and leaned the mop against the wall. "Not since yesterday, but if you're looking for him, you're on the wrong floor."

"But 2D is what the tag says in the foyer."

"Yeah, I guess it does. Been meaning to change that. He moved to the first floor a while back. Trouble with one of his legs, so he couldn't climb the stairs too well."

I decided to come back later when I could avoid the manager, so I thanked him and turned to go.

"Let's just go see if he's in."

He led the way down the hall to 1C and knocked on the door. No answer, thankfully. I wasn't quite sure what I'd say if he answered.

"What are you wanting Harold for? Friend of yours?"

"No, not exactly." I tried to look concerned. "He didn't show up for work this morning, so they asked me to check up on him. He's usually pretty dependable."

"Yes, he loves working at the park. All he talks about is driving that train. Gives him something to look forward to. Most of these fellows in here don't have anything important like that." He shook his head sorrowfully, and I wondered if he was talking about himself.

"Why don't we take a look," he said. "Just in case."

I had a really bad feeling in the pit of my stomach.

The manager knocked again and then pulled out a set of keys and opened the door. There wasn't much light in this room either, but there was enough to throw a yellow pall over a body sitting in a chair with his head rolled back. The manager gasped. I stopped myself from asking if it was Harold. The assumption would have to suffice. Harold's eyes were wide open, and his tongue hung out under a graying moustache. There was a red welt around his neck and stubble on his chin. I looked around for a phone, but there was none.

I asked the manager to go call the police and say that Spencer had told him to call. I gave him Stosh's direct number. While he was gone I did some snooping. An envelope on the dresser contained several slips of paper, one of which was an IOU to Joey Mineo for two-hundred-twenty dollars. Certainly not enough to die for, but an odd coincidence.

The manager came back but wouldn't come in the room. "They're coming," he said.

I nodded and thought about Harold's train. You never knew about other people's lives. As I looked at Harold, I thought something as simple as a train was all some people needed to bring some happiness. And it could be taken away so easily.

Twenty minutes later, Lt. Powolski followed two uniformed cops down the hall. I introduced him to the manager, and he asked one of the uniforms to get his statement.

"I assume you wouldn't listen to me if I suggest you go up to Wisconsin," he said.

I took a deep breath and let it out slowly. "Trouble would still be here if I left, Stosh."

"Yup. Not going to lose my job anytime soon. But your stirring has opened the barn doors. I'm not worried about the trouble… I'm worried about you. Who do we have here?"

I explained what had brought me to Harold's room.

He bent and looked closely at Harold's neck. "Looks like a rope burn. Not clean like the woman. He must have struggled. Examiner should be here shortly." I nodded to a detective whom Stosh had taken aside for a chat. The usual procedure. Two more made for a crowded room, and I asked Stosh if I could leave.

"You have anything to add to this that you're going to tell me about?"

I didn't and told him so. The only thing I had was the IOU to Joey, and his men would find that.

"What's next?" he asked with a wary look.

"I have a few stops to make. I'm worried about Harvey. I think I'll stop by and warn him."

He took a step toward me and pointed his finger. "That park is the last place I want you. We've got three corpses because you've been putting your nose in where someone doesn't want it. You want to protect Harvey? Stay away from him."

I squinted at him. "I wonder who doesn't want me there."

"I'm sure as hell going to find out. Do you get my message?"

"Got it. I'll see you tonight. But I need a couple of favors."

"Which are?"

I handed him a copy of the list of employees and asked if he'd check them for records. He agreed and asked what the other favor was.

"I need to think about it some more. I'll let you know tonight."

He sighed and went back to work.

***

I stopped by the office after lunch to check in and plan my afternoon. All but one of the addresses were on the north or northwest side. Jeanette Kimball lived in Streeterville, a few blocks from the lake, still technically on the north side, but not by much. I got out a map and wrote all the names in red and made a roadmap for the afternoon. But my first stop would be to pay a visit to Joey Mineo.

Chapter 24

Joey Mineo's office was just a storefront, and he was never there. A secretary who was in her seventies answered the phone for his legitimate business. The last time I needed Joey I was given an address on Belmont which turned out to be an ice cream parlor, so that's where I headed. The front was a soda fountain and the back, where I had been directed after stating my business, was a plush room I would almost call a den where Joey entertained guests. A formidable fellow about twice my weight had sat at the back table. I had needed a password to get past him—*upset*."

The sun was casting longer shadows as I parked in front of the parlor. I was hoping they hadn't changed the password.

The same moose was sitting at the same table reading a paper. He watched me as I walked up to him. The only thing that moved were his eyes. I told him I wanted to see Joey, and he asked for the password. *Upset* just got me a blank stare. After deciding that he could stare forever, I told him who I was and that I'd like to see Joey about a money matter.

He got up and knocked on the door to the back room. A small, horizontal panel in the door slid open, and he told whomever was on the other side that I wanted to see Joey and that I had an old password. A few seconds later the door lock clicked, and the moose held out his hand.

"What?" I asked.

"I'll take your gun."

I gave him the gun after a hard stare that told him he could have my gun, but I was still a tough guy.

He held the door open and another fellow who looked like a milk-toast showed me in. But looks were deceiving. I knew this guy could handle a gun better than most or he wouldn't be in the room.

Joey was sitting in a plush red chair in a dark room with a thick carpet, paneled walls, and no windows. I knew there were extra layers of brick on the back wall. I figured the mayor's office wouldn't look much better... but would have windows.

Joey spoke first. "Spencer Manning. I enjoyed our chat at the park. What brings you here?"

Our chat at the park had involved very few words, but it was always nice to know someone enjoyed spending time with me.

"Accounts receivable."

I had his attention.

"Yours or mine?" He wasn't smiling.

"Yours."

He just waited—a man of few words. The milk-toast was sitting on a couch against the back wall. He wasn't smiling either.

"I'm working on a case that looks to have crossed your path."

"And what case would that be?" Joey asked.

"Missing kids."

He sat straight up in the chair and grabbed the arms. "Hey! I got nothin' to do with kids!"

"Not saying you do, Joey. Just saying there's maybe some things in common."

"Okay. You remember that. I got a soft spot for kids, and I don't want nobody sayin' otherwise."

"Good to hear." I paused long enough for him to ask questions, but he didn't so I continued. "I'm a big picture guy, Joey. This case has lots of little pieces that seem to make no sense. But I'm thinking that if all the pieces are put together they might make a nice picture."

"And I'm one of those pieces?"

I nodded.

"And you're here because…? You mentioned accounts receivable."

"I did. Looking for some help to put the pieces together and maybe give you some help along the way."

I glanced at the milk-toast who hadn't moved a muscle. He didn't take his eyes off me and didn't blink. But I was sure he would move pretty quickly if he had to. Joey pulled out a cigarette, and milk-toast was instantly there with a match.

"You have my interest, Manning. What are the pieces?"

"It started with a missing boy from the south side who worked at Riverview. The last place he was known to be was at work more than a week ago. He didn't go home. I started asking questions at the park, and two days later Benny Parker is found dead in the Tunnel of Love. Then Saturday you show up and have a talk with Meyers. I put Benny into that picture, and I come up with Benny on your receivables list."

He reached for the ashtray and settled back in the chair. "That's a nice story, Manning. But why would I be interested? I can't get money from a stiff."

"No, you can't. And I figure you wouldn't bother for small change. So it must be a nice sum, say in the thousands… maybe ten." I wasn't going to tell him how I knew how much it was… let him think I was a genius. "And for a sum like that you'd want some answers."

He just looked at me, took another slow puff, and let out a cloud.

"And how do you figure this is giving me some help?"

"That isn't. But this might. Benny is only one of the pieces. Two more are dead. The latest is Harold Dejan."

"So whadda I care about a Harold Dejan?"

"I have reason to believe he's also a receivable."

Joey glanced quickly at the milk-toast who nodded.

Looking back at me, Joey asked, "And why would you think that?"

I smiled. "Just a hunch. But I'm good at hunches."

"And let's say that's true. So what?"

"So, people on your list are dying. I'm wondering why. Just thought you'd want to know." Actually I didn't think it had anything to do with Joey. The sign on my wall about coincidences isn't written in stone. I was pretty sure this was an exception and that Joey's involvement was just a coincidence, but I firmly believed in one of my other rules that *was* always true—it never hurts to shake the trees and see what falls out. The more trees you shake the better.

The milk-toast had gone back to being a statue. Joey stubbed out the cigarette. "Okay, you have my attention."

"And I have another question. Is Gertrude Morgan a client?"

He stared at me and then looked at the milk-toast who shook his head once, which was when I knew that the milk-toast, besides being protection, was also the accounting department. And the exchange I just saw was why Joey was walking around in fancy suits instead of wearing stripes in a cell somewhere. He didn't have any books—he had the milk-toast, who had all the books in his head. And he got a gun man for the same price. He looked like a milk-toast on the outside, but I was guessing that was where it stopped.

"No, she is not. Why do you ask?"

"Because she's dead too."

Joey was not one to show emotion, despite his soft spot for kids and ice cream cones. He was all business. But he always paused before responding and always responded calmly. There was a thought process going on that no one else would ever know.

"Pardon my questioning your case, Manning, but for looking into missing kids you got a lotta bodies piling up."

I nodded my agreement. "That's what makes this job so fun. You open a door, you never know what you're going to find."

He nodded back. "I wish you'd find out soon. Dead clients are bad for business."

"I'll keep that in mind," I said as I stood up. "One more question."

He gave me a look bordering on controlled anger. I knew I was wearing out my welcome, but he didn't say no.

"Meant to ask you last time. The old password was *upset*. That seemed strange to me. I'd think you'd not be a fan of upsets."

"Agreed," he replied with a slight smile.

"Meaning?"

"Meaning I got hooked on horses when I was a kid. I had an uncle who told me stories. My favorite was about the Sanford Stakes in 1919. It was the only race that Man o' War lost. He was named by the wife of August Belmont, who the Belmont Stakes was named for, because August was overseas fighting in World War II."

This was a side of Joey few had ever seen. He looked almost wistful.

"Back then there weren't no starting gates, just a piece of webbed material that was raised. The horses would circle behind it and then line up. When it was raised, Man o' War was still circling with his rump to the web. Even though he got a late start he only lost by a half length… to a nobody named Upset." The smile had grown.

"Interesting. Do you bet on upsets?"

Now he grinned. "I've never bet on *anything*, Manning."

My look of surprise made him laugh.

"I don't like giving away money, Manning," he said as the smile disappeared.

"I have another question. Why the hell do you have passwords?"

He shrugged. "Uncle Al had a password. Good enough for him… good enough for me."

"Uncle Al? Al Capone?"

"There's another Al?"

"He was your uncle?"

"No."

I was going to ask the next question, but his look said he didn't want to hear it.

The milk-toast opened the door.

I turned back as Joey said, "Hey, Manning. I hope you find the kids."

My nod ended our chat.

The moose handed me my gun and returned to his table in the corner.

I had no idea where the last half hour had left me, but it was always interesting talking to Joey. The insight into his other side gave me shivers. I had seen him buy the kid an ice cream cone, and I had just seen him slip back into his childhood. But I also knew he would break somebody's legs without giving it any thought.

Compared to the dark office, the sunlight was blinding, and I had to squint to check the list for Barbara's address. A light breeze brought a wave of car exhaust.

Chapter 25

I listened to the Cubs as I drove west. The game with the Pirates was just going into extra innings. North of Lawrence, the homes on Kimball changed from multi-family to bungalows. Barbara's was typical with red brick and decorative stone insets. The built-out attic overhung the front porch where a large picture window looked out on the small, grassy front yard. The house was narrow and long, with little space between the houses on either side. Some of Chicago's bungalows were built just after the turn of the last century, but this one looked newer. If it wasn't, it was certainly well kept. I rang the doorbell and waited.

After a minute I rang the bell again. A few seconds later I caught a flutter of drapes at the corner of the picture window. I tried one more time and was ready to give up when the door opened a crack.

I could only see part of a woman's face. She tentatively said, "Yes?"

"I'm looking for Barbara Reid."

"Yes?" She was hesitant.

Not exactly the answer I was expecting. I assumed I had found her. "If you're Barbara, I have a few questions."

"And who are you?"

I held out my card. She didn't take it, or look at it. "Spencer Manning. I'm trying to find a missing boy who worked at Riverview and would just like a few minutes—"

"We were all told not to talk to you. Please leave," she said in a shaky voice.

"Who told you not to talk to me?" I already knew the answer.

"You need to leave, Mr. Manning."

As she started to close the door, I gave it one last try. "It won't hurt just to answer a few questions, Miss Reid."

"It would hurt. They're watching. You've been here too long already." Before she closed the door I dropped my card inside. A few seconds later she closed the drapes.

Glancing up and down the street I saw no one. She was paranoid, but her paranoia was real, even though the surveillance wasn't, and she was afraid inside her own house. A knot in my stomach told me I was doing something I didn't really want to do. That was one of the bad parts about my job. As I walked down the steps, I thought about Harold. He was one of the *all* Barbara had referred to, but instead of opening the door and telling me that, he had stared at me with eyes that no longer saw what they were looking at. Why was he dead and Barbara still here to open the door? Maybe he was just first on the list. And maybe she wasn't wrong to be paranoid.

***

I pulled into Stosh's drive a little after five. He wasn't home yet, so I used my key to let myself in and turned on the game. The Pirates had scored and taken a four to three lead after eleven and a half. Larry Bowa led off the Cubs half of the eleventh with a single. Two outs later I saw Stosh pull into the drive. I knew he had the game on. He closed his door as Ryne Sandberg lined a fast ball into the left field bleachers just inside the foul pole. I would have waited in the car. He had heard me yell.

"What the hell did I miss?"

"Sandberg line drive homer to left."

"He's the best. This is the year, Spencer. I can just feel it. Time for a World's Series pennant on the north side."

I laughed. "I recall you feeling it several times before."

"But not like now. If they don't make it this year it'll be a hundred before they do."

I laughed. "That'll never happen."

"Yeah, well we'll see. You hungry?"

"Sure, how about Italian?"

"Good by me. I'll change and wash up."

We talked baseball and weather on the way to Mama Abella's and were seated at our usual table in a back corner.

Luigi brought a bottle of dry red wine and asked if we wanted the usual lasagna. We did. We were in a rut—a very nice rut.

After a sip, Stosh asked if I had made any progress.

"Not much."

"If you haven't discovered any more bodies, I'd call that progress."

I ignored that and told him about Barbara.

"Sure is something going on to scare her that much."

I agreed. "Anything on your end?"

He took a deep breath and shook his head. "So far the lab has nothing on the pipes but a lot of smudged prints. They're about half done. I've got personnel walking the park, and we've talked to a whole lot of people who know nothing."

"You're not going to find anything on the pipes."

"No shit."

"But you have to look anyway."

He just stared at me with a frown.

"Lots of wasted time."

He agreed. "Part of the job. We have to cross all the Ts."

"And whatever it was could have been tossed in the river."

"Thanks. I never would have thought of that. We have divers going in tomorrow."

Figuring I had pissed him off enough, I said, "This sure can't be just coincidences."

He nodded. "I'd still feel much better if you'd go up to Door County and spend some time with Aunt Rose."

"It's tempting. Been too long since my last trip. Have you heard about the meeting at the park tonight?"

"Nope. How did you hear about it?"

"Harvey. He got an invitation to attend."

"What's it about?"

"No clue. We're having breakfast again in the morning. I'll let you know."

"And you don't think you're putting him in jeopardy with all these meetings?"

"Don't see how anyone would know about them."

"And you're staying away from the park?"

I hesitated.

He looked disappointed. "Spencer." He shook his head slowly. "I agree with shaking the trees once in a while, but you've done enough. When were you there?"

I told him about my quick visit with Harvey to find out about who showed up for work.

"And how do you know nobody saw you?"

"Baseball cap and sunglasses. And I was in and out. I saw Walters' stooge, Mooney, but he didn't see me."

"You sure? You're taking a chance. Stay away from there."

"I'll try."

"Jesus."

The food came, and we ate in silence for a few minutes, listening to the strolling violin player.

As Luigi refilled the wine glasses, I said, "I did find out something about Benny." He kept chewing. "He told Harvey a few weeks ago that he was going to be free."

"From what?"

"Don't know. Harvey couldn't remember what they were talking about."

He finished the last bite of lasagna and wiped the plate with bread dipped in oil. "Well, whatever it was, he sure is free now."

***

B ack at the house, Stosh put on a Count Basie record, and I set up the card table for gin. I was ahead by almost three bucks when the phone rang a little after ten. He listened and then closed his eyes.

"Be there in fifteen," he said.

"Watcha got?" I asked.

"Broken window."

"I'm on a hot streak. You've gotta go for a broken window?"

"Yup, and so do you. Your hot streak is over."

Tossing down the cards, I asked, "Why do I have to go?"

"Because it's your window. Close your mouth."

"The one with my name on it?"

"Don't know, but if I was going to send you a message, that'd be the one I'd shoot at."

"Who reported it?"

"A concerned citizen."

I rode with him in his unmarked cruiser. The concerned citizen turned out to be Carol, and she was standing in front of the window talking to an officer when we pulled up. The officer introduced her, and she started from the beginning.

A little before ten she had heard what she thought was a car backfiring, but then there were several more bangs and she thought it was strange. She looked out and saw my shattered window and called the police. She hadn't seen the car. Two officers had been talking to neighbors who had all heard the shots but hadn't seen the car either. We spent a little more time waiting for the board-up company.

On the way back to my car, Stosh said, "So both our points are probably valid."

"And those are?"

"None of these are coincidences, and you should head north and spend some time with Aunt Rose."

"Well, I agree with the first."

"I think you should agree with the second."

"I know, and I appreciate it, but you don't really think I will, do you?"

"Doesn't hurt to try. Three people are dead, and you've been sent a pretty clear message. This isn't a game, Spencer."

"Agreed."

"They're trying to scare you."

He turned into the drive and stopped next to my Mustang.

"They're just pissing me off." I thought about Barbara. "These guys are just bullies."

"Bullies who are killing people. I'd pay attention."

"And run away?"

"Nope, but I'd be careful."

I agreed that they had my attention and assured Stosh that I could take care of myself and would be careful.

He nodded slowly. "You're pretty good at it, but you don't have eyes in the back of your head, and whoever is doing this isn't likely to play fair and challenge you to a duel. They're just going to put a bullet in your back."

"I don't have a death wish, Stosh. Quite the opposite. And I have friends in high places."

He got out and leaned on the roof for a few seconds before saying goodnight.

Chapter 26

Harvey was sitting across from our usual booth, sipping coffee and reading the paper.

"Morning, Manning. I don't see your name in the paper so you must be behaving yourself."

"I always do, but I tend to get involved with people who don't." I told him about the window.

He shook his head. "Pretty clear warning... and yet here you are."

"Hey, I wouldn't want you to have to pay for your own breakfast."

The waitress brought the coffee, and we ordered.

"So what was the meeting all about?" I asked.

He laughed. "Just Walters explaining what was going on around the park... at least their version of it. He warned us again not to talk with anyone, especially you. We're supposed to refer anyone asking questions to him and tell him if we see you. You're not on the top of his guest list."

"I'll try not to take it personally. Was Meyers there?"

"Yup. She didn't say a word, but she was paying close attention to the crowd. I felt like she was taking attendance and making mental notes."

"Do you feel unsafe?"

He smiled. "I'm not worried. Walters is just a bully, and bullies don't scare me."

"Three people are dead, Harvey. Somebody helped them get that way."

He took a deep breath. "Well, we all gotta go sometime."

The food arrived and I started on the eggs.

"You still thinking about having me arrested?"

I finished a bite of toast. "If you were arrested Walters would be able to threaten your employment unless you cooperated with him."

"Cooperated how?"

"That's what I'd like to find out. It sure looks like people are being hired who have something that would look bad on a resumé." I got the waitress's attention and asked for some Tabasco.

As he ate his pancakes, Harvey said, "I've been thinking about it too. I kind of set a goal of never seeing the inside of a jail cell."

"You wouldn't have to. We'd work it out."

"I hope so—I don't look good in stripes." He smiled. "Where would I be arrested?"

"At the park. It would have to be obvious. If Walters didn't actually see it, word would get around pretty fast."

He sipped his coffee and sat back in the booth. "Still wondering… arrested for what?"

I took a drink of coffee and set the cup down carefully before answering. "Well, how about murder?"

He looked shocked and I didn't blame him.

He opened his eyes wide and said, "I guess if I have to ruin my record I might as well do it right. When is this going to happen?"

"Don't know yet. How about breakfast again on Saturday?"

He shrugged. "Okay. See you Saturday, same time, same place. Thanks for the grub."

He walked out while I paid the bill. I didn't want another broken window, but the pot needed some more stirring.

***

I was in the office when Samantha came in the back door and stopped, her eyes wide with amazement.

"What in the world happened?"

"A little run in with a few bullets."

She set her purse down and stared at the plywood. "Oh my God, Spencer. What does this mean?"

"It means I got someone's attention."

"My friends just send cards."

The phone rang as I was trying to think of a comeback. Realizing I had a secretary, I walked into my office.

"It's for you, Spencer," Samantha said. It was a cheap intercom system.

I picked up the phone. "Hello?"

"Mr. Manning?"

I didn't recognize the female voice. "Yes."

"This is Barbara Reid."

That surprised me. "Yes, Miss Reid."

She was obviously nervous. "I really don't know what to say, but I'd like to talk to you about the… well, what you asked me about."

I tried not to sound excited. I needed to find something besides dead bodies. "Go ahead."

"Not on the phone."

"I can be there in fifteen minutes if you—"

"No, not here. I'm sure someone is watching."

I could hear the fear in her voice. "Then where would you feel comfortable? You can come to my office."

"I really don't know. I feel like we should meet in a bookstore or something."

Samantha appeared in my doorway with a questioning look.

"Whatever you say, Barbara. But I think my office would be fine."

"They're probably watching your office too. They had a meeting last night that…"

"I know about the meeting. I think you're safe here with me."

She was silent for a minute before answering. "Okay, but what happens when I come home? I don't feel safe here."

I didn't have to think at all about my next suggestion. "Can you take some time off?"

"Yes."

"Then pack a bag with enough for a week, and I'll get you somewhere safe."

"I don't know. I don't even know you. I…"

"I understand. I'll do anything you want. But we need to talk."

"Where is somewhere safe?"

"You ever been to Door County?"

She hadn't, but she knew about it. I explained about Aunt Rose's inn. She asked how much it was going to cost and didn't believe me when I told her it was free. Eventually, she accepted. I thought she must be pretty worried to trust a complete stranger.

"Would you like me to come and get you?"

She quickly answered no. "I'm taking a chance just calling you. I don't really know you're who you say you are. You could have been sent by them just to test me."

Her mind had dug a deep hole.

"Well, if that's true, Barbara, you're already in trouble by making this call. Since you took that chance you might as well trust me."

"Okay, but I'll take a cab. I can be there in an hour. How can I be sure it's a real office? I might be walking into a trap."

I rolled my eyes at Samantha. "Here's another suggestion. If you'd feel better we can meet at a police station where I'm pretty well known."

"No, that's okay. I'll just come to your office." She sounded a little less frightened. "Do you have a sign on your office?"

I started to tell her my name was on the window, but it obviously wasn't. I explained that it used to be but the glass cracked, and it had to be boarded up. I was sure the truth would have meant the end of our conversation. We hung up with me wondering if she'd really show up.

From the doorway, Samantha asked, "What the heck was that all about?"

I briefly explained and told her I'd be gone for a bit. "The glass company is coming sometime this afternoon. Would you stay till they get here?"

"Of course. I'm looking forward to having something to do."

"Great. And the stenciling person is coming tomorrow morning."

"Okay." She hesitated. "Spencer, is it safe here?"

"Yes. The people who did this are cowards. They're allergic to daylight."

I took care of some case notes while waiting for Barbara. When the phone rang again ten minutes later I worried that Barbara had changed her mind.

"Spencer, it's Lieutenant Powolski," Samantha said.

I picked up. "Hello, Lieutenant, a fine day for—"

"Yeah, can it. I've got something on those names. All of them have a record."

The first piece of what I was trying to put together clicked into place. "That's what I was hoping."

"Okay. I'm not gonna ask, but see if you were hoping for this. All of them except for one have the same arresting officer—detective Bringman."

"Okay, but lots of people have the same arresting officer."

"Uh-huh. Guess who Walters' partner was."

"How many do I get?"

"None. Come on over tonight and we'll chat."

"I can't." I told him about Barbara.

"Thank goodness for Aunt Rose. It's like an underground railroad you've got going on up there. Be here for breakfast at eight." He hung up.

The rest of the hour dragged by with me wondering if any of Barbara's paranoia was real. I was relieved when a cab pulled up almost exactly an hour later.

A middle-aged woman who looked like she hadn't slept in days got out and hesitantly looked at my boarded up window. I met her at the door and took her suitcase. It didn't look big enough to hold a week's worth of clothes. She was obviously nervous but seemed to relax a bit when Samantha introduced herself. Her eyes darted around the room.

I told her we had a six-hour drive and asked if she needed the washroom. She said she didn't, but I was willing to bet she wouldn't make it all the way without a stop. My friend Maxine needed two. I was looking forward to seeing Maxine and Aunt Rose. I hadn't been up to Door County in months.

I asked if she had let the park know she wouldn't be in. When she looked flustered, I suggested she call and tell them she was feeling sick and would be off for a few days. I offered the phone in my office.

We left after I gave Samantha a few more instructions.

***

In the car, Barbara stared straight ahead and held onto her purse with both hands. Short brown hair to just below her jaw framed a thin face with a scar on the left side of her chin. Her jaw was firmly set, and I could see muscles in her neck. It was like a face carved in granite. She certainly wasn't relaxed, but she had no reason to be. I felt sorry for her. If trusting a complete stranger was your best option, your options weren't that good.

I had no idea what to talk about. How do you make small talk for six hours with someone you just met who is afraid of her own shadow? I decided to just say what was on my mind.

As we turned onto the expressway, I said, "So, I'm wondering why you called me."

She glanced at me quickly and then looked back to the front. I thought she wasn't going to answer, but then tears welled up in her eyes.

"I thought about it a lot, Mr. Manning. I just couldn't bear it if something bad has happened to those kids." She paused, turned her head away from me, and wiped her eyes with her fingers.

I had several questions but thought it best to let her talk at her own pace. But when she didn't continue, I asked what she knew about the kids.

After a big sigh, she said, "I work at the Skee Ball booth. There was a boy there named Terrence Jacobs. Nice kid, polite, nice smile. He told me he lived in a foster home with six other kids. It was his fourth since he was eight. Before that he lived in a county home. Over a few weeks we talked about what that was like." She tensed and stopped again as a car switching lanes cut right in front of me.

When we both recovered, I asked, "So, how was it?"

Shaking her head, she said, "Not good. Lots of yelling and anger. Why would anyone take on six kids?"

"Because they get paid by the kid. It's not a good system but better than being on the streets."

She rolled the window down a bit. "I suppose."

Out of the corner of my eye, I watched her looking out at the scenery rolling by. She had a strength about her, but also hesitation and fear.

"So what happened?" I asked.

"Meyers came up to me one day and told me she wanted me to bring Terrence to the little office under the Bobs roller coaster. I asked why, and she told me he was going to work on one of the other coasters, the Fireball. That's every kid's dream who works there. I was thrilled, and so was Terrence."

We merged onto I94 and continued north. I settled back into the right lane.

"Sounds great," I said.

"Yeah, I thought so too. But I stopped at the Fireball the next afternoon, and Terrence wasn't there. Gerry, the fellow who runs it, said he didn't know any Terrence, and no kid had showed up for work."

"Maybe it was his day off."

"I didn't think so, but I thought maybe they changed it, so I stopped the next day and the next, but no Terrence. So I went to the police station and asked Mrs. Meyers. What do you think she said?"

I had a guess. "What?"

"She didn't remember any Terrence and said she had never asked me to bring anyone anywhere."

That was my guess. "So what did you say?"

"I told her she was mistaken and wondered what was going on. She told me to mind my own business and that if I continued she'd have to check my file. Then she asked if I had ever had any problems with the police."

"And had you?" I knew the answer to that too.

"Well, yes." She held her hands tightly together on her lap. "I had some trouble a few years back, but I was let go. The policeman was very nice. He even offered to help me get me the job at Riverview. He said he knew the chief there."

Another piece fell into place. "So that's how you got hired?"

She nodded. "But Mrs. Meyers said that old case could always be looked into if I didn't cooperate."

"So you cooperated by shutting up?"

"Yes." She looked down sheepishly at her hands. "Then a week or so ago we got told about missing kids and that we weren't supposed to talk to anyone but Walters... and especially not you."

"Nice to be special." I smiled. She didn't.

"But I really wondered about Terrence and if something bad had happened to him."

We passed the exit to Kenosha, and I resisted the urge to head east and take the scenic route along the lake. I had a lot of driving to do before the day was over so I stayed on the expressway.

"What did you think happened?"

"I thought he had an accident. They're really proud of their 'no accidents' record, and I figured they'd cover it up if something happened. But I figured they'd take care of Terrence. I forgot about it until last night when we had a meeting after work by the carousel."

"Yes, I heard about that. What happened?"

"Walters and Meyers were there, but Walters did all the talking. He just told us again not to talk to anyone, especially you, without talking to him first. And he made it seem like we were all being watched." She ran her fingers through her hair, pulling it away from the side of her face. "He doesn't like you."

I smiled. If someone doesn't like you, you're doing something right. "I got that impression. Was that all he said?"

"It was going to be, but then someone asked about Benny, the guy who died in the Tunnel of Love." She tilted her head and pursed her lips. "Walters seemed flustered. He said the police had looked into it and not found anything so it must have been an accident."

"Do you believe that?"

She shrugged. "I don't know what to believe. But it's probably not going to be anything Walters has to say."

"Probably a wise choice." I passed a semi and slowed down to sixty-five.

"Do you mind if I ask you some questions, Mr. Manning?"

"Not at all."

Turning sideways in the bucket seat, she asked, "You said you knew about the meeting. How did you know?"

I was impressed. She had paid attention. But I also felt put on the spot. I wasn't sure I wanted to share that information, but I also realized that if I wanted to keep her at ease I couldn't appear to be hiding anything.

"I've been chatting with a few people at the park... one in particular."

She nodded slowly. "Yes, I know. Harvey."

I tried to hide my surprise.

She laughed. "Not many secrets there. Word spreads fast."

As we approached Racine, a food sign caught my attention.

"Are you hungry?"

She was.

I pulled off 94 and into a McDonald's. She suggested we go through the drive-through and eat in the car. We picked up a chicken sandwich for her, hold the mayo, and two cheeseburgers and fries for me.

As I handed her the bag of food, she said, "Do you know that Harvey is Mrs. Meyers' cousin?"

It was a good thing she had a grip on the bag because I would have dropped it.

We were back on the expressway in three minutes. Four hours to go.

Chapter 27

After we got the food arranged, fries between my legs and Barbara in charge of the drinks, she said, "I'm guessing your answer is no."

"Correct. How do you know that?"

"The place is a great gossip factory. Like all gossip, you have to weed through what's true... but that is. I take it he didn't mention that."

"No, he didn't."

We finished eating in silence, but my thoughts were racing. Cousins! This threw a whole new wrinkle into whether or not I trusted Harvey. But since he hadn't told me, he would have no reason to think I knew, so I could just keep playing it like I trusted him. This certainly increased the chances that he was a stooge for Walters and Meyers.

After Barbara collected the trash, I spoke. "You said you have questions... you've only asked one."

I noticed that she had relaxed since getting into the car. I could no longer see her neck muscles.

"Okay. How did you get involved in this?"

I explained about Martin and gave her some background about Johnny and the Blue Note. Talking about jazz for a few minutes relieved some more tension. She was a John Coltrane fan and suggested that *Giant Steps* was the best jazz album ever made. I said she'd get some arguments from Miles Davis fans who swore by *Kind of Blue*. We agreed to make it a toss-up.

"So you're working for Mr. Ray?"

I laughed. "Well, working isn't quite the right word. That implies pay. But if I heard about this I'd probably be involved even if I hadn't been asked. I played Don Quixote in *Man of La Mancha* in high school."

She laughed. "Knight in shining armor, eh?"

"Well, a bit tarnished perhaps."

We were silent for a few minutes.

"Do you think Benny's death is connected to the kids?"

Rule number three—pay attention to coincidences... they usually aren't. "I'd be very surprised if it wasn't. That happened after I started asking questions." I decided not to tell her about Gertrude and Harold. That would only scare her. As I started to tell her more, I looked over, and she was asleep with her head back on the rest and her mouth slightly open. I figured she hadn't had much sleep lately and was happy she dozed off... I needed to think about what was going on.

My dad had a list of rules and each one had a number. When I was a kid I thought he was just making up numbers as he told me the rule. But after I started paying attention, I remembered the rules, and they always had the same numbers. I asked him for a list, and he told me the list was in his head. There were over twenty, but I only remembered the ones that had the most significance for me. And I had added some to the list.

***

Barbara woke up with a start as we crossed over the canal at Sturgeon Bay and entered the peninsula of upper Door County. Only a half hour left.

"Well, you had a nice nap."

She glanced at the clock. "I guess so." Looking out at the rolling farm land, she said, "This is lovely."

I agreed. "Wait till you see the inn."

"When will we be there?" she asked as she stretched.

"About a half hour."

She nodded. "I have another question, Mr. Manning."

"Okay. I'll let you ask if you call me Spencer."

She looked concerned. "Do you... are you...?"

That much hesitation between two relative strangers usually meant something personal, like are you married or do you kiss on the first date. "Try just spitting it out."

She took a deep breath. "Do you have a gun?"

That surprised me. "I do."

"With you?"

"Yes." It was in the glove box but I didn't want to tell her that.

"Do you think it's necessary?"

I smiled. "Well, I've tried saying bang, but it just doesn't have the same effect."

She just stared out the window, leaving me wondering why she had asked, and why my wit had fallen flat. I finally asked.

"Just wondering. I guess I wanted to know how serious this all is. Must be pretty serious."

I took a left fork and continued on Highway 42 toward the west side of the peninsula and Green Bay. "I think it's serious, and so do you—you were a prisoner in your own house."

She nodded quickly. "Are you a good shot?"

"Yes. If it's me or the other guy, the one on the ground will be the other guy." I was hoping that would make her feel better. "But I don't like to carry a gun. I rarely do."

"If you do dangerous things, why wouldn't you carry it?"

I laughed. Wasn't the first time I'd been asked that. "Pretty uncomfortable... and not easy to conceal." I was hoping she'd drop it.

"What kind do you have?"

Talking with her about guns made me uneasy, but I decided to answer. She must have been asking to make herself feel better.

"I have several. I have a Smith and Wesson .357 Magnum, a Smith and Wesson snub-nose .38, and a 9mm Glock."

"Why all the guns?"

"Do you know anything about guns?"

"I know they kill people."

"Well, we could argue that point, but remember my statement about me or the other guy."

"So why all the guns?"

I took a deep breath. "Well, the .357 is heavy, but it'll shoot through a brick wall. I mostly have it because it's a showpiece... blued-steel barrel and engraved grip. It was my dad's. The other two are working guns."

"Why two?"

"Because sometimes two are better than one."

That seemed to satisfy her, but I was still wondering why she was asking. Maybe she just wanted to know that she was protected. And maybe she wanted to know my armament for some other reason. I had asked her to trust me, a person she didn't know. But I was in the same boat. Maybe I was being set up. Maybe she was a Walters plant. As 42 turned to the north, I wondered if there were two paranoid people in the car. Still, there was a difference between being paranoid and being aware... I just wasn't sure where the line between them was.

* * *

I gave her some history as we drove, and she admired the little towns we passed through. But she was most impressed when we pulled into Peninsula State Park and the bay came into view. Sailboats with furled sails bobbed on slight swells. I parked in the lot by the ranger's office.

She looked afraid and asked, "What are we doing here?"

"The inn is on the other side of the bay. I have a couple more questions. Do you mind?"

"Okay," she said hesitantly.

"Do you know anything about the tunnels under the park?"

She relaxed. I had no idea what she thought I was going to ask.

"I do. They're for moving supplies and people so they're not seen by the customers."

"Ever been down there?"

"Sure. Lots of times. Why?"

"I'd like to see them."

"Well, you'd need someone to show you how to get in. But Walters would not be happy."

"Walters wouldn't have to know."

She had been looking out at the bay. She now turned to face me. "Walters knows everything."

"You give him more power than you should."

"I don't have a gun, so I assume the worst and hope that keeps me safe."

"Well, I think you're safe up here. You didn't tell anyone you were coming did you?"

"Just my daughter."

I nodded. "Do you know anyone who would be willing to get me into the tunnels?"

After thinking for a minute and looking out at the bay some more, she made a suggestion. "There's a woman who hates Walters and Meyers... Sadie Peterson. She's also afraid, but I think she'd love the chance to get even with him."

"Get even? For what?"

"For beating her."

"Pardon?"

"He took her down in the tunnels after work and beat her. The official story was she had some kind of accident."

"How do you know what happened?"

She gave me the most determined look I've ever seen and uttered the strongest four words I have ever heard. "Because she told me."

"Why did he beat her?"

"He said she stole food."

"Did she?"

"I think so."

"Why would she do that?"

"We don't get paid much, Spencer. Many of us work other jobs."

"Doesn't justify stealing."

"No, but she can't work an extra job. She takes care of her invalid mother."

I sighed. Life is never easy. "And you think she'd help me?"

"You could ask."

"If she's afraid, she probably wouldn't talk to me. Would you call her?"

"I don't have her number. But take this." She slid a ring off her baby finger. It was a sapphire set in a plain silver setting. "This was my mother's and Sadie loved it. She was always admiring it. Tell her I had it on the wrong finger. She'll know you talked to me."

I took the ring. Another job for Samantha—find Sadie. As I turned around and headed out of the park, I realized I trusted Barbara. No one could have planned the ring this far ahead.

I had described the Harbor Lantern Inn, but when I turned into the drive just around the bottom of the bay and pulled up the hill, Barbara was surprised.

"Oh my, Spencer… it's lovely. I'm staying here?"

I laughed. "You are. If you try real hard, you might enjoy it."

Maxine came down the steps of the porch and met me with a hug when I got out.

"Do you greet all your guests this way, ma'am?"

She crossed her arms and said, "Yup. It's in the manual."

I gave her another hug and, after opening the trunk, introduced Barbara to Maxine. I had filled in Aunt Rose on what was going on, and I knew she had shared it with Maxine.

"Rose is shopping for something special for dinner," Maxine said. "Come with me, Barbara, and we'll get you settled. And you, fella, you can say hi to Amelie."

They headed into the inn, chatting like old friends. I sat on a rocker on the porch and had a staring contest with Amelie, the stray black cat Maxine had found in the woods. I won as Amelie lost interest and slowly closed her eyes to continue her nap on the railing in the late afternoon sun.

As I looked out at the bay I thought about Walters. The boss doesn't beat people… he has other people do that for him so his clothes don't get dirty, unless he's crazy and then all bets are off. I needed to have another chat with Stosh about Walters.

Maxine was back ten minutes later.

"Nice lady, Spencer."

"Yes. I have pretty high standards in the women I bring up here."

She smiled and reached over and patted my arm.

We caught up and watched the boats in the harbor.

"How you doing with running lights?" I asked.

A while back I had taught Maxine navigation rules and showed her how to tell how boats were moving at night by looking at the lights.

"I'm a pro. I actually do enjoy sitting here and watching the boats at night. The lights are relaxing and kind of magical." She paused and lost her smile. "I'm sure you didn't tell Rose all that's going on, Spencer. But what she told me sounds dangerous."

"Could be. Missing kids and dead bodies are never a good thing."

She touched my arm again. "I'm worried about you."

I took her hand. "Thanks, but I can be dangerous too."

"I know, but still…"

Aunt Rose pulled up the hill and parked in the spot farthest from the inn. She always said spots at the front were for the guests. The lot was about half full. We helped her carry groceries into the kitchen and sat down at a butcher block table. There was, of course, a cherry pie cooling on the counter.

"Are you staying here or at the cottage?" Rose asked.

I sighed. "I shouldn't even be staying for dinner. But if pie is for dessert, I'll force myself."

"You don't mean you're driving back tonight!" said Rose with motherly concern.

"Wish I wasn't… but I am. I have a meeting with Stosh at eight in the morning."

Dinner was wonderful as always. Fresh salmon, mashed potatoes, and asparagus, topped off with pie. Barbara spent the whole dinner asking questions about life up here. She seemed surprised that such a place existed.

I offered to clean up, but Rose said I'd better get on the road. I reluctantly agreed. Rose gave me a hug and started to rinse dishes. Maxine and Barbara walked me to the car. I got a goodbye hug from Maxine and orders to stop if I got sleepy.

Barbara asked how long a girl had to know me to get a hug.

"What time is it?" I asked.

She started to look at her watch and then stopped, laughing. I gave her a hug and told her to just forget about everything and enjoy the inn. She said that wasn't going to be a problem.

I really wanted to stop at the cottage on Moonlight Bay and watch the sky darken from my deck, but I only had another hour before losing the sunlight and wanted to put on as many miles as I could before dark.

Chapter 28

Martin watched the cat sitting in the corner by the door. It was watching him. Once in a while it blinked. He hadn't been sleeping well and had given up counting the marks on his arm. The ceiling light had already turned off, but there was just enough light coming in the boarded up window for him to make out the shadowy shape of the cat. When he sat up in bed the cat opened its eyes wider and gradually grew to twice its normal size. When he woke up the cat was gone, and a tray of food was on the table. It looked like breakfast.

Chapter 29

It was ten minutes after eight when I pulled into Stosh's driveway. The sun was just starting to burn off the night chill. I had stopped at a rest area just north of Milwaukee and taken a ten-minute walk in the chilly air. It woke me up enough to make it home safely and get in four hours of sleep. Stosh was waiting for me on the porch.

"Where the hell you been?"

"Nice. Four hours of sleep and I get an attitude."

"Don't get out of the car." He stood next to the door.

"Come on, Stosh. I need sleep, not abuse."

There was no sympathy in his look.

"I got a call fifteen minutes ago. We found Samantha's father."

"Thank God. Where did they find him? How is he?"

It took him a few seconds to respond. I knew it wasn't good news.

"There was a fire last night... abandoned building just north of Broadway and Foster. Search of the building found a body."

"Oh no. Are you sure it's him?"

"They have the ring."

I closed my eyes and tried not to think about Samantha. "I guess she'll have to ID the body."

"Spencer, there's nothing to ID. He was totally burned. Dental records might do it, but it's not something you want her to look at. All that's left is a cinder."

"Jesus… life sucks sometimes. I wonder what happened."

"My guess is he was lost and found the empty building to sleep in and somebody torched it… insurance maybe. We'll find out. The arson squad is good at what they do."

"But it's not just arson."

"No, it's not. You want me to come with you to tell her?"

I took a deep breath and let it out slowly. "No, thanks. I'll head over there."

"Okay. She can pick up the ring at the morgue."

* * *

I thought I could catch Samantha before she left for work, and I did. I thought about what to say on the way to her apartment but had no real plan. I could certainly empathize after losing my folks, but I had no way to make it easy.

She looked happy to see me, which made me feel even worse. But the happiness disappeared quickly as she saw the look on my face.

I barely managed to get out, "I'm so sorry, Samantha," before she collapsed into my arms.

I led her to the couch, and she sat sobbing with her head in her hands. After a few minutes she stopped crying and asked what had happened. I told her in the gentlest way I could. Somewhere along the way she had taken my hand. I put my arm around her, and she leaned on my shoulder.

"He died alone, Spencer. That's so horrible." And she started to cry again.

A little before nine she pulled away and told me she'd better finish getting ready for work. I told her not to worry about work, just to stay home and attend to whatever she needed to attend to.

"Thanks, but I'd rather be busy. I need to make some phone calls, but if it's okay with you, I'd rather do that from the office. It's so lonely here."

I'd never seen such a sad, lonely look and knew how she felt. I had felt the same way in my parents' house for quite a while.

"Sure, I don't mind."

"Can I have the ring back?"

"Of course."

"Do I have to...?" Her soft voice trailed off.

I shook my head. "No. But you can pick up the ring." I didn't need to tell her there was nothing left to identify.

"Thanks, Spencer. You're wonderful." She gave me a kiss on the cheek, and I wiped away some tears.

I asked what the funeral arrangements would be.

"He wanted to be cremated."

I nodded and tactfully avoided the obvious remark. "Okay, let's take a ride and get the ring. Do you have a power of attorney?"

"I do."

She got a folder full of papers and asked, "What are you doing today?"

I stood up and offered her a hand. "I have a couple of stops to make and another address to find."

"I'll do that for you."

"No, don't be—"

"Spencer..." She started to cry quietly. "I need something to do."

I understood and nodded. "Did the window get replaced okay?"

"Yes," she said as she washed a dish and set it next to the sink.

"Good. The stencil guy is coming later this morning."

"Okay, I'll take care of it."

"Thanks, Samantha. If there's anything I can do..."

She gave me another kiss and said I'd be the first person she'd ask.

"Would you drop me at the office after...?"

"Of course."

As she gathered her things I looked around the apartment. I thought it had looked lonely before. I held the door and followed her down the stairs.

I tried to make small talk as we drove, but it was obviously a tense situation. As we waited at a light I asked her to adjust the side mirror.

"The inside knob is broken so you need to roll down the window and push the mirror."

A couple of small adjustments took care of it.

***

The new office window looked just like the old window. Back to normal. As I looked at it I thought about the warning and considered the new information that Walters had beaten Sadie Peterson. I decided I still wasn't afraid but should step up my level of awareness. I also knew I should stay away from the park, but I really wanted to see the tunnels. I knew there was probably nothing down there that would help, but the kid in me was looking forward to the adventure. It would be even better than exploring the limestone caves up in Door County.

When we got back it only took Samantha a few minutes to find Sadie Peterson's address.

"Thanks, Samantha."

Her eyes filled with tears again as she looked at the ring. She looked at the inscription, and her hands started to shake.

I put my hands on her shoulders and asked if she wanted me to stay with her.

"No... no thanks, Spencer. I've been getting ready for this. I still had hope, but it has been so long. I'll be okay."

"Well, how about I bring back lunch?"

She nodded and wiped her eyes.

"I'll get subs from the deli down the street."

"Thanks. I'll be here," she said with a slight smile.

***

Sadie lived on a quiet side street in a wood-framed, two-story house that had seen better days. White paint was peeling everywhere, and one window was cracked. Almost all the houses on the block were of the same construction, but most were in better shape. If Sadie took care of her mother, I understood why she didn't have money to take care of her house. A golden retriever lay in the sun on the porch next door and quietly watched me walk up the steps. Two pots of geraniums were on the porch next to two wooden chairs.

I pushed the bell but didn't hear a ring. I rang again and then knocked. A minute later a large woman in a white uniform came to the door, opened it a crack, and asked what I wanted. The door was chained. I asked if Sadie Peterson was home. The woman matter-of-factly told me she was at work and wouldn't be home until dinner. I said I'd stop back. She asked if she could say who called and I told her a friend.

I walked back to my Mustang and wondered how much the lady in the white uniform cost. Sadie had enough trouble without Walters.

The low purr of the engine was always soothing, and I listened to it and thought for a few minutes about the sadness this morning had brought. Not a good way to end the week. I hoped the afternoon would improve the day.

Twenty minutes later, I pulled into the police station and parked next to the lieutenant's cruiser. Rosie's car wasn't in the lot. Must still be working nights.

Stosh wasn't in his office, but the sergeant told me he was in the building so I sat on a wooden chair and closed my eyes.

"I thought I already had my quota of you for today."

Without opening my eyes, I said, "This'll take care of tomorrow."

He dropped a pile of folders on his desk and sat. "How'd it go with your secretary?"

"About as you would think. Pretty damned sad."

"Yeah, pretty tough, kid. You okay?"

"Sure."

"And how is Aunt Rose?"

"Hard to be anything but wonderful living in paradise. Cherry pie for dessert."

"You get your friend settled?"

"I did. Rose and Maxine will make her feel at home."

He nodded. "That was a wonderful thing you did for Maxine."

"Well, she deserved it."

I had met Maxine on a prior case. She was a hooker and a wonderful lady who needed a break. And Aunt Rose needed help at the inn. So when the case was over, I drove Maxine up to Door County.

A knock on the door got his attention, and he held up a finger.

"Got a meeting, Spencer. Anything else?"

"Just a couple of interesting facts." I told him about Barbara and Terrence Jacobs, the last kid reported missing.

"So what happened to the kid after he was brought in to meet Meyers?" he asked.

"The million dollar question. I know you're not going to like this, but we could set them up."

"Correct, I don't. But just out of curiosity, how would you go about doing that?"

"They seem to like orphans, Martin being an exception. We could plant a kid with an orphan history, and you could have somebody watching."

"Use a kid for bait. I don't see *anything* wrong with that. What about that did you think I wouldn't like?"

"Well, I'm not fond of it myself, but I got nuthin' else… except for Sadie Peterson."

"I hate to ask. Is it as brilliant as your last idea?"

"Brillianter. Barbara told me about a woman who was beaten by Walters—Sadie Peterson." I told him the story and about the tunnels. "I'm going to have a chat with her tonight."

"I know those tunnels are like a siren calling to you, but remember the rock that siren was sitting on."

"I know. But this is one rock that needs turning over."

He stood up. "My advice is to stay away from there. You can fix a broken window, but other things aren't so easy. Let us take care of it."

"Understood. But unless you find something to justify a warrant there's nothing for you to take care of. And Walters hasn't left a trail of bread crumbs. I don't need a warrant."

He shook his head. "Don't do anything dumb."

I had been wondering whether to tell him about Harvey. I was glad I didn't—he wouldn't have let me out of the office.

Chapter 30

I rang Sadie's bell at seven-thirty. After a quiet lunch with Samantha, I had walked across the street and spent an hour with Carol, who wanted to know what was going on at Riverview and if anyone had called because of the posters. They hadn't. She told me Billy was still talking about the Cubs game, and I told her we'd go again before the season was over. She said Billy was sure they were going to win the pennant. I told her that many had said the same thing over the last seventy-six years. She laughed... improving my day.

I rang the bell again before someone came to the door and opened it, pulling the chain tight.

"Yes?"

"Are you Sadie?"

"Yes," she said hesitantly.

"My name is Spencer Manning. I spent most of yesterday with Barbara Reid. I'm looking into what's going on at the park, and she suggested I have a chat with you."

"Do you have identification?"

I showed her my license.

"Okay, but I'm just getting my mother settled for the evening. If you'll give me five minutes, I'll come out."

"Sure."

I was apprehensive. After what had happened to her, I'd been partly expecting her to tell me to get lost.

The sun had dropped behind the houses when Sadie came back with two glasses on a tray. She wasn't as big as the caretaker. Except for a limp, though, she looked sturdy and strong.

"Would you like some lemonade, Mr. Manning?"

"Sure, thanks." I felt a little guilty taking something from someone who had to steal food to eat. She placed the tray on the table between the chairs and sat down.

I told her about Martin and asked if she knew him.

"No, I'm sorry. It's a big place. There are lots of kids working there, and the faces change pretty frequently."

"Do you know about the missing kids?"

"Only what Walters told us. Before that I wasn't aware of the problem." She took a drink and held the glass in both hands. Looking out over the street, she said, "But I did know Benny."

"How well did you know him?"

"Nothing serious… just had lunch when we were both off at the same time. I don't think his death was an accident."

"Why do you think that?"

"Benny wasn't careless. He worked on the coasters… you know, fixing them and doing maintenance. And he had no reason to be in the Tunnel of Love."

"Well, you're correct. The blow to his head wasn't made by a boat."

She nodded. "Not surprised. I hope they catch whoever did it."

"They're trying."

She set the glass down and turned toward me. "So why are you sitting on my porch?"

I smiled. I liked Sadie. "I need some help. Barbara suggested you."

She looked surprised. "Me? How can *I* help?"

"I'd like to get into the tunnels."

"I can't imagine why. Would you like more lemonade?"

"No thanks. I don't know why myself. But there's something going on, and when I found out about the tunnels it sparked my curiosity. You've been down there?"

"Yes. Quite often."

"What for?"

"I work the concessions. We move food and supplies through the tunnels when the park is open so the guests don't see."

The sun had disappeared behind the houses, and a cool breeze blew from the north. I wished I had brought my jacket. Sadie had on a sweater and didn't seem to be bothered by the breeze.

"Sadie, would you tell me about what happened with Walters?"

Her eyes followed the cars that passed the house. As a beat-up Chevy went by, she said, "I called Barbara when I got home—she didn't answer."

I let that hang there until she turned and looked at me.

"If she was home sick she would have answered," she added.

I didn't want anyone knowing where Barbara was but thought it best to be honest with her. "She was concerned about being watched. I moved her to a safe place."

"And I'm just supposed to take your word that she's okay?"

I reached into my pocket and pulled out the ring and handed it to her. "Barbara said to give you this and to tell you she wore it on the wrong finger."

Sadie laughed. "Okay, only Barbara could have told you that." She watched another car. "This is all so bizarre. You asked about Walters. He asked me to stay after work… said he would pay me overtime to take inventory down in the tunnel's storage rooms. I could really use the money. I was walking ahead of him in one of the tunnels when he hit me in the back of the legs with a baseball bat. As I curled up on the dirt floor he told me he knew I had stolen some food, and he needed to teach me a lesson."

I let out a deep breath.

"He told me to get up but I couldn't. My legs weren't working, and the pain was horrible. He ordered me again to stand up and then hit me in the side and asked if I was done stealing. I said I was. He smiled and said he was glad because he really didn't like this part of his job, and he wanted to report to Mrs. Meyers that the problem was taken care of." Her eyes no longer followed the cars. She just stared out at the street.

"Why didn't he just fire you?"

"He told me he could have me arrested and then I wouldn't be able to get another job. He said he could fire me, but he thought we could work something out."

"What?"

"I don't know. He just said he'd forget about what happened if I'd help him when he asked. He said he owned me."

When I didn't respond, she said, "He hasn't asked."

Sadie was another person Walters had something on. He was running a prison camp.

"I'm so sorry, Sadie. If it helps any, I don't know what's going on yet, but I'm going to get him."

She nodded slowly. "I'd like to be there when you do."

"I bet. I'll figure out how to get in the tunnels some other way. You've had enough trouble."

Her eyes narrowed, and her hands shook a bit on her knees. "I want to help. I need some revenge. And I'd feel safe with you there."

"I won't always be there. And revenge isn't always a good thing."

She thought for a minute. "Have you ever wanted to kill someone?"

"Yes."

"And did you?"

"Yes."

"And was that a good thing?"

I saw her point, but it wasn't that simple. I took a deep breath. "The world is better off with some people not on it. But I don't take pleasure in pulling the trigger."

"Well, Mr. Manning, you got your revenge. I want mine." She turned to face me. "Charles Dickens said in one of his books, 'He would make a lovely corpse'."

I tried not to show my surprise at her literary knowledge, but she laughed as she watched me.

"What book was that? Who was he referring to?" I asked.

"Oh, I don't remember the book, but I'm thinking Walters fits nicely."

There was a lot of hate in her voice. I didn't blame her. "I'll buy that."

"Excuse me for a minute," she said. She went back inside and a few seconds later the porch light came on.

"So, are the tunnels the only thing you need help with?" she asked as she sat back down.

"At the moment, yes. You have anything else in mind?"

She raised her jaw and said, "If you're planning on killing him, I'd like to help."

I expected her to smile but she didn't. I didn't either.

"Well, just for the record, planning to kill people is illegal. Sometimes killing them without planning is illegal too."

"I know. But also for the record, I wouldn't mind seeing him dead."

"I don't blame you, Sadie. But behind bars is pretty good too."

"Sometimes pretty good just doesn't do it, Mr. Manning."

I couldn't argue with that. As I started to ask her about the tunnels, the dog on the porch next door started to bark, seemingly at nothing.

Sadie laughed when she saw my perplexed look. "That dog's not too bright—probably a squirrel."

I nodded. "So are you willing to help with the tunnels?"

"Sure, but I'll have to give it some thought. I assume you don't want to be seen, and I'd rather not be seen with you."

I agreed. "Tell me about the police force."

"What do you want to know?"

"How many are there?"

"Well, you know about Walters. He and Meyers are there Tuesday through Saturday but their hours are sporadic. They show up late or leave early. Then there are two that have the title of sergeant—Mooney and Phelps. All but Meyers have guns. Mooney and Phelps cover all the shifts. Then there are six officers. Do you want their names?"

"Maybe later. I've met Mooney."

"Lucky you. He's a clown."

"But a clown with a gun. So maybe the best time would be on Sunday when Walters and Meyers aren't there. I'm assuming we can't do this after hours."

She shook her head. "Don't see how. The place is closed and locked. There's a night watchman, and you never know where he is… probably sleeping somewhere. I'll think about it."

I sat up in the chair. "Well, please call me when you figure it out. And if Walters contacts you, call me. The phone at my office forwards to my house at night, and I have an answering machine. If there's no answer, call my pager and put in 911 and your number, and I'll call you right back."

She said she'd call for sure and looked like she had something else to say. I waited.

Looking back out at the street, she asked, "Barbara's really okay?"

"Yes. She's scared, but she couldn't be in better hands."

She turned to me with a look that was powerful and steady. "Good. There are lots of scared people there Mr. Manning." She sighed. "It used to be a fun place to work."

"So I've heard. But you don't seem scared, Sadie."

"I'm not afraid of bullies."

"Good for you. But you should be afraid enough to be wary. These are dangerous people. You are proof of that."

She was quiet.

"And there's Benny."

She didn't respond.

I didn't want to tell Barbara about Harold, but I thought Sadie should know. "And Harold."

That got her attention.

"Harold?"

"Harold Dejan ran one of the trains. Did you know him?"

"I did. Why are we talking in the past tense?"

"I found him dead in his room Wednesday."

She dropped her head and closed her eyes. "And you think it's connected?"

"Yes, I do."

She took a deep breath and nodded. "Okay, I'll be more… wary."

"If you want to forget about the tunnels, I understand."

"Nope. You just keep giving me more reasons to get the bastard." Her determined look was back.

"I'll listen to whatever plan you come up with, but if it doesn't sound safe I won't do it. I'm not putting you in jeopardy. And Walters may not be the only one to watch out for."

She nodded. "If you mean Meyers, I already know."

Sadie was pretty smart. She wanted revenge, but she wasn't just acting on emotions. She was thinking pretty clearly.

"Of course you'll have to take a pill," she said with a sly smile.

"Pardon?"

Her smile turned into a laugh. "Marcel, the barker at the castle, is from Louisiana. He has everyone convinced that the tunnels are full of evil spirits and you need protection to go down there."

I gave her my best skeptical look. "What kind of protection?"

"Well, he just happens to sell voodoo pills that he guarantees will do the trick."

I rolled my eyes. "Of course he does. What do you mean by *everyone*?"

"Well, maybe not everyone, but close to it."

"Including you?"

She was still smiling. "Including me. I'm from New Orleans. My mama used to see a voodoo priestess, and I've seen some things I just can't explain logically. I know Marcel is just working a scam, but a part of me says it can't hurt."

I shook my head with a smile. "And I was just thinking how sensible you sounded."

"Covering all your bases sounds pretty sensible to me."

"Okay, but don't be offended if I decline."

"Hey, it's your soul."

I knew she was mostly playing with me, but there was some childhood indoctrination there too.

"I'll wait for your call." As I straightened and grabbed the arms of the chair to get up, I told her I had one last question.

"What?"

"Feel free not to answer. I'm wondering what you stole that resulted in that attack."

She smiled. "A package of hot dogs."

I had no words.

When I didn't respond, she continued. "I knew it was wrong, but I was out of money and out of food, and it was three days till payday. I was going to replace them."

"How did he find out?"

She slowly shook her head. "I have no idea."

"A package of hot dogs isn't going to get you in much trouble, Sadie."

"No, but he said there were other things missing, and he said he wouldn't be surprised if I stole them too."

"Nice guy."

"Yeah, a real prince."

I got her phone number, we shook hands, and I got halfway down the steps before I turned back. "Do you need some money, Sadie?"

"We're okay. I just got a little behind last month. My mother... But thanks for the offer. I appreciate it." She held out the ring.

"Why don't you keep it. You can give it back to Barbara."

"Okay. It can be a good luck charm."

I nodded and headed for the car. After a couple of blocks I turned on the heater and wished for warmer weather.

***

I was close to the lake, so I drove back to the beach where Rosie and I had sat on the rock a week ago. It seemed like years. A light breeze was blowing offshore, and the lake was flat and peaceful. Behind me was a city that was majestic but not very peaceful. The lake wasn't always either, but I knew how to deal with it. You could survive a storm with the right skills. I knew how to deal with people who were willing to kidnap kids too. It was a different skill set, but first I had to find them, and I wasn't having much luck so far. I found it ironic that the darkness out over the lake was far safer than the brightly lit city behind me. I watched running lights twinkling on the lake for an hour before heading home.

Chapter 31

Martin ate the food on the tray—meatloaf, mashed potatoes, and peas—but he wondered how the food had made it into his mouth now that his thumbs were twice their normal size. As he walked back to the bed, he heard a knock on the wall. He climbed onto the bed and listened. He had no idea how long it was before he heard it again. He reached out and knocked back, and it was only seconds before he heard the knock again. That continued for what seemed like hours. Martin thought it was fun but had no idea why the wall was knocking at him.

Chapter 32

Saturday promised to be a beautiful day… temperature in the seventies and clear skies. The Cubs were in St. Louis for an afternoon game, and the only plans I had for the day were to have breakfast with Harvey and watch the game with Stosh.

Harvey was back in our old booth reading the paper.

I sat down, and he asked with a grin when he was going to be arrested.

I laughed. "Not everyone seems so happy about the prospect."

"Not everyone gets a paid vacation out of it."

As I sat, the waitress brought coffee. I had thought about his relationship to Meyers and decided to be less trusting. "Well, hate to spoil your vacation, but I talked to my contact in the department, and he didn't go for it." That seemed like a good white lie.

He looked disappointed as he folded the paper. "Oh well, back to my boring life."

"Sorry. If you want to get arrested you're on your own."

"I think I'll pass."

Breakfast went by quickly. He asked when our next breakfast would be. I told him I'd call him.

***

I was taking care of chores when the phone rang at about eleven. It was Sadie.

"Hello, Spencer. I only have a minute. I'm at a pay phone at the park. I'm thinking tomorrow about four would be a good time. The park closes at six, so everything is winding down for the day by then, and the tunnels should be empty."

"Nobody will be moving anything?"

"No, they stock up after lunch and then before the park opens in the morning. And Walters and Meyers won't be here."

"Do you know which sergeant will be there?"

"I don't, but we can hope for Phelps."

"How do I find you?"

Suddenly all I heard were screams from people on the roller coaster. When they stopped, she said, "Come to the hot dog stand by the Parachute Drop. I'll be there and we'll play it by ear. I may not be able to get you in, but I'll try."

"All I can ask. Thanks, Sadie."

"Sure. Bye."

She hung up before I could respond.

I had no idea if a walk through the tunnels would help, but I was excited to have the chance. Most big cities had tunnels, including ancient Rome. They had figured out even back then that it was easier to move all sorts of things without having to deal with the people on the surface. I knew Chicago had tunnels beneath the downtown section for utilities and moving supplies. There was an element of danger in our exploration, but Walters and Meyers wouldn't be there, and I was carrying a gun so I felt pretty confident.

***

Stosh was already working on a beer when I got there, and bowls of chips and pretzels were set out on a table. He knew how to live.

As he set down the bottle he said, "You look like hell."

"Good afternoon to you too." I went to the kitchen for a beer but came back with a glass of ice water and stretched out on the couch.

With raised eyebrows, he asked, "You on the wagon?"

"A beer will put me to sleep in five minutes. That may happen anyway. I haven't had a good night's sleep in a week. I can't stop thinking about Rosie, I don't know why kids are disappearing, I know Walters and Meyers are involved in something but I don't know what, and three people are dead and we don't have any leads. We can charge Walters with assault, but the victim won't talk, and the guy I trust the most is a loan shark."

"Is that all?"

"If I don't fall asleep I'm sure I'll think of something else."

Stosh left the room and was back in a few minutes. Five minutes later I smelled coffee brewing.

He sat on the edge of the recliner, muted the TV, and said, "The last time I was so confused trying to follow something was when I tried to read *Ulysses*. There were some items in your stream of con- sciousness that are news to me."

I arranged the pillows behind my head on the arm of the couch. With my eyes closed, I asked, "You read Ulysses?"

"I said tried. I gave up. Let's run through your list."

"I'm in no mood for the third degree."

"Doesn't matter. First, you can call Rosie anytime you want. You're just being stubborn."

I sighed. "It's not that easy."

"Sure it is. Second, we, as in the police force you support with your tax money, do have some leads and are following up. Your case is Martin... we'll take care of the murders."

"They're connected, Stosh."

"Maybe. But even if they are, you worry about Martin and let us do our jobs."

Before I could respond, he unmuted the TV as Sandberg was rounding third with a two-run homer. We watched the replay and then he muted it again and went to the kitchen and came back with coffee. I let it cool a bit.

"Third—assault?"

I told him about Sadie.

"So you're using her as bait? I thought we ruled that out."

"She refuses to report the assault. By doing that she silently agreed to do Walters a favor when he asks."

"And what do you think that favor will be?"

I shook my head, took a deep breath, opened my eyes, and looked over at him. "I'll let you know when she tells me."

"What if she can't get ahold of you?"

"She has my phone and pager numbers, and I'm planning on staying near a phone."

"And what if she can't get to a phone?"

I watched as the Cubs ran off the field at the end of the fourth with a two to nothing lead. "Then she lets me know after whatever happens. It's not a perfect plan."

"Not even close. If she calls you, you call me."

I agreed and continued our chat. "Walters and Meyers have hired people who have something to lose if they don't follow directions, whatever those are. And you have that ex-partner of Walters involved in the arrests. All this is connected, and the connection is Walters or Meyers or both. We're just missing a few lines to connect the dots."

Stosh leaned back in the chair and unmuted the TV after the commercials were over. "There's also the question of who the killer is."

"And is it the same killer for all three?" I asked. "I'm betting on Walters for Benny. We know he likes baseball bats."

"And the other two could be anybody. You have any ideas?"

"I'm not a fan of Frank Knight... Meatstick. He runs the booth where Martin worked and has to know more than he's saying. He certainly looks tough enough to strangle someone. And there's a little runt who rubs me the wrong way—guy named Marcel. He *doesn't* look tough enough to strangle someone."

"That would be Marcel Rateau. Both of them are clean. And just because someone rubs you the wrong way doesn't make them guilty. Sometimes you rub *me* the wrong way."

"And just because they have no record doesn't mean they're not involved. Every criminal has to start somewhere."

"Bring me facts, Spencer."

I held the coffee cup in both hands and took a drink. The warmth felt good on my hands.

"Something else keeps bothering me," I said. "Remember Benny told Harvey that he would be free?"

"Yup. Probably had something to do with the loan from Joey."

"Probably. But why is he dead?"

"Lotsa whys, Spencer. Walters was probably paying off his debt in exchange for something."

"But what? And if Benny holds up his end of the bargain he doesn't have to die."

"Maybe he decided not to hold up his end."

"Could be. But it would have to be something pretty bad to over-power ten grand."

We were both quiet, not wanting to think about what that could be.

Stosh broke the silence by asking what I was doing with the rest of the weekend.

I had debated telling him about the tunnel plan and decided I should, if for no other reason than he would know where I'd been if I didn't show up. He wasn't in favor of the plan. I wasn't surprised.

I thanked him for the coffee and headed home to man the phone. I threw a burger on the grill, ate on the deck, and fell asleep on the chaise lounge. I woke up at eleven and went to bed. The phone hadn't rung.

Chapter 33

I didn't get out of bed until ten. Sunday was almost half over. I spent the day around the house on chores and bills, trying not to think about the tunnels.

The parking lot at Riverview was pretty empty when I got there at a quarter to four. I joined a group of three adults and three kids as they walked down the Midway toward the Parachute Drop. I was carrying my .38 under a windbreaker. I felt better after passing the bottle booth and the Freak Show where Marcel and Meatstick knew me by sight. It was a few minutes after four when I got to the hot dog stand just north of the Parachute Drop. Sadie and another woman were working the stand.

I got in the short line and ordered a hot dog from Sadie. As she was making it, she told the woman next to her that she needed a fifteen-minute break. She told me with a nod that she'd meet me at a bench a few yards away. She joined me there and, as I ate my dog, explained the plan. We were going to walk around the other side of the Parachute Drop where there was a wooden shack. Inside the shack, as in several others, there were stairs going down to the tunnels. She gave me a brief description of the layout, told me that any stairs would lead up to one of the shacks, and told me how to get to the river in case I needed an escape.

I wasn't quite as excited now as I had been.

When I was done eating, I suggested she walk ahead in case we ran into someone who knew me. As we rounded the corner of the Parachute Drop, I saw Mooney about fifty yards ahead. I knew he saw me too.

"Mooney ahead, Sadie. You keep walking. I'll call you tonight."

She ignored him as she passed him. I tried to do the same, but he stood in front of me.

"Well, well. Who do we have here?" Mooney said.

I didn't respond and stepped to my right.

He stepped to his left. "You must really love amusement parks."

I still didn't respond.

"Tell you what, Manning. I'll give you the VIP treatment… special tour. I'll walk with you and make sure you get treated special."

"Nice of you, Mooney. But that's not necessary. Don't want any special treatment."

"I insist. I'm sure the boss would be upset if I didn't offer someone important like you the special treatment." He gave me a big grin that looked a lot like the Cheshire Cat's.

"Who's the boss?"

He kept the grin. "Where to? Wanna try the Parachute Drop? I'll wait for you at the bottom."

"No thanks." I wasn't going to shake him, so I decided to walk around the park so he'd have to waste time escorting me. He asked if I wanted to go on every ride we passed. When we got back to the front gate I turned toward the exit.

His grin reappeared. "You didn't have much fun, Manning… not one ride."

"But fun nonetheless, Mooney. You gonna be okay if I leave you?"

The grin disappeared. "You were told, Manning. You don't listen well."

"Depends on who's doing the telling." I turned and headed for my Mustang.

I probably could have lost Mooney somewhere along the way, but that wouldn't have led to anything good. The tunnels would be there another day. And if I believed in signs from heaven, and sometimes I did, there was a good reason Mooney showed up. Some unknown fate awaited me in the tunnels. I'd sure like to know what that might have been.

***

Sadie answered on the first ring. It was a little after eight.

"Thank goodness, Spencer. I've been worried."

"Thanks. But no problem… he's harmless."

"Probably, but he knows people who aren't."

"True. Did he connect you to me?"

"Not that I know of."

"Good."

"Do you want to replan the tunnels?"

"Maybe. I'd still like to see them. But let's wait a few days… I'll give you a call."

"Okay."

"And remember to call me if you hear from Walters."

"I sure will. Whenever I think of him I get so angry. Have you heard from Barbara?"

"That's my next call. But the only problem is she may not want to come back."

Sadie laughed. "Say hi for me."

"I will. Get some sleep."

"Good night, Spencer."

"Good night, Sadie."

***

Aunt Rose answered the phone, and we chatted for twenty minutes before she put Barbara on. She assured me Barbara was having a great time and looking more relaxed each day. She had insisted on helping out around the inn. Maxine was at a movie.

"I worry about you, Spencer."

"I know, but I'm a lot smarter than the morons I deal with. I'll be okay."

"You be sure to call Lieutenant Powolski if there's any trouble."

"Yes, ma'am. Is Barbara available?"

"She's out on the porch. I'll get her."

I thought she had left without saying goodbye, but after a pause she said, "You need to come up for a visit. It's been too long."

"I promise. As soon as this is all over."

"Okay, I love you, Spencer."

"I love you too."

Barbara came on a minute later. We chatted for ten minutes, and she thanked me several times for bringing her to the inn. I passed along Sadie's hello, and we talked for a bit about her.

After I hung up I thought about calling Rosie, but I walked away from the phone.

Chapter 34

I was fixing breakfast when my doorbell rang around eight o'clock. I turned off the gas burner on the stove and wiped my hands. Lieutenant Powolski was at the door with an officer behind him.

I was smiling. He wasn't.

"Well, what an unexpected pleasure," I said, opening the screen door.

"Unexpected, yes… pleasure, no."

"What's the matter?"

He took a deep breath. "I'm here to arrest you."

I laughed and asked him to come in.

"I'm not kidding, Spencer. You're under arrest for assault and battery." He asked the officer to read me my rights.

"Hang on, I…"

He held up his hand and I stopped.

I waited rather impatiently. When he was done, I asked, "Who am I supposed to have assaulted?"

"Belva Meyers."

My mouth dropped open, but I quickly closed it and nodded. I stepped outside and let the screen door close.

"I'm guessing your little tunnel adventure didn't go so well," Stosh said.

"It didn't go at all. I ran into Mooney who insisted on giving me a personal tour and didn't leave my side."

"Yeah, and then made a phone call. Jesus, Spencer, I told you to stay away from there."

"You did, yes. We're really doing this?"

"I have a complaint from a citizen who said you threatened her and then pushed her."

"That's crap and you know it."

"I do, but I'm not a judge. A coupla lawyers will have to battle it out."

"This is nuts."

"I agree. But the wheels of justice have started turning, so do you come peacefully or do I have James put you in cuffs?"

"I have a choice?"

"Yes."

I sighed. "Okay. Can I call Ben?"

"From the station."

"Okay. Let me lock up… I'll be right with you." As the screen closed I heard James ask if he should follow me in case I tried to slip out the back.

And then a much louder, "Shut the hell up."

I managed a chuckle.

As we walked down the sidewalk, Stosh said, "There's a good side to this."

"Dying to hear it."

"I'll know where you are for the next coupla hours."

"How nice for you."

***

I got my phone call. Praying that he'd answer, I called Ben Tucker, who got me started on my second case and then retired from the Illilnois State Attorney's Office when it was done. He answered on the fifth ring.

"Hey Ben, Spencer. Glad I caught you in."

"You just barely did. I have a ten-twenty tee time."

"Would you mind missing it?" I explained.

When he stopped laughing he said, "Had to happen sooner or later. I'll go find a judge and be there in an hour."

It was two hours, but all I had to do was sign a Recognizance Bond and buy Ben lunch. As we stood outside the door of the station, he explained the procedure and told me the court date. Basically, I couldn't leave town and most importantly, he said, there was a restraining order against me. I had to stay away from Meyers and since she worked at the park, I had to stay away from the park.

"I know this is bogus, Spencer, but the restraining order is serious. If you ignore that, you've got real problems."

"But that's bogus too."

"I know. But not until the court says it is. Until then, you stay away from her."

I nodded with a frown. "I hate being played."

"Don't we all."

We went to Molly's. When we were seated he asked for details. I gave him the short version over burgers.

"I had some cases with Walters," he said in between bites. "I cringed when I saw his name. He never did me any favors... loose ends and shaky evidence. So if he's the brains behind this, he'll make a mistake sooner or later."

"I'd rather it were sooner. There are kids missing."

"Yeah, I'll cross my fingers. I'd like to see him in jail just for the trouble he caused me."

"But you managed to win anyway."

"Well, usually the bad guys are so dumb it doesn't take much."

I asked for a Coke refill. "I also ran into someone you never managed to beat."

He smiled. "How *is* Joey?"

"As fashionable as always."

"Yeah, I think the juries were distracted by his clothes."

"Right. Whatever excuse works for you."

He laughed. "In my defense, no one else got him either. The man doesn't make mistakes."

I told him about his reminiscing and the incident with the ice cream cone. "You never know about people. Not surprising he has the ice cream parlor as a front. Do you know he gives out free ice cream to the neighborhood families?"

"Really." he said. "That doesn't surprise me. Long tradition going back to Capone, who took care of the neighborhood."

"Al would be proud."

We both finished. I thanked him for his services and told him to send me a bill. He said I just paid it. We promised to have a beer soon.

I headed for the office, all the more sure that I was getting close to something at Riverview. They were certainly serious about keeping me out of there. And I guess they had found a way to do that. About a block from the office I remembered Sadie and wondered what I'd do if she called.

***

I got to the office a little before two. Samantha wasn't there. Thinking that she might have gone for a late lunch, I busied myself with paperwork for an hour and then realized she should have been back by now. I thought of calling her but decided to give it some more time. After another half hour I drove to her apartment.

She didn't answer the bell. As I was thinking about picking the lock, another resident came in, and we had a chat. She knew Samantha but hadn't seen her all weekend. That wasn't so strange… people in apartments keep to themselves and usually don't notice their neighbors. She suggested I knock on the door.

I did, but softly enough so that the other people on the floor wouldn't hear. If she didn't answer, I was going to pick the lock. I got more concerned as I thought about what she might have done. She had nobody, and the loss of her father to deal with.

The lock was simple, and it only took a minute to get in. I opened and closed the door quietly with lots of apprehension. The main room was empty, and there were no sheets on the couch, but with Samantha's father gone she may have moved to the bedroom.

That was empty too… as were all the drawers and closets. She didn't live there anymore.

I stood in the middle of the room for a few minutes thinking, then decided it really didn't matter one way or the other that she was gone, except that I owed her a week's pay, and I'd have to find another secretary.

On the way back to the office, I remembered the hell I went through interviewing candidates and cringed thinking about doing it again.

I looked through her desk, and it was empty too. I hoped she would find some peace. I walked outside and watched the rush hour traffic for a few minutes. As I turned to go in, Carol came out of her building and waved. I waved back, waited for a lull, and walked across the street.

"Hi Spencer!" she said with a big smile.

"Hey, Carol. How's life?"

"Just fine. Billy's at my sister's overnight, and I'm off to get some groceries. Are you done for the day?"

"I am. Heading home."

"Can I interest you in a home-cooked dinner?"

"Sure. That'd be great. Is an hour enough for you to get back?"

"Sure is. You like lasagna?"

"Absolutely. Sounds wonderful."

"Good. See you in an hour."

She headed west toward the neighborhood grocery store. I turned east and took a walk toward the lake. A car honked at a taxi cutting into traffic. Pigeons rummaged in the gutters at the edge of the street, fighting with the crows for dinner morsels.

The day had been warm, and the late afternoon sun still made for a pleasant walk. I walked for a half hour and then turned back. As Carol opened her door, the rich smell of sausage and sauce filled the hallway. She pointed to a bottle of red wine on the counter and asked me to pour.

We talked as she cooked. I told her all about the case, ending with my arrest. She was shocked.

"They can do that?"

I took a bite of sausage and a drink of dry wine. "They can. You can accuse anyone of anything, and the accused has to defend himself."

"Well, what if it's just not true? Like with you."

"Then, hopefully, you win in court and the lawyers make money."

"That's insane." She asked me to stir the sauce.

"It is. Some states have laws against frivolous lawsuits. If you bring a suit and lose you have to pay the defendant's court and legal fees."

The lasagna was delicious. I thanked the cook and washed the dishes. Then we moved to the couch with our wine.

"How's your secretary doing?"

I took a deep breath. "I don't know."

Her eyebrows raised into a confused look, and I explained about Samantha's father.

"That's horrible, Spencer."

I reached out and took her hand. We had both lost parents. She looked at me with understanding and held my hand.

"I felt so badly for her. She had no one to turn to. I offered to talk anytime she wanted, but she never called."

"It's a very personal thing. People react differently," Carol said.

I nodded. "But I think I need a new secretary." I told her about my visit to Samantha's apartment.

"Maybe there's another explanation."

I smiled. "Like what?"

"No clue. Just trying to be optimistic."

My laugh brought a smile from her that changed quickly to a frown. I waited for her to tell me why.

"Spencer, you say she had no one here, right?"

"Right."

She looked thoughtful. "Actually, there was a man."

I let her think.

"I saw him three times. Twice he walked into the office, and they left together."

"Probably someone she met in the neighborhood."

She nodded. "Could be. But they were pretty friendly. With those big picture windows you have I can see into the office pretty clearly. There were some pretty passionate embraces."

A chill went down my back, and I thought back to the time I saw her on the phone but she told me there had been no calls.

"You said three times."

"Yes. The last time was Friday. But this time she came out and got in the guy's car. And she didn't look sad. She looked very happy." She paused. "You look confused."

"I am. That's not the Samantha I knew. I wonder what the hell is going on."

"Maybe she stole from you."

I shook my head. "No. There's nothing to steal. I even owe her a week's pay."

"Well, you'll probably get a call telling you where to mail it." She got up and rinsed her glass at the sink.

"Probably." But I thought probably not... there was something I was missing. I thought back over all of my interactions with Samantha. I had liked her as soon as we'd met, and I had decided to hire her almost immediately. She was friendly and smart and easy to talk to. I had called her two references. One was a lawyer and the other was a jewelry store. They were the only connections I had to Samantha.

I joined Carol at the sink and handed her my glass. "Thanks for the dinner. It was delicious, and your company was as wonderful as usual."

"You can't stay for a bit?"

"I'd love to, but there's something I need to take care of."

I gave her a quick hug and headed across the street to make a couple of calls.

Back in my office, I found the referral numbers and called them again. Both had been disconnected.

After staring out the window for a quarter hour I decided to go back to Carol's. I wanted to talk with someone, and she was prettier than Stosh.

She was surprised to see me and even more surprised when I told her about the calls.

"This gets stranger by the minute, Spencer."

I agreed.

She went into her bedroom and came back a minute later. She handed me a slip of paper. I unfolded it and saw an Illinois license plate number.

"What's this?"

"Well, I was intrigued by the hugs in your office. When he drove away on Friday I got the license number."

I was thrilled. "You are amazing, Carol. I could give you a big kiss."

She smiled and tossed her hair back over her shoulders. "Nobody here would stop you, Mr. Manning."

I leaned over, took her face in my hands and gave her a kiss on the forehead. I was so excited about the plate number I didn't realize until later that she had looked a bit disappointed.

"Did you also get the car make?"

"I did. Red Chevy Impala… fairly new."

"You're the best. Thanks!"

Now I needed to talk to Stosh.

Chapter 35

It was close to ten when I got to Stosh's house. He was asleep in his chair with his large volume of Sherlock Holmes stories open on his lap. He had read it many times. When he got to the end he'd start over. I'd only read it through once, but I had read some of my favorite stories several times. I didn't want to just let myself in. After all, he was a cop with a gun. It took two rings of the doorbell before he woke up and answered the door.

"This better be the end of the world to wake me up in the middle of the damn night," he said gruffly as he walked back to his chair.

"First of all, it's hardly the middle of the night, and second, the world is fine. But I think it's worth interrupting your beauty sleep—which, by the way, isn't helping."

He yawned. "What's so important?"

"Samantha's gone."

"Meaning?"

"Meaning wasn't at work today, apartment is cleaned out, and there's no note."

"Tough being the boss. Maybe better benefits."

"Carol, the lady who reported my broken window, saw her get into a car Friday afternoon with a man she had seen several times in the office hugging Samantha."

"So? No law against that."

"She had told me she knew no one in Chicago. It was just her and her father."

"Well, she met someone."

"The first day she worked I saw her on the phone as I drove away, but she later said there had been no calls."

"She could have called someone… maybe the hugger."

"Are you done being a pain in the ass? Because there's something else. I called her two references an hour ago. Both numbers have been disconnected."

That he had no answer for. I continued. "Something's wrong here, Stosh. Who is Samantha George?"

"And who was her father?" he added.

"And why did she come to work for me?"

He was silent.

"Any suggestions?" I asked.

"I'll get a print team to your office in the morning. Will you be there at ten? Let's find out who she is. Then we'll go from there. What's her apartment address?"

I gave him the address. "I'll be there at ten. One more thing you can do. Carol got the license plate of the car. Newer model, red Chevy Impala." I gave him the slip of paper.

"Sounds like Carol's doing more work than you are." When I didn't respond, he continued with a smirk. "And she hasn't been arrested."

"Nice. When can you get the plate run?"

"As soon as you stop talkin'."

He made a call and then turned on the TV. We watched Johnny Carson while we waited. Twenty minutes later the phone rang.

The car was a rental. Stosh said he would have someone check with the rental company in the morning. After a reminder about the restraining order I headed home.

Chapter 36

Sometimes Martin would start the knocking and the wall always knocked back. Martin couldn't remember how many days it had been going on. He still had no idea why it was happening, but it gave him something to do. When he got tired of knocking he sat on the bed and saw that the cat was back… with a purple kitten sitting next to it in the corner by the door, ten feet away. Both were watching him intently. As he moved around on the bed their eyes followed him. He reached out to pet the cat, and his arm stretched toward it. It kept stretching longer and longer, but it never reached the cat.

Chapter 37

A clear sky at sunrise had quickly turned gray, and a light drizzle started a little after eight. Forecasters were calling for rain all day. I liked gray days... good for reading and napping. I wasn't so sure about looking for fingerprints.

The print team arrived at a little after ten, leaving wet trails on the linoleum floor. I spent ten minutes with Detective Parks, making a list of people's prints he might find. There were a number of secretary candidates but none of them had made it past the front desk. The only other person who had touched anything was Carol, and I had told her to stop by to be printed when she saw activity in the office.

Parks took Carol's prints ten minutes later, and she stood outside chatting with me while the team worked. The main target was the desk in the main office.

"This is all so crazy, Spencer."

"It is that."

"Do you have any idea what's going on with Samantha?"

I shrugged. "Maybe nothing. People do strange things. Trying to make sense of someone else's behavior can be a full time job."

She laughed that pretty laugh. "You're thinking she isn't who she said she was?"

"It's possible."

"I wonder why."

"Me too."

As we watched a Plymouth trying to squeeze into a parking space, the sky opened, and a downpour made seeing the costume shop across the street difficult. We went inside and watched people scurrying for cover. It only lasted a few minutes, but the gutters were running with water that had overwhelmed the sewers.

When Parks called me over a few minutes later, Carol left after asking me to let her know what happened.

"Our job just got easier, Spencer. The desk and chair out here have been wiped clean. Same with everything on the desk. Not even a speck of dust, so that happened pretty recently."

Samantha had anticipated us looking for her prints. There *was* something going on. But what the hell was it?

"Have you done the phones? I may get a call." I hadn't forgotten about Sadie.

"The phone on this desk has also been wiped clean, so you can use it. We're working on your office. There are prints on your desk. Was she in there?"

I thought back. The only time she had come close was when I was talking to Barbara, and Samantha had stood in the doorway. "Not while I was here. But she was usually here by herself. The bathroom is probably a good possibility."

"Right. Adams is working in there."

I nodded and then remembered something. Barbara had used the phone in my office. I told Parks he'd find another set of prints on my phone.

Ten minutes later the phone rang. It was the lieutenant.

"Print team there?"

"Yup. The reception desk and chair and phone were wiped clean."

"Interesting. Parks is good… if there's a print there he'll find it."

"Maybe she's good too."

"Hopefully not *as* good. We found the car abandoned on Randolph just west of downtown. The rental registration is bogus."

Not a part of town you wanted to bring tourists to.

Stosh continued. "I've gotta get him over to the car. I think I'll have him do that before they head to the apartment. Do you have any guesses about what she was doing, Spencer?"

"I've thought about it. Doesn't make sense."

"Nothing she said that seemed strange?"

"Nope. Just all the events with her father."

"Well, keep thinking. Put Parks on."

I had been awake much of the night thinking about it. There had been nothing strange about her behavior except for the bare apartment. But even people who had lived somewhere for years sometimes had bare walls. And it was hard to tell what was normal after what had happened to her father. What really didn't make sense was her being so sad when she was with me, and acting so oddly as reported by Carol. Which was real?

Parks handed the phone back to me. "Lieutenant wants you."

"Yup."

"You got plans for dinner?"

"Nope. My only plans are to stay away from Riverview."

"Good to hear. Come over at six… we'll figure out where to go."

"Will do."

The team left an hour later. They told me the bathroom had also been wiped clean. Parks commended my excellent cleaning service. The only prints in my office were mine and an unknown on the phone. There were prints on door jambs and knobs, but they were mine also. Samantha had done a good job of leaving no trace. Too good.

***

Waiting wasn't something I did well. And waiting for the phone to ring when I didn't know when or if it would was the worst.

I had been awake a good part of the night thinking about Rosie, and I realized that I might be using my heart as an excuse. I realized that a part of me was happy with things the way they had been. Maybe it was better that way.

I had also wondered what to do if Sadie called. I couldn't let her down, but there was that restraining order. And I had told Stosh I would call if I heard from her. I decided that if she called I would go, but if I told Stosh he'd lock me up. Without a call I didn't have to worry about it.

But something else was bothering me so I took a drive, and at a little past one I was standing in front of Joey's Ice Cream Parlor. This time I had left my gun at the office. It was a friendly visit. I walked past the counter where a woman with short brown hair was sitting with a banana split. I watched her eyes follow my image in the mirror on the back wall. After the customary pat down I was ushered in.

Joey was sitting back in his chair with a big grin on his face. "Manning, I'm thinking I should put your name on the door. What brings you back?"

"I'm writing an article for a fashion magazine... wondered what color your handkerchief was."

"You coulda called."

I nodded. "I'm wondering what brought you to Riverview last week."

"Are you now? Marty... did you hear that? He's wondering."

Marty didn't respond, and Joey didn't continue.

"I know some of it, but some gaps could use filling in."

Joey looked at me with his head slightly cocked to the left. Cigar ash was collecting in a glass ashtray.

"I gave you some news during our last chat. Your IOUs are being buried with your clients. I gotta figure you're not happy about that. I figured that before I saw you at Riverview."

He still looked at me with no reaction.

"And when I saw you, I figured you were following up on Benny. Ten grand is a lot of money. I was at the park because of missing kids, and when I started poking around, Benny was killed, and then Harold, who was also holding an IOU to you. So I figure both of us are there because of the same people. I'm guessing Walters and Meyers are part of my missing kids case, and you're having a long chat with Meyers."

He knocked off the ash. "That's a lot of figuring, Manning."

"Yeah. And I figure I'm right. What I don't know is what you were chatting about."

"And you'd like to know?" He balanced the cigar on the tray.

"I would. It might help with the missing kids, who I hope are just missing and not dead."

"Me too, Manning. But I don't see the two being related."

"They're related because of Walters and Meyers, and the more I know about them the better chance I have of putting this puzzle together."

He took another puff and blew a smoke ring. "Okay. You helped me out in the past. I think you're a standup guy. Walters took over Benny's note."

"That was my guess. Do you know why?"

He spread his palms wide. "Don't know, don't care."

"That's a pretty cavalier attitude."

He shrugged. "To be frank, all I care about is the money. I get paid, I don't care who writes the check."

"Have you been paid?"

He squinted slightly and then glanced at Marty who very slowly shook his head.

Joey didn't need to answer.

"You said Walters picked up the note," I said. "But you were talking to Meyers."

"And how do you know that?"

"That's what I do for a living… I detect things," I said with a smile.

Joey didn't return the smile. "If it wasn't for the kid angle you would have left ten minutes ago, Manning. I don't mess with kids, and I don't like people who do."

I nodded.

"Walters had told me to work out the details with Meyers."

"But you're not paid yet."

"I gave her till Friday to walk in my door with ten grand and change."

"Or what?"

"Joey Mineo doesn't need an *or what*, Manning. I have an excellent track record."

I didn't doubt that. But I knew that whatever had preceded the excellent track record hadn't been pretty. Joey didn't make threats... he foretold the future.

"One thing doesn't make sense, Joey."

"Only one? Ya hear that Marty? This guy has life all figured out except for one thing. What would that be, Manning?"

Marty still didn't care.

"I like Walters for killing Benny. The only reason I figure Walters takes the note is that Benny is worth something to him. Why kill a guy worth ten grand to you?"

Joey shrugged. "Maybe Benny welched. And maybe Walters got his ten grand worth and then Benny became expendable. And maybe you're all wrong about Walters. But after I get my check I could care less about all the maybes."

I nodded again and asked, since I was a regular visitor, if I should get the password. He told me the passwords weren't for guests.

"Thanks for dropping in, Manning. Always a pleasure. Get a cone on the way out... on me."

I did. Butter pecan. The woman was gone.

I liked being right about my hunches, but this one got me nowhere. I could explain a lot of things that would get me nowhere. I was getting lots of pieces, but they didn't seem to fit together.

***

Stosh and I went out for pizza. The drizzle had stopped, but the sky was still gray. He filled me in on the car. It and the apartment had been wiped clean.

"No other place her prints could be?" he asked.

I shook my head. "Nope."

When the beer came, he asked, "So how's your relationship with your buddy Harvey?"

I about choked on a mouthful of beer. "Where the hell did that come from?"

"Trying to make a point. What's the answer? You still seeing him for breakfast?"

"Not since Saturday. But since I've been banned from the park there's nothing to talk about."

He took a long drink. "You trusted him... right?"

I got his point. "Yes."

"Based on nothing but a gut feeling... right?"

"Right."

"And you trusted Samantha enough to hire her and give her a key to the castle. Right?"

"Right. I get it. But the castle had nothing in it worth anything."

"Not the point."

"I know. If it makes you feel better, I stopped sharing with Harvey. Some new information came to light."

Garlic bread arrived and we each took a piece.

"And that would be?"

"Harvey is Belva's cousin."

It was his turn to choke on the beer. Once he got it down he started laughing.

"How did you find out?"

"Barbara."

"Doesn't mean you can't trust him."

I put down my glass. "I don't trust him, I do trust him... which side are you on here?"

"No side. That's my point... so be careful who you trust."

We finished the pizza talking about the Cubs. Stosh was sure we'd still be watching them when the World Series rolled around.

The day ended with no phone call. I figured if Walters had some use for Sadie it would be during park hours, so I relaxed and fell asleep to Johnny Carson talking with George Burns, a great example of why Hollywood people changed their names. Nathan Birnbaum would never have made it big.

Chapter 38

I went to Molly's for breakfast Wednesday morning. I wanted to see if I could manage to eat alone. I did fine. I detoured to see if the office was still there. It was. So were all the windows.

I had just picked up Sherlock Holmes when the phone rang.

"Hi, Spencer, it's Sadie."

I froze for a brief few seconds. "Hi, Sadie. You okay?"

"I am, and I have an assignment."

I waited.

"He wants me to bring a boy, Vincent Prather, to the shack under the Bobs. He works in one of the hot dog stands. Walters says he has a better job for him."

I took a deep breath. Exactly what Barbara had said.

"Do you believe him?"

"Not at all," she said with hate in her voice. "What do you want me to do?"

"When is this happening?"

"Nine tonight."

The park would be emptying, and the rides and stands would be getting ready to close.

"I wish we could arrest him for what we think, but we have to catch him at it."

"Okay, so…?"

"So, if you're willing, go ahead. I'll be there with help. We'll be right behind you."

"What if they see you?"

"They won't."

"They have before."

"Yes, they have. But they were looking for me. I'm betting they think they've taken care of me." I told her about the restraining order. "I'll be more careful."

"I don't want Vincent to get hurt, Spencer. We're taking a chance here."

I moved the phone to my other ear. "If you weren't talking to me what would you do?"

"I'd do what Walters said. Next time he'll kill me."

"Okay. So we're several steps ahead. We'll get him."

"What are you going to do?"

"First, make sure Vincent and you are okay. Then we'll deal with Walters. How? I won't know until it happens. But I'm good at improvising. And if at any time you feel in danger, take Vincent somewhere else and call the police."

"Okay. I hope you're right."

"Me too, Sadie. Tell me about the shack."

"What do you mean?"

"What's inside? From the front it looked bigger than the others. Just one room? Layout? Furniture?"

"There are two rooms. You walk into the main room, and there is a door to the left in the middle of the wall that leads into a storage room that's about half the size. There are a few boxes in there, but at the back of that room are the stairs down to the tunnels. There are boxes along the wall of the main room and open shelves as you come in the door before you get to the desk. And there's one desk that Meyers uses against the back wall in the right corner."

"Any windows?"

"No. None of the shacks have any."

"Thanks, Sadie. Remember, take Vincent somewhere else if you feel in danger."

"I will."

We hung up. I sat on the couch and wondered what Sherlock would do. He was a master at disguise and setting traps. I needed a disguise, and some help.

I was at the crossroads of calling Stosh or not. Once I had decided to show up at the park, that meant I wouldn't call Stosh. I felt pretty bad about that... he wasn't going to be happy. But I had done things in the past that hadn't made him happy, and they had turned out okay because in one way I was like Walters—I didn't exactly do things by the book, but I got things done. In this case the potential reward was well worth the risk.

But I did need help. I wasn't going into this alone. There was only one person I could count on, and he had been willing to help me bend the rules in the past. I called the station and asked for Steele.

Chapter 39

I met Steele outside the park by the motorcycles. I fit in well with my leather jacket sporting a skull and crossbones on the back, a bandana on my head, a bushy moustache, and dark shades, all of which I had picked up at the costume shop beneath Carol's apartment. Steele walked past me and looked around. I tapped him on the shoulder and he jumped.

"You gotta be kidding," he said with a grin.

"Worked, didn't it?"

He admitted he had no clue it was me even though he was looking for me.

We were an hour early, so we went over the plan. It would have been nice to know who would be in the shack, but we had no way of knowing. We were going to take up spots on either side of the Bobs and wait for Sadie and the boy. Walters or Meyers would either be inside or would show up right after Sadie. We would watch and see if anyone showed up, and agreed to wait fifteen seconds before going in. If no one had shown by then, they were probably already inside. I hoped fifteen seconds wasn't long enough to do whatever they were planning on doing. We sat in the Mustang to pass some time.

"Something about this isn't right, Spencer. If these guys are involved in something, why would they continue when they know the heat's on?"

I rolled the window down halfway. "Because they don't *think* the heat's on. You guys certainly aren't putting any pressure on them. The only one they're worried about is me, and they think they've taken care of me with the restraining order."

He nodded. "Maybe. But it's not too smart."

"Nobody said criminals are smart."

"Thank goodness… makes them easier to catch."

I agreed. "How many bank robbers do you think you'd catch if they just robbed one bank? There are many cases where some guy was caught after the tenth robbery. Quit after one and spend your money."

We were both silent for a few minutes.

"Hard to wait for time to pass, isn't it?" Steele said.

"Yeah, each minute takes forever."

"You nervous?"

"Not really nervous… more like excited. You?"

"Nope. It's just a job… and I'm good at it. If you're good at something you just get it done and move on."

I nodded. When I had decided to call Steele I thought hard about it, given the history with his son. I knew Stosh had told me Steele assured him he'd have no problem if the cases overlapped, but people tend to tell their bosses what they want to hear. My conversation with Steele on the phone, and what he just said, left me with no qualms about him being able to think clearly.

I used the rest of the time to fill Steele in on the layout of the shack and give him a description of Sadie. At twenty to nine we paid the admission and entered the park under the sign that told us to *Laugh Your Troubles Away*. Neither one of us was laughing.

***

The shack was under the first drop of the Bobs. I left Steele fifty feet before the shack, then walked past it and stood in the group of people at the ticket booth for the roller coaster. Steele looked relaxed. I was aware of everything that was going on around me as I watched for Sadie. It was two minutes past nine when I saw her coming with a sandy-haired boy a little taller than her. The kid looked very excited. They were walking quickly.

Sadie was looking around, perhaps looking for me, perhaps looking for Walters or Meyers. I didn't see either of them, and if Steele didn't notice me I knew she didn't either.

Steele saw them coming and started walking leisurely toward the shack. Sadie held the door for Vincent, and they disappeared inside. I wondered about Riverview, where very little was as it seemed, and thought about the screen doors in the Fun House that had no handles. This door had a handle, but what was inside was just as mysterious.

By the time I had counted to fifteen both of us were near the door with our guns out and pointing down. Steele nodded at me, and I opened the door as a coaster started its descent on the first drop, covering the sound of the door opening.

The room was dark with only one dim lamp on a desk, but I could see Belva sitting at the desk looking down at some papers. Walters had ahold of the boy by the collar and was pushing him toward the desk with his right hand. He held a rag in his left. Sadie was standing with her back to me. The kid almost fell as he was pushed roughly to the front of the desk. The screech of the roller coaster was deafening, so Walters didn't hear me approaching as I made my way slowly along the shelves that were four-foot-wide units open on both sides. Walters blocked Belva's view of me. I knew Steele was behind me and prayed Sadie wouldn't see us and give us away.

Still next to the shelves, I inched closer to Walters as the coaster reached the turn at the bottom of the drop and the noise built to a roar. I had no idea how these people stood the noise, but it was a blessing to me.

Walters bent over the desk, wrote something with one hand, and held the kid by the collar with the other. The white rag was in his pocket. The kid was shaking.

Sadie saw me, and her mouth opened slightly. I put my finger to my lips. Both Walters and Belva were looking down and didn't see her reaction. I inched my way behind the shelf until I was only three feet from the desk.

Steele must have bumped into the shelf because something fell off and hit the floor with a thud. Walters looked up, saw me, and reached into his jacket.

I hit him on the head with the butt of my .38. He went down and crumpled against the desk. His eyes were open, arms at his sides. There was blood where I had hit him, but he was conscious.

Belva grabbed the boy and moved back toward the wall with her arms around him. She didn't have a weapon.

"Belva, move away from the boy."

"I'm just protecting him," she pleaded.

She very well may have been, but I needed to be sure. "Move away, Belva… now!"

She dropped her arms, and the boy ran over to Sadie. Walters was still lying on the floor.

With a determined look, Steele stepped up and raised his gun.

"He's done, Steele. Put your gun down."

Steele just stared at the man on the floor without responding.

"Steele!"

He moved closer to Walters, his gun aimed at his chest.

"Steele. I know how you feel. He deserves to die, but he's our link to the kids."

Steele moved closer and placed the barrel of his gun against Walters' forehead, probably thinking about his son.

"Steele. Remember when I wanted to shoot that bastard Vitale? You told me he wasn't worth it and that one day I would feel guilty about it from a jail cell."

He didn't answer. His gun didn't move.

"Put it down, Ronnie. It might make you feel better for a minute, but tomorrow won't be so pretty."

He didn't move a muscle. I wanted to take his arm but was afraid that he would twitch his finger.

"Ronnie. It's cold-blooded murder. Think. You'll get a death sentence."

Steele just stared at Walters. And more surprisingly, Walters was just staring back with a slight smirk. I couldn't imagine that eyes could look so empty. There was no fear, no pleading, nothing human. He was on the edge of dying and had no reaction besides arrogance.

I tried once more and softly said, "Ronnie, I'd have to testify at your trial, and I can't lie."

In a calm voice, he said, "You won't have to."

I relaxed and took a deep breath. As I was letting it out slowly, the tiny room was filled with the explosion. The hole in Walters' forehead was neat and round, but the floor under his head was covered with pieces of his skull and a spreading pool of blood and brains. Walters' eyes were still staring at Steele, but the smirk was gone.

Sadie stood with one hand over her mouth and the other arm around the boy.

I lowered my gun and sighed as I wondered if Belva *was* on our side. If she was, our only lead was gone.

Steele's look hadn't changed. His face showed no emotion—only determination.

I stepped toward the body as Steele moved away. "Jesus, Steele. You just shot the guy who knows where the kids are."

As he glanced at me, Belva said, "I know where they are."

Steele gave me a two-finger salute and walked into the adjoining room.

I turned to Belva. "Whose side are you on? And if you're on my side, how do you know where the kids are?"

She just stood against the wall as I heard the sound of the next coaster clanking up to the top of the first hill. I got ready for the deafening screech. But before the clanking stopped, another explosion filled the tiny shack. It came from the other room, and it was all I could do to keep my knees from buckling. As the coaster screech faded, I started to move toward the back room and heard, "Drop the gun, Manning."

I turned toward the voice and saw Marcel, the Freak Show barker, standing next to the shelving. I also thought I saw a flicker of a shadow move at the end of the shelves, but it was hard to be sure in the dark room.

"Drop it, Manning. Last time I ask." He was pointing a gun at my chest, and at ten feet away I didn't think he'd miss.

I dropped my gun.

"Kick it to me."

As I did, I thought I saw something move on the other side of the shelves. In some places there were spaces on the shelves, and I could see the wall on the other side. A part of me hoped it was Steele, but I knew it wasn't. I didn't want to go in the back room.

"Put down the gun, Marcel," I said. "You can't kill everybody." Belva had moved over to Sadie and Vincent.

"I'd be happy just killing you, Manning. If it wasn't for you none of this would have happened."

I wanted to keep him talking to buy time. "And kids would just keep disappearing?"

"Hey, nobody cared about those kids. You had to go and butt in."

I heard the clanking of the next coaster. As the screech started to build, one of the shelving units fell into the room. Marcel turned and wildly fired a shot into the shelf. A second shot exploded and Marcel staggered back with a surprised look, his free hand on his chest. As he fell to the floor, the shadow stepped out from behind the shelves. It had been two weeks since I had last seen Rosie.

We both walked over to Marcel. He was dead. We just looked at each other—I had no words.

"Where's Steele, Spencer?"

"In the other room, but I don't think you want to go in there. I heard a shot just before Marcel came in." I picked up my gun. Vincent and the women were still standing frozen against the wall.

Rosie closed her eyes for a second and lowered her head. "What the hell was he doing here?"

"I asked him."

"Oh, Spencer." I've never heard two words filled with so much despair. For a brief moment she looked overwhelmingly sad, but then regained her detective composure. "Let's get this under control. I have to go look."

"Before you do, would you put some cuffs on Belva?"

Belva looked shocked. "Why? I told you I'm on your side!"

"I hope so," I said. "But until we know for sure, I'm not taking any chances."

Rosie cuffed her and left the room.

I took Walters' gun out of his inside jacket pocket and took the rag out of his outside pocket. It smelled of chloroform. I turned to the women.

"Sadie, take Vincent and go call an ambulance and the police. Tell them Detective Lonnigan was involved in a shooting."

"What about Meyers?" she asked.

"Good question."

As Sadie and Vincent moved away from her, Belva said nervously, "I'm on your side. I need to explain."

She told me about a house where kids were kept and a factory where they worked. I told her she'd have to repeat it to Lieutenant Powolski when he arrived.

Rosie came out of the back room with tears in her eyes and the saddest look I've ever seen. She just shook her head.

"Did he kill Walters?" she asked.

I nodded.

"I can't imagine," she said. "All these years with all that sadness and hurt."

I walked over to her and tried to put my arms around her.

She pushed me away. I thought it had something to do with us, but she shook her head quickly and said, "If you do that here, I'll lose it. And I can't lose it here." She bit her lower lip.

I moved away and realized I would have lost it too.

"What now?" Belva asked.

Rosie answered. "We get this sorted out. But let's get outta here."

Chapter 40

It was almost ten and the park was closing. As we stood outside the shack, tired happy people walked by on their way out... just twenty feet or so from a horrible tragedy. They'd read about it in the morning papers and be shocked.

Belva sat on a bench. Rosie and I stood next to her.

"Glad to see you, Rosie," I said with one eye on Belva.

She nodded.

"I thought you had night duty."

"I did. You were it."

"Pardon?"

"The lieutenant assigned me and Pitcher to follow you around."

I was confused. "To protect me?"

She scrunched up her face. "Maybe partly. But more because you tend to find trouble, or trouble finds you. Our best lead in this case was you. So I followed you to the park. Nice outfit. I was about to enter the shack when I heard the shot. I started to move, but then I saw Marcel running toward the shack. He must have heard the shot too."

I could hear faint sirens. "That's ironic."

She looked at me with raised eyebrows.

"The lieutenant questioned my idea to use people as bait, and I'm the biggest bait in the bucket. He warned me several times to stay away from here, especially after the restraining order. Speaking of which…"

We turned to Belva who was sitting slumped over on the bench. This was a different Belva than the hard, tough woman in the police station. She had tears in her eyes and looked defeated. Perhaps that was because she had been caught. I needed some convincing to believe she wasn't one of the bad guys.

"Belva, there's a little matter of a restraining order."

She looked startled when I mentioned her name. "Pardon?" she asked.

I repeated the sentence.

"Yes, I'm sorry about that. He made me. He—"

I stopped her. "Save it. The police will be here soon." The sirens were loud.

It struck me that Belva was in a pretty good position if she was involved. She could blame it all on Walters, and he couldn't deny it.

I looked out over the crowd of people moving up the Midway and saw Harvey. He watched for a minute and then joined the crowd walking north.

A fire department ambulance was the first to arrive. It pulled into the park and drove down the Midway. Two police cars were not far behind. I told the paramedics what they would find inside.

I turned back to Belva. Tears were streaming down her face.

"Mr. Manning. The kids…"

"Hold on a few more minutes, Belva. The lieutenant will be here soon."

She nodded and wiped her eyes on her sleeve.

Five minutes later the Midway was filled with official vehicles. Ambulances and police cars, both marked and unmarked, were lined up farther than I could see.

Sadie made her way through the crowd with Vincent.

"I called Vincent's parents and told them what was going on and that Vincent might have to talk to the police. I told them someone would call them."

"They'll want to get a statement. You and he will probably have to go back to the station."

"Okay. We'll wait over there." She pointed at the cotton candy stand. I watched to make sure Sadie was going to be okay.

I looked for Rosie and found her talking to a sergeant as Lieutenant Powolski walked up. They talked for a minute and then she pointed in my direction. I had no idea what to expect from the lieutenant, but it probably wasn't going to be a pat on the back. Steele was the worst part, and Stosh was the one who had okayed Steele's involvement. But it was me who had brought him into this. He headed in my direction with a very strange look on his face.

"Rosie filled me in. I'll want a statement from you too."

I nodded.

"We have a lot to talk about."

"Yes." I couldn't imagine how he felt about Steele. "But first, this is Belva Meyers. She says she knows where the missing kids are."

"Mrs. Meyers, what's going on here?"

She looked exhausted.

"The boys are being kept in a big house. Every day they're brought to a factory building to work. At the end of the day they're brought back to the house."

Stosh gave me a confused look. I returned it.

"What kind of factory, Belva?" I asked.

She shook her head and her eyes welled up. "I don't know for sure, but it has something to do with drugs."

"Do you know where it is?"

"No, but I know where the house is."

"Where?" the lieutenant asked.

"It's at 1212 Division."

Stosh glanced at me again. That was a high crime area known for gangs and drugs.

The lieutenant asked Belva to come with him.

"There are a lot more questions, Mrs. Meyers. We need to get a full statement at the station."

"Am I under arrest?"

He motioned for her to get up. "Not at the moment. We just need more information." He walked her over to an officer and asked him to bring her to the station. Stosh said he wanted to be in on the questioning and would be there shortly.

He let out a big sigh as he turned back to me. "I have questions for you, too, but you're on the bottom of my priority list at the moment. I want you in on the questioning since you have more information than we do. Meet me at the station."

"Okay." I slowly shook my head. "Stosh, I'm so sorry about Steele."

"Yeah, me too. It's always hard losing part of the team, but this…"

I'd never seen Stosh cry, even when Francine died, but I knew how badly he felt.

"He had me convinced that he was okay. We'll talk about that too." He started to walk away and then turned back to me with that strange look again and said, "Lose the moustache."

I had forgotten about the disguise.

I found Rosie and told her what Belva had said and that I was heading for the station. She said she would be there soon.

We looked at each other. My look was serious. I wanted to say something about us, but this wasn't the time or place, so I just looked. Her look started out as serious, but then a tiny smile crossed her face.

"What?"

"If you want me to be seen with you in public, don't ever grow a moustache."

"I'm glad I can provide some comic relief."

She touched me on the arm. "Me too. I needed some."

I held out my hand and she took it. "Thanks for having my back, Rosie."

"Protecting the taxpayers… that's what we do." She turned back to an officer.

When I got into my Mustang I peeled off the moustache. As I backed out of the parking space, I noticed that the passenger side mirror needed adjusting again. A light bulb immediately went off in my head.

Chapter 41

Stosh, Belva, Pitcher, and a stenographer were in an interview room when I got to the station. They were collecting Belva's personal information. Stosh took me out of the room and told me that Belva had waived her right to an attorney for the moment. Whether or not she needed one depended on the rest of her story. He also told me he wasn't sure whether she had been involved or not, but based on what she knew it looked like she was. He didn't trust her and asked me to pay attention to any discrepancies in her story and ask any questions I thought were pertinent. Based on the Belva I knew at the park, I wasn't sure either. She was a great actress. The Belva in Walters' office was a different person from the one tonight. I just needed to find out which was the real Belva.

Pitcher offered her something to drink. She asked for water.

The lieutenant started with questions about what Belva had already told us.

"You know a lot about what has been going on, Mrs. Meyers. How is that?"

"I'm in charge of personnel at the park. A while after Walters became the chief I noticed that the turnover in kids was higher than normal, and they didn't stay as long. Usually kids kept their jobs for the whole summer. It's a fun job for them."

Stosh nodded.

"One day I was out on the Midway and saw Marcel walking with a boy. Something about it seemed odd. I followed them to the shack where we were tonight, and they went inside. Not thinking much of it, I followed them in."

Her hand holding the glass started to shake.

"Take a drink, Mrs. Meyers," said Stosh. "Take your time."

She continued. "The boy was passed out in a chair, and Marcel was standing over him with a rag in his hand. Walters was seated at the desk." She paused with a quivering lip. "I immediately knew I shouldn't be there and tried to leave, but they wouldn't let me."

"What did they do?" Stosh asked.

"Walters told me they couldn't let me go and that I had only two options. One was to join them and help."

"Did they say what the other was?"

"They didn't have to."

I started to say something and Stosh stopped me. "Mrs. Meyers, you may be incriminating yourself. Would you like a lawyer now?"

She shook her head. "No, I need to tell you. I've been living with this a long time. It's been killing me."

"So you helped them?" Stosh asked Belva.

She just nodded with a very sad look.

"I need you to answer verbally, Mrs. Meyers."

Looking down, she very quietly said, "Yes, I did."

"I have to ask why."

Tears welled up in her eyes again, and she started to shake. "Because he threatened my son." She paused and took a deep breath. "Walters said if I didn't do as I was told my son would end up like the others."

The door opened and Rosie joined us.

"How did he know you had a son?" We already knew the answer to that, but it would be a good check of her story.

"My son, Albert, had been arrested for theft. Walters got him off. I was very grateful. But then Walters came to me when the chief job opened up and told me if I didn't get him the job he would have to look back at my son's case and he would go to jail."

"So you got him the job?"

"I recommended him and that was enough. Mr. Block doesn't like dealing with those kinds of things."

I knew that was true. Mr. Block didn't seem to like dealing with *any* kinds of things.

"You had no problem recommending him?"

Her forehead creased. "Yes, but he was a policeman, so I figured he would do a good job. I had no idea all this would happen."

"And what happened?"

She shrugged. "I don't know much about how it happened. I only know what's going on now, and that there are others involved."

"Do you know who?"

She shook her head.

"Verbally again, please."

"I do not."

"You gave us an address for the house, but not the factory. How do you know the address?"

"Walters wanted me to know exactly what would happen to my son if I didn't go along with them. One Saturday morning Marcel drove me to the house. We sat in the car for ten minutes before a van pulled up in front. A few minutes later five kids came out with two men and got into the van. They put a blindfold on me. When they took the blindfold off we were inside a building. They led me to a room that had two rows of tables with people sitting there filling tiny packets with white powder. Most were kids." She started to shake again and then regained her composure. "I have gone to sleep every night with the image of my son sitting at that table. Some nights I didn't sleep at all."

"You could have come to the police and told us about Walters. We would have protected you."

She shook her head. "No, I don't think you could have. Walters was a cop. And he said he still had friends on the force. So who would protect me and my son?"

We were all very quiet. I was glad the lieutenant didn't respond because I would have agreed with Belva. Stosh and I had talked a lot about the things the police couldn't do because their hands were tied by the law. They sure couldn't give Belva and her son personal bodyguards. A heavy blanket of sadness hung in the room.

I broke the silence. "May I ask a question, lieutenant?"

"Yes."

"Belva, you're wearing a diamond bracelet. Where did you get that?"

She violently shook her head, took off the bracelet, and placed it on the table. "It's from him."

"A present?"

"That's what he said. But he wanted me to have something that would remind me to not say anything."

"So he bought you off?"

She sighed. "I guess, but he didn't have to after threatening Albert. If it wasn't for Albert I wouldn't have done this."

"You could have not worn the bracelet."

"No, he made me wear it. One day I forgot to put it on, and he said if I forgot again Albert wouldn't like it."

I still wasn't sure whether Belva was acting. "The day before Benny was killed I was in the Fun House and someone behind me asked me to meet him at the hot dog stand. He didn't show up. Were you there in the Fun House?" I had no proof, but I had a suspicion based on the flash I had seen when I looked back in the darkness. Everything depended on her answer.

Belva started to cry and buried her face in her hands. "It's my fault Benny is dead," she said with a shaky voice. "If I… I didn't know…"

I knew what she meant, but had to ask.

"So you were there?"

She nodded and then looked up at me. "I was. Walters told me to follow you and report where you had been and who you talked to."

"I didn't see you."

"There are walkways for the workers behind the maze. I saw you go in and then saw Benny go in after you." She paused and looked confused. "How did you know I was there?"

"I didn't for sure. But I saw a sparkle of light that I thought may have been from your bracelet."

She was quiet.

"So it *was* Benny who wanted to meet me?"

"Yes."

"Do you know who killed him?"

She looked down and then back up with half-closed eyes. "Walters took him down in the tunnels to teach him a lesson. He brought his baseball bat. He made me come with… to show me what could happen if I didn't cooperate."

"You can't teach someone a lesson by killing them, Belva."

"No. He didn't mean to. But Benny put up a fight, and Walters hit him in the head." She started to sob. "I didn't help. I just backed against the wall and froze. I felt so awful."

There wasn't anything any of us could say to help her with that.

"How about the others?"

She shook her head. "Well, there's Marcel. He was meaner than Walters."

"One more question, Belva," I said.

She looked up at me.

"Harvey is your cousin. Is he involved in any of this?"

"No. He knows nothing about it."

I looked over at Stosh and winked.

He narrowed his eyelids ever so slightly and took over the questioning. "Who else is involved, Mrs. Meyers?"

"I don't know any of the people outside of the park. Walters and Marcel and I were the only ones at Riverview. There were probably others who brought the boys to the shack, but they had no idea what was going on."

"Last question. There were three people killed before tonight— Benny, Harold, and Gertrude Morgan, Mr. Block's secretary. Do you know anything about Harold?"

She shook her head. "Poor Harold. I overheard a conversation between Walters and Harold. Walters didn't know I was there. Harold evidently saw something and said he was going to the police.

Walters said that wouldn't end well for him and he should think it over. I guess he didn't get the chance to do that."

Rosie raised her hand halfway.

"Go ahead, Lonnigan," Stosh said.

I said I had a question too.

"Why was Walters doing this?" Rosie asked.

Belva shook her head. "Money. Why else? Someone was paying him a lot of money for each kid."

Stosh nodded at me.

"Belva, Gertrude Morgan was Mr. Block's secretary."

She started to lose her composure again as her lips started to quiver.

I continued. "She had been a loyal secretary and then suddenly didn't show up for work one day. Do you know anything about that?"

"Yes. Walters told me to call her and tell her she didn't have a job anymore. He would pay her to stay home as long as she said nothing to anyone." She gave me a forlorn look. "She asked why. I didn't know, but I told her not to worry about it since she would be paid to do nothing. She agreed."

"You seem upset, Belva."

She lowered her head and said very quietly. "I figured it had something to do with what was going on, but it was a good deal for Gertrude." Tears started to run down her cheeks. "I didn't think any more about it until Walters told me to call again and tell her she had to leave town. I called her in the middle of the night. And then... I..." She sobbed through the rest. "I read about her in the paper. I..."

"Do you know who did it, Belva?"

She shook her head. "Not for sure. Probably Marcel."

I thought about the cheerful barker enticing people into the Freak Show. He was the biggest freak of them all.

"Okay, Belva," Stosh said. "Thanks for answering our questions."

"Am I under arrest?"

"No, but we're going to hold you until we can talk to the District Attorney in the morning."

She looked like she was going to cry. Stosh didn't look too happy either.

"I'll get a matron to take care of you."

"Can I call my son?"

"Certainly."

I told Stosh I needed to hit the head. He told me we weren't done talking. I already knew that.

On my way back to the room I ran into Sadie and thanked her for her help.

"I couldn't have imagined, Spencer. Remember when I said I wanted to get the bastard and I wanted to be there when it happened?"

"Sure."

"If this happens again, I don't want to be there."

"I don't blame you."

"I hope you get the kids back."

"We will."

We said goodbye, and I headed back to the interview room, not knowing what to expect.

Chapter 42

I sat down next to Rosie. It was awfully quiet in Stosh's office. I joined in the uncomfortable silence until I couldn't stand it.

"I'd like to know how much trouble I'm in," I said.

"Cumulatively, or for each of the twelve things?"

I didn't answer.

Stosh stood up and sat on the corner of his desk. "Things were done wrong. We'll let Internal Affairs tell us which. The biggest is me. I never should have let Steele anywhere near that case."

"But he—" I started.

"No buts. It's on me. He was very convincing… enough so that I didn't see the problem. The police shrink will probably tell me why my judgement was bad."

I tried again. "If I hadn't—"

"Nope. Me. I green-lighted him, and you didn't question that." He folded his hands in his lap. "However, I do note that you called him and not me. I would wonder why if I didn't already know. I wouldn't have let you do it. Then there was that restraining order. And I still would love to know what happened in that basement last year and who the mystery man was."

"There wasn't any myst—"

He held up his hand. "Right. I'll never find out. And now the only other person who knew is dead. But you got Pitcher back and the bad guy ended up dead. Again we have dead bad guys and some answers."

"Then there's Steele," Rosie said.

"Yeah, sad as hell. But maybe he's better off. I can't imagine what he's been carrying around inside all these years that made him do that. Must have been awful."

"I wonder how he got through the psych evals," I said.

"Aw, what the hell do those guys know?" said Stosh. "Anybody with half a brain can give them what they want to hear and be back on the street. And Steele had more than half a brain."

He stood up and stretched. "I'm beat."

"We all could use a good night's sleep," Rosie said, stifling a yawn.

I glanced at my watch. Almost one.

Stosh sat back in his chair. "So, where do we go from here? We have an address for the house and none for the factory."

"Want my two cents?" I asked.

"Of course."

"We could pick up the kids and whoever is running the house now. But that doesn't get us the guys at the factory."

"The people at the house might tell us," Rosie said.

"Might. And might not. And they might not even know. I say we wait for the van to show up in the morning and follow it to the factory. We can make a better decision on how to proceed once we have more information."

"And we have no idea how many kids and guards are inside that house and what weapons they have," Rosie added.

"We'll put surveillance on the house," Stosh said.

"Better to get the kids from the van than the house," I said. "More control. And we have another problem. This is going to be all over the news in the morning."

"How about if we get the press to say there was some kind of big accident at the park?" Rosie asked.

Stosh picked up the phone and called the desk sergeant. "Powolski. Find Walsh and get him up here."

"I have another question," Stosh said. "Meyers said it was just an ordinary house… no bars or fences. So how come none of those kids escaped?"

"Not too hard," Rosie said. "Keep them locked in their rooms and have several people in the house to control them."

Stosh nodded.

"Or," I said. "Walters had a rag in his pocket that smelled of chloroform. I'm guessing he used it to put the kids out. Remember Meyers said she saw a kid unconscious in a chair? And she saw white powder at the factory. Not hard to figure this is about drugs. So maybe they've got the kids drugged. Maybe they don't even know they're prisoners."

"Lots of maybes, Spencer."

"You have a different explanation?"

Stosh shook his head. "Not that makes any more sense."

There was a knock on the door, and Walsh came in.

"Walsh, can you get the news people to sit on this for a day, maybe two?"

"How do I do that? That neighborhood was lit up with red lights."

"Gotta be some kind of security issue."

I chimed in. "How about a bomb scare? And we've had more threats."

Stosh nodded. "Walsh?"

Walsh shrugged. "I can try."

"Try real hard. We need to buy some time."

"Okay, Lieutenant."

"You two get some sleep. I'll arrange for a couple unmarked cars to watch the house in the morning. Be back here at ten."

Rosie stood up.

"I have one more thing," I said.

"Can it wait till morning?" Stosh asked.

"It could, but I'd rather it didn't."

"Go home and get some sleep, Rosie," he said.

She sat back down. "I'll wait."

"Suit yourself. What's so important, Spencer?"

"I remembered where there might be a print from my mysterious secretary."

That got his attention. "Where?"

I told him about the mirror she had adjusted.

He picked up the phone again and asked for a print man to meet me in the parking lot.

"Now get outta here before you think of something else."

I followed Rosie out.

***

R osie waited with me in the parking lot and introduced me to the print guy. I showed him the mirror, and ten minutes later he had two nice prints. He said he'd see how fast Lieutenant Powolski wanted them run. They were backed up for several days. I told him it wouldn't be a problem.

"Well, that was a helluva night," I said.

Rosie put her arm around my waist and suggested I walk her to her car. She leaned against the door.

"Rosie, I wanted to call you, but..."

"It's okay, Spencer. Let's just get some sleep and talk about it when we're..." Her lips quivered and tears streamed down her face.

I pulled her to me and put my arms around her as she started to sob.

With her head buried in my chest, she said, "I'm going to miss him so much, Spencer."

"Me too." I could barely hear her. Her words in between sobs were muffled in my shirt.

"Rosie, do you remember when you transferred up here and you got Steele for a partner?"

I could feel her nod. "I forget who his partner was before you, but they told you the new person in the department got Steele because he was such a pain in the ass."

"Sure... I remember." She pulled away a bit but kept her arms around me. "And I soon found out that the new person didn't get

Steele because he was a pain in the ass. They got him because he was the best. If somebody new was going to learn the job, Steele was the guy to teach them."

"He taught me a lot too, Rosie."

She smiled briefly through her tears. "But he *was* a pain in the ass."

I returned the smile. "Yes, he certainly was."

She started to cry again. "And I loved him."

I pulled her back to me.

When she moved away she said, "Spencer, would you have...?" She slowly shook her head with a confused and sad look on her face. "I'm sorry—I don't know how to say..."

I put my arm around her shoulders. "It's okay. I know. Would I have done what Steele did?"

She just nodded.

I took a deep breath and let it out slowly. "I've thought about that. I really don't know. Dad and Stosh have said that we're not judge and jury. You guys just arrest someone and let someone else make the tough decisions. But Steele had a lot more to deal with because of his son. We can't put ourselves in his shoes."

We were silent for a bit.

"What actually happened in there?" she asked.

"It was almost like it was happening in slow motion. Walters was lying on the floor on his back. Steele then slowly walked up to him and put the barrel of his gun on his forehead. He was calm and seemed to know exactly what he was doing. I thought he was just trying to scare Walters."

"Did he?"

"I don't think so. There was a smirk on Walters' face... like he knew a cop wouldn't pull the trigger. Maybe that's what got him killed. Maybe if he had shown fear Steele wouldn't have done it."

More silence.

"I tried to talk him out of it... pointed out that it was cold-blooded murder and that he would end up in court and I'd have to testify against him. He said not to worry, that wouldn't happen. I took that to mean he wasn't going to shoot, and relaxed. Then he pulled the trigger. I hadn't considered the other meaning to his 'that wouldn't happen.'"

"That must have been awful, Spencer."

"I think I was in shock, but I didn't have time to think about it at the moment with Marcel showing up."

A squad pulled into the lot and parked two spaces away.

"You haven't answered my question," she said.

"I know. I don't think there's an answer. The easy answer is no, I don't think I'd do it. But if my son had disappeared and I had those emotions to deal with… I just don't know. How about you?"

"I don't think I'd pull the trigger, but you're right… you just don't know."

She got out her keys. "I can't believe he's gone, Spencer."

I stepped over to her and put my arms around her.

"And when I think about his son and what he has lived with all these years, I feel so…"

"I know. Sometimes life really sucks."

I don't remember what time it was when we finally let go of each other and headed home. It seemed like hours had passed.

Chapter 43

There wasn't much time for sleep between three and nine, even if I *had* been able to. I knew we were taking a chance by not getting the kids out of there right away, but there were probably more kids and guards than we knew about. We could use more knowledge about conditions inside the house. Part of my not being able to sleep was anxiety over what the police would find in the morning.

When I got to the lieutenant's office it was empty. I sat and closed my eyes and fell asleep. When I opened them Stosh was working at his desk.

I yawned and stretched.

"Have a nice nap?"

"Nicer than the sleep I got last night. Why didn't you wake me?"

"Figured I'd let you sleep till Rosie got here."

I looked at my watch. "She's late."

"She's getting coffee for you. And Tanner, from this morning's surveillance, is going to join us."

"Did you get anything?"

"Yup."

That was all I was going to get, so I closed my eyes and was almost asleep again when Rosie came in and handed me a cup of coffee. Stosh already had his.

"Morning, Spencer."

"Hi, Rosie. Thanks."

"What about the prints, Stosh?" I asked.

"They're working on it."

Tanner walked in and took a seat. I hadn't seen him since the last case. We nodded at each other.

Just the aroma of the coffee helped to wake me up. I turned to Stosh.

"So?"

"First, the news people are going along with the story, but that won't last long. Give us a review, Tanner."

He straightened in the chair. "A plain white van pulled up to the house a few minutes past eight with a driver and passenger. Six kids came out a few minutes later with three men. They walked straight to the van and got in. My partner said they looked like robots."

"Did they look okay?" Rosie asked.

"Other than the robot thing, they looked fine."

"What happened to the men?" I asked.

"They went back into the house. We followed the van to a building on Adams, about ten blocks to the west. The van pulled into the alley behind the building, and after a series of honks, an overhead door opened and the van drove in."

"Series of honks?" I said.

"Yes. Short, long, short."

"A signal."

"Yes."

"Did you look for cameras?" Rosie asked.

"We did. Nothing. And there's no bell outside the overhead door."

"So," I said, "the honk was the doorbell. What about other buildings?"

"Except for gangways and recessed rear doors, solid buildings down the alley."

"Other doors besides the overhead?" Stosh asked.

"Just regular entry doors in the alley and the front."

"Did you see anyone?"

"Nope."

"Was there a name on the building?" I asked.

"Sign on the front says Metco."

"Windows?" Rosie asked.

"None in the alley. Several in the front."

Something was niggling at me. "Stosh, can I get the folder on the Simmons Gallery case last year?"

"Why?"

"I want to check something."

He picked up the phone, and a few minutes later an officer came in with the file. I leafed through while they talked and found what I was looking for.

"What is it?" Stosh asked.

In the folder was a list of businesses owned by Larry Maggio, the crime boss in Chicago. Metco was on the list.

"Metco is owned by Larry Maggio."

"Well there's a surprise," Stosh said sarcastically.

"Agreed. If it's a drug operation, Maggio's involved. But I bet he doesn't know about the kids."

"Why do you say that?"

"I got the impression from something Maggio said last year that he doesn't mess with kids and doesn't like people who do. Neither does Joey, who gives out free ice cream." I told them about the kid at the park.

"Salt of the earth," Stosh grumbled with a frown.

"I'm not defending them. Just saying I bet this was Walters' doing."

"Why?" asked Rosie.

"Belva said there was a lot of money changing hands. Certainly enough to buy a diamond bracelet. Illegal or not, you have to pay employees. If you can get them for free it cuts down on your overhead. And these kids are free. You pick on kids without families and no one notices. If he's running the operation and giving Maggio a cut, less overhead means more profit."

"Except Martin has a family," Stosh said. "How do you explain that?"

"You've said many times that we're lucky criminals are so dumb. They screwed up."

He nodded. "So?"

"So, maybe this leads to Maggio."

Stosh humphed. "It might lead there, but based on past trails it'll be a dead end. If we ever get him it'll be because of something dumb, like tax evasion. Did you follow the conversation while you were looking through the folder?"

"I did. You decided to go in tomorrow morning, but you hadn't figured how to do it yet."

We all talked for another thirty minutes and decided on a plan. The police would intercept the van after it left the house with the kids and have several ambulances nearby to take the kids to a hospital. I'd stay with the kids along with other officers. I wasn't happy about that, but now wasn't the time to bring it up. Stosh would alert the nearest hospital and the feds. Another team would address the house.

Stosh's people and the feds would man the van and two more vehicles. Since we had no idea how many people were inside the building, they hoped that fourteen people would be plenty... four in each car and six in the van. Men from the cars would take up positions on foot against the back wall and follow the van in.

Stosh pushed back in his chair. "Okay, let's meet back here at two. I'll make some phone calls and have a chat with the captain."

* * *

I walked out with Rosie.

"Well, you do know how to stir things up," she said.

"I guess I do. I've lost a lot of sleep lately... and some of that was because of you. I've done a lot of thinking, and the truth is I'm not sure *what* I want."

She smiled. "That's a start. Let's continue from there after all this is settled."

"Fine by me. But I am sure of one thing. You're a friend I don't want to lose."

"Me either. We'll figure it out."

Chapter 44

We all met in the captain's office. Rosie, me, Pitcher, Tanner, two other detectives, and two FBI agents. One was the head of the newly formed Hostage Rescue Team that was only about a year old. They would have drug agents standing by outside. I figured we had enough people to fight a small war, which might be what we were doing.

The FBI had the lead, and Tanner reviewed everything he had seen that morning. Basically the plan stayed the same. The FBI wanted to know if we could get more information about what was going on inside. That would be hard without tipping our hand.

The FBI said that we would meet a block away from the house at seven and wait for the van. I suggested staging a fake accident. That would put police cars and ambulances on the scene and stop the van without arousing suspicion. Stosh got a map, and Tanner located a spot to stage it.

Stosh ended the meeting with a suggestion to get to bed early. He asked me to meet him in his office.

***

After we had sat down Stosh let out a big breath. "I hate waiting. I'd much rather just go get those kids."

"We'll get them." I wondered what he had on his mind. I didn't like the look on his face.

"Three things, Spencer. Belva is out on bond. The DA charged her as an accomplice on five counts. But she obviously cooperated and seems to be an unwilling accomplice, so he thinks most of the charges will be dropped, and she'll get probation on what's left. We don't think she's a flight risk so bond was pretty low. She has agreed to cooperate and testify if we find others who are involved."

"You mean like Walters' ex-partner? There has to be something there."

"We're looking at it. He's off today. We have someone watching his house, but he hasn't shown." Stosh fidgeted in his chair and looked pained. "And the second... I don't know quite how to say this, Spencer."

I knew I had some kind of lecture coming, but I didn't know how serious it would be. "Well, at least you can't fire me," I said with a little smile.

"What?"

"I said—"

"I heard what you said. What the hell are you talking about?"

"I figure I'm in trouble for any number of reasons, and—"

"Oh Jesus. You probably should be, but nobody's complaining."

"Then what...?"

"We got a hit on those prints." He looked worried. "Her real name is Cheryl Wallace, and she's wanted in three states for insurance fraud."

I just stared at him in dismay.

"Spencer?"

"Yeah, I got it."

He opened a file. "Florida, Georgia, and Tennessee. She and a fellow by the name of Joseph Stone are wanted for insurance fraud for setting up and collecting on phony deaths of her father."

I couldn't believe what I was hearing. "So her father isn't dead?"

"Oh, her father's dead." He turned a page. "Died when she was six. They make up new identities for her and a father and buy an insurance policy. We're still waiting to hear from Georgia, but in the other two they created an identity and then reported him missing."

Nothing about this made much sense, especially the part about my being taken in. "How did the insurance companies not pick up on the scam?"

"It's actually pretty slick. If you look at what happened here, without those prints on your mirror you just have a strange story to tell. They wait a while, file a claim, and cash the check."

"I wonder if someone in the insurance companies was involved."

"Certainly a possibility. We're following up. Lots of people are talking." He handed me a photo of a man. "Would you show this to the lady across the street and see if it's the same guy?"

"Sure." I looked at the photo. "Missing person in all cases?"

"Yes."

"They're wanted for fraud?"

"Yes."

"So that wasn't a quick process. They'd have to wait for the missing person to be declared dead."

"Yup. We're talking fifteen years since the first one."

"How much were the policies?"

"A million dollars."

"Jesus. I could wait fifteen years for millions of dollars."

I looked down at the photo and then back up at Stosh. "Our case is murder."

He nodded. "It is. I guess they got tired of waiting years for the payoff."

"Holy crap, Stosh! They burned someone."

"They did."

"I felt sorry for her and gave her a hug!"

"Well, that's because you're one of the good guys."

"It's because I'm a gullible jerk, who just happens, by the way, to be a private detective." I thought *Belva* was a good actress. She was nothing compared to this monster.

"Something you're pretty good at. Chalk this up to another lesson about gut feelings."

"Thanks. Just what I needed." I stared at the photo some more, hoping it would give me some answers. It didn't. "That's one ballsy woman. She picked a private detective to use as her dupe." I just shook my head.

He closed the folder. "Like I said... not a bad plan. Who's going to question a death that a PI is vouching for? If your mirror isn't broken, they get away with it."

I let out a short laugh. "I almost had it fixed a month ago. I don't remember what meaningless chore kept me from doing it."

"Sometimes you don't know what things are going to matter later."

"I assume you're looking for them."

"Yup. All the normal channels in multiple states."

"How about putting their photos out on the news? Someone might see them."

"That was suggested. We don't want to spook them. They think they got away with another one. We're contacting insurance companies to give them a heads-up."

"Were the others all the same company?"

"Nope. All different."

"Amazing."

"Wipe that forlorn look off your face and forget it. Let's go get those kids."

"I don't know about the look, but we *will* get the kids," I said.

"And Spencer... don't stop having gut feelings. Just look for a few more facts before you make decisions."

"Thanks. I'll tell that to Harvey when I see him."

He smiled.

"You said three things, but I have one for you."

"I figured you would. That's my third thing." He took a deep breath and let it out slowly. "The fake accident is a good idea but after we get the kids I'd really like you to go to the hospital."

I was sure my look told him what I was thinking.

"Spencer, you've done a lot, but bottom line is you're a civilian."

"A civilian who pretty much handed all this to you."

He sighed.

I shook my head. "That's not going to happen, Stosh."

He shrugged. "Didn't figure it would, but I had to try. Okay, you go in with the foot crew, and you're the last one in."

I knew that was the best I was going to get and agreed.

Chapter 45

I caught Carol as she was starting to cook dinner. Billy was watching cartoons, but not the great cartoons I grew up with. Yogi Bear, Quick Draw McGraw, and the Flintstones were far better than anything I saw today.

I told her I had a story she wouldn't believe and offered to take them out for dinner. She accepted. Before we left she identified the man in the photo as the one she had seen. Billy wanted to go to McDonald's, so we went to one with a Playland. After dinner, he played while I told Carol the story. She was shocked.

As we sipped coffee, I said, "That leaves me without a secretary. I'm dreading going through that again."

"You don't have anyone you already saw that you could call back?"

"Well, there's one."

"Great, that'll save you a lot of trouble."

"It will if she accepts."

"Why wouldn't she?"

"She didn't exactly apply. She has a little boy to take care of and may not want the job."

She set her cup down and looked at me with a furrowed brow. "Do you mean me?"

I smiled. "I do. You were great. If I hadn't already hired Samantha I would have begged you to take the job."

She looked at me with her mouth half open.

"So, I'm begging you now."

Billy came running in and asked for ice cream. Carol started to get up.

"My treat, Carol. We'll be right back. You think about how you're going to say yes." I gave her my best smile, which hadn't worked on anyone in the last few weeks.

As Billy licked, we talked.

"So, how do I twist your arm?"

"Actually you don't have to twist my arm. I could use the money, and it would be fun."

"Is there a *but* coming?"

"Yes." She nodded toward Billy who was about halfway through the cone.

"Not a problem," I said.

"You like to explain that?"

"It's a pretty flexible job. I'm basically looking for someone to be around sometime during the day to do some paperwork and check the mail and be there if someone is coming in. I don't much care when that is. Being right across the street you could even work at your place. And if you had to, you could bring Billy to the office."

"Well, I don't know about that. Are people done shooting out your windows?" Her eyes twinkled.

I laughed. "I'd say that was a once-in-a-lifetime event." At least I hoped it was. "Why don't you think about it overnight and let me know."

She shook her head. "I don't want to risk losing the opportunity. If you're willing to be that flexible, I'll take it."

"Great!" We shook on it.

"When do you want me to start?"

"Why don't you come over Monday morning about ten, and we'll get it worked out."

"I'll look forward to that."

Billy finished the cone and asked if he could play some more.

"That's enough for one night. We've got some chores to do at home," Carol said.

On the way to the car, Carol thanked me for dinner.

I held the door while she and Billy climbed in.

Following Stosh's orders, I was in bed by ten and asleep by ten after.

Chapter 46

It was raining Friday morning—one of those gentle spring rains that lasts all day. Nice day for a car accident. By seven thirty we had set up the accident scene. The front right bumper of one car was touching the driver's door of another at a little less than a right angle. Unless you got right up to it you couldn't see that there was no damage. Two ambulances were parked next to the cars with lights flashing. Two police cars were parked at the curb, and officers were directing traffic. When we got word that the van had left, they would shut down the area for a block in all directions. Officers had already walked the neighborhood and told people to stay in their houses. I was excited.

I had my gun but had been told to stay away from the van. The police would take care of the heavy lifting. I was in charge of the kids and making the transfer to the ambulances.

At five after eight we got word that the van had left the house with six kids. We had three minutes. I saw the van coming from the east. It slowed when it approached the accident scene, and an officer stopped it and approached. There was another man in the passenger seat. The officer neared the van, and I could see both men in the van watching him. I also saw two officers approaching the van on the passenger side. As the driver rolled down his window, the officer on the driver's side and one on the passenger side yanked open the doors and pointed their guns at the two men. It was over in seconds.

The two men in the van followed orders and put their hands on the dash. With guns still aimed at the men, two other officers pulled them out of the van and cuffed them. Two other officers rolled open the side door and went in with me. Six boys were seated on bench seats. One was Martin. They just stared at us but did as they were told, which was to climb out of the van. I called to Martin, but he didn't react to his name. We led them to the ambulances, which took off for the hospital.

***

I followed the van and two unmarked cars to the factory, and we all pulled into the alley. The van stopped in front of the door, waited for the rest of us to take positions against the wall on either side of the door, then honked the signal. After ten seconds, the door slowly rose.

The van pulled into a dock area, and as the door started down we all moved in as agents jumped out of the van. There were guards inside the building, but they obviously weren't expecting trouble. The only one in the dock area was the man who had opened the door. The lead FBI man motioned for everyone to spread out.

The dock was filled with cardboard cartons stacked on pallets. Through large windows I could see a large open space filled with lots of kids seated at long tables. The man who had opened the garage door was against the wall being patted down.

As the officers made their way to the big room, someone came through the open door and saw the man against the wall being frisked. As he raised his gun I shot him in the chest, and five seconds later all hell broke loose.

I picked up the man's gun as four men came running from the other room. When they entered the dock the man against the wall yelled, "They're behind the cartons!"

The four spread out along the glass windows and moved out of my view. Shots were fired almost continuously from both sides. The

FBI and cops had to be careful because the kids were on the other side of the windows. I saw four cops move into the big room where several more men simply put their arms in the air.

As I slowly made my way down the row of cartons, praying that a bullet wouldn't come through from the other side, one of the drug men came around the corner with his gun pointed down. He paused a second too long. I'm sure all he focused on was my .38.

"Make one move, please," I said.

The only move he made was to drop his gun. I ordered him to the floor, picked up his gun, and stood over him. Shots stopped a few seconds later, and the FBI man yelled for a status report.

Three of the four men were dead, and I was standing over the fourth. The guy who had opened the door was in cuffs.

Someone opened the overhead door, and the drug agents came in. I could hear sirens in the distance.

I told the lead man I had shot one of them and asked if he needed me. He didn't but told me the police would want my gun. I stayed until the ambulances arrived and made sure the kids were being taken care of. Then I headed back to the station.

Chapter 47

Stosh was on the phone when I walked into his office. He waved me to a chair. His conversation didn't have anything to do with the case, and I could tell he wanted to get off the phone. Two minutes later he did.

"All over, Spencer. Three dead… not ours. Seven under arrest. One injured… one of the hostage team. He'll be okay."

I laid my gun on his desk. "One of the dead guys has my bullet in his chest."

He frowned at me. "So much for going in last."

"It was *because* I went in last. I was the only one who could see the guy who was about to take out one of yours."

He nodded.

"How are the kids?" I asked.

"Doc says they were full of some pretty strong stuff. They'll be okay, but it might be a long road."

"Any of them able to talk?"

He shook his head. "Sounds like the staged accident went off without a hitch."

"Just as planned."

"Nice when plans work out."

"Yup." I thought for a minute. "We have to be missing some people."

"Okay, why do you say that? But first, we found Bringman, Walters' ex-partner."

"Where did you find him?"

"Hiding in a closet at the factory."

We both laughed.

"He's been spilling everything he knows, and probably some he doesn't, hoping for a deal."

"He going to get one?"

"Not if I have anything to say about it."

His phone rang.

"Powolski."

He looked over at me. Now what?

"Yeah. Thanks."

I was looking at him with raised eyebrows.

"Four kids are ID'ed. We're getting ahold of families for those we have contacts for."

"That's great." I'd have to drop in at the Blue Note.

"So who's missing?" he asked.

"Maybe only one. Something was bothering me last night."

Stosh just looked at me and waited.

"How did Walters get his money?"

"Good question."

"Direct deposits to his account would be easy enough to find. So let's assume he was smarter than that. So how does he get his money?"

"Riverview."

"Exactly. I wonder who writes the checks."

Stosh hit the intercom button and asked his secretary to call Mrs. Meyers.

While we waited, I asked if he thought Maggio was involved in this.

"Of course he is."

"Can we get him?"

He shrugged. "I doubt it. But this was all about getting the kids back, so it's a success. And we shut down that operation."

"Yup, a good day's work."

Stosh's phone rang a few minutes later.

Chapter 48

I walked into Block's office at two. Randel looked at me with disgust and told me he was busy. I told her that only worked once. As I told her I was going in whether she helped or not, I pulled aside my jacket and showed her the reason that was going to happen. She called Block on the intercom and said I was here and coming in. She didn't bother getting up.

As I walked toward the door I heard the announcer on WGN mention they had breaking news. I knew what it was.

"Mr. Manning, I'm very busy this morning. You really need to make an appointment. I don't know if you're aware, but there has been a lot going on at the park. We had a bomb scare."

I stopped him. "I'm not aware of any bomb scare."

"Don't you listen to the news? It's been—"

"Turn on your radio, Mr. Block. WGN."

He turned to the credenza behind his desk and turned on the radio. A newswoman was talking about what she called the amazing story coming out of Riverview. As she talked about three dead people and kidnapped children, I watched Block's face. He looked confused and worried. She then switched to the drug raid this morning and the kids who were freed, and Block opened a drawer and reached down. I reached inside my jacket and grabbed the butt of my gun, but he came out with a Kleenex and blew his nose.

When he started to talk, he said he was shocked. He had no idea. I found it hard to believe that. Nobody could be that dumb.

I asked him about sizeable checks going to Walters. He had no idea. I asked him about kids being drugged at the park and forced to work in a factory. He had no idea. He had no idea about anything.

"Mr. Block, are you trying to tell me you ran that amusement park and had no idea that all these things were going on?"

"Well, it does sound a little implausible, but it's true. I know I'm not a good manager." He shook his head. "I didn't know about those things."

I had met enough good actors to start a Broadway show.

The door to his office opened and Tanner stuck his head in.

"Got her, Spencer."

I nodded.

"Who's that?" Block asked.

"Chicago Police."

"Police? What's going on?"

"Come with me, Mr. Block."

He followed me out of his office, through the reception area, and into the hall where Pitcher was putting handcuffs on Miss Randel. Block stood outside the office looking shocked.

"What's going on here?"

"Mr. Block," I said, "there's going to be an audit of your books. I think you'll find that someone has been funneling large checks to personal accounts. That's either you or Miss Randel. What's your guess?"

He looked at her with dismay and said, "Miss Randel?"

"Shut up you old fool."

I stopped Pitcher as she moved away with Randel. "Pitcher, do me a favor. When you get her booked, let me know what her first name is."

"Go to hell," said Randel.

Pitcher smiled.

I left Block to his confusion.

Walters needed someone on the inside of the office to funnel the money and keep an eye on things, so he had arranged for Morgan to be replaced by Randel. And when it started to fall apart, he had to get rid of people who knew too much. Gertrude Morgan was just an innocent pawn.

Chapter 49

I slept in until a little after nine Saturday morning. I had been out until two a.m. with Rosie at the Blue Note, celebrating. We had a wonderful evening of dancing and conversation, some of it serious and some of it not. Drinks were on Johnny.

I could have slept longer, but I wanted to stop by Riverview and spend some time with Harvey. A sunny morning was forecast to turn to rain in the afternoon.

Before I left, I called the inn and gave Barbara an update. She was relieved and overjoyed.

"I'm going to drive up there tomorrow to bring you back home."

There was silence on the other end.

"Barbara?"

"Yes, I'm here. I was just thinking maybe I don't want to come back… at least not yet."

"Can't blame you for that."

"I was thinking, Spencer." Again silence. "I wish there was some way Sadie could come up here for a bit. She really needs a break."

"She does," I agreed.

"But there's her mother, and she doesn't have any money and…"

"I think it's a good idea, Barbara. She was a huge help. Let me see what I can do."

We chatted for a few more minutes, and I told her I'd get back to her.

***

I pulled into the Riverview parking lot, paid, walked through the gate, and strolled leisurely down the Midway without having to worry about who would see me. The shack under the Bobs was padlocked and taped off. I paused in front and spent a moment remembering Steele.

Happy faces and screams from people on the coasters were exactly what an amusement park is about. None of the visitors knew what had happened at this wonderland for kids.

Harvey saw me coming and waggled his fingers at me. He was all alone in front of Wonderland.

"Morning, PI. I must say, when you put on a show, you put on a show. I didn't know there were so many vehicles with red lights."

I smiled. "Morning, Harvey."

"Read about it in the paper. Amazing. Glad the kids are okay."

"Well, not quite okay, but they will be with time."

He nodded, jingling the bells on his hat.

"I want to thank you for all your help with this, Harvey."

"I didn't do anything."

"You were a big help, providing some of the pieces to the puzzle."

"Well, glad to help. If I ever want to get arrested I'll call you."

I glanced at the wall behind him covered with all the Alice characters, so strange and wonderful. What a shame that an amusement park had been turned into a place of terror for some by Walters and his cronies. My gaze settled on the Cheshire cat with its ominous grin, and I realized that for all the grinning that cat did, it never laughed.

***

After arranging with Carol to handle the office for a week, I picked up Sadie at eight Sunday morning. I had told Sadie she was getting an all-expense-paid vacation in Door County. It was a nice change to see tears of joy. She told me all the reasons she couldn't go, the main one being her mother, and I told her I had already taken care of that. All she had to do was find someone to stay with her mother. She said she couldn't afford that. I told her I had taken care of that too. She then said she had already used her vacation time to be with her mother. I sat her down and explained.

It hadn't been hard to convince Block that Sadie needed a week off with pay. I explained to Sadie that all she had to do when she found someone to be with Mom was to give me their contact information—the bills would be taken care of. She asked who was paying them. I just told her not to worry about it. Block didn't know it yet, but *he* was. She finally gave in.

A light drizzle was falling until we passed Milwaukee when the sky started to clear. As the sun came out, she reached into her purse and pulled out Barbara's ring.

"I brought the good luck charm," she said with a big grin.

***

I had invited Rosie, but she had a court date on Tuesday. So I had the cottage all to myself until she drove up and joined me on Wednesday. I was very much looking forward to watching the moon rise out of Moonlight Bay.

If you liked this book, please post a review
on Amazon.com.

To be notified of other Rick Polad books, go to
rickpolad.com and click "Contact "

"Like" Spencer at Facebook.com/
SpencerManningMysteries

www.ingramcontent.com/pod-product-compliance
Lightning Source LLC
Chambersburg PA
CBHW022009010726
47494CB00003B/967